❧ LONESTAR HOMECOMING ❧

OTHER NOVELS BY COLLEEN COBLE INCLUDE

❧ LONESTAR HOMECOMING ❧

COLLEEN COBLE

THOMAS NELSON
Since 1798

NASHVILLE   DALLAS   MEXICO CITY   RIO DE JANEIRO

Published in Nashville, Tennessee. Thomas Nelson is a trademark of Thomas Nelson, Inc.

Thomas Nelson, Inc. books may be purchased in bulk for educational, business, fund-raising, or sales promotional use. For information, please e-mail SpecialMarkets@ ThomasNelson.com.

Library of Congress Cataloging-in-Publication Data
Coble, Colleen.
  Lonestar homecoming / Colleen Coble.
    p. cm.
  ISBN 978-1-59554-734-7 (pbk.)
  1. Single mothers—Fiction. 2. Texas—Fiction. I. Title.
PS3553.O2285L64 2009
813'.54—dc22
                                                  2009029197
                    Printed in the United States of America
                    10 11 12 13 RRD 5 4 3 2 1

For my husband and real-life hero, Dave.
When I first met him, he was in an air force uniform.
Is there anyone more handsome than a man in uniform?
Love you, honey!

There are two kinds of people: those who say to God,
"Thy will be done," and those to whom God says,
"All right, then, have it your way."

—C. S. Lewis

1

IN A FEW MINUTES, SHE'D BE A MARRIED WOMAN. GRACIE LISTER TUGGED
at the silk encasing her hips and drew a deep breath that did little to
calm the flutters tapping against her ribs. San Diego traffic rumbled
past her small rental house, but she blocked out the noise and focused
on the way her life was about to change. Things would be better now.
Cid had changed. She was sure of it.

Hope tugged at her hand. "Mommy, we should pray," she whispered. The dimples in her round cheeks flashed before her expression
turned serious again.

Gracie smoothed her five-year-old's dark curls, so unlike her own
fine, blond locks. She might not love Cid, but her daughter did. She
couldn't disappoint Hope, who wanted him for her daddy. "Okay,

honey." God didn't answer her prayers anymore, but praying would pacify the child. She sat on the edge of the bed and gathered her daughter onto her lap.

Hope folded her hands and closed her eyes. A smile tugged at Gracie's lips as she did the same. "Jesus, you know Hope needs a daddy. And we both need a home. May this day bring the fulfillment of all our dreams. Amen."

"Amen," Hope echoed, her eyes popping open. "I have to potty."

"Hurry, we need to meet Cid in fifteen minutes." Gracie smiled when she saw her daughter hiking the hem of her ruffled pink dress before she reached the bathroom. "Shut the door," she called. "Someone might come in."

Gracie rubbed her perspiring palms together and wished the ceremony were over. Soon this dump would be just a memory. Hope would have a princess room with ruffled curtains in the window that overlooked a park. Their furniture would be better than this mismatched collection of things from the Salvation Army. Hope could hold her head high at school in new clothes that weren't hand-me-downs.

When the knock came at the door, she glanced through the window and saw two men in suits standing outside. She lifted the hem of her dress off the floor. The dress rustled in a delicious manner as she went to the door. When had she last worn something so beautiful?

She opened the door. "Hello," she said, smiling. "Can I help you?"

The tall blond man flashed a badge that identified him as Roger Hastings. "Federal officers, ma'am. We'd like to talk to you a moment."

Every muscle tightened as her vision blurred. She stepped aside to allow them entry. "What's this all about?"

The younger one glanced her way with something that looked like pity in his eyes, but Hastings kept his expression impersonal. "We'd like to talk to you about Cid Ortega."

Goosebumps raised on her arms. "My fiancé. Can't this wait? Our wedding is in just over an hour. I have several things to attend to before the guests start arriving." The guests would be Cid's family and a few of her coworkers. "What's this all about?"

"I'm afraid it can't wait. Have you observed him transferring any-thing to others? A box, a briefcase, a bag?"

She needed to sit down. "No," she said. "What is it you suspect him of doing?"

The two men exchanged a glance. "Think," Hastings urged in a harsh voice. "Maybe in the park?"

"What is this about?"

"We have reason to suspect he is turning a blind eye to gun-and-drug traffic through his district."

Gracie took a step back and put her hand to her throat. Cid had not changed after all. The fact that she didn't spring to Cid's defense told her more than she wanted to know about their relationship. Her main priority had been to make Hope happy, no matter the cost.

"We'll know more when we talk to your fiancé. I suggest you let us take you into protective custody. When he's arrested here, the car-tel will assume you helped us and may retaliate."

Protective custody. "But wouldn't that make me look even more guilty in their eyes? The minute you let me go, they'd come looking for me."

Hastings shrugged. "Then you'd better get out of town until this blows over."

The news had been full of the Mexican violence that had spilled over into the United States. Beheadings, mutilation. The list was long

3

and horrific. Every impulse told her to grab her daughter and flee now, but did she owe Cid the courtesy of listening to his side?

Tires squealed outside, and Gracie turned to peer out the window. "It's Cid."

Hastings pulled a paper from his jacket and headed toward the door. "Stay back, ma'am, in case it gets dangerous."

"He doesn't have a gun," she protested.

"That you know of," Hastings said. "Stand back."

Gracie backed away from the door as the men exited and approached Cid's car. With the door partially shut, she peered out into the street. Cid exited the car and turned toward the house. The younger agent pulled out handcuffs. A battered brown van veered to the curb with a shriek of brakes, but she barely noticed with her attention focused on the exchange between Cid and the federal agents.

When the first *pop, pop, pop* came, she thought a car had backfired. Then she saw three men, their guns smoking, spill from the van. The men weren't familiar to her. She slammed the door and locked it, then peeked through the open window in the entry. Cid's car blocked her view. She didn't see the agents at first, then she noticed a shiny pair of black shoes by Cid's back tire. And a second pair of shoes. There was no sign of Cid. Was he dead too?

The men glanced toward the house. Gracie ran to the bathroom and grabbed her daughter's hand as Hope exited. "Be very quiet," she whispered. Keys, she needed keys. She snatched her bag from the top of the dresser.

Hope's dark eyes were huge. "Mommy, what's happening?"

Gracie put her finger to her lips. Her pulse stuttered as she led her daughter into the hall. Where could they hide? The voices grew closer. They'd be in the house any moment.

The steps to the attic were only a few feet away. Maybe she could trick them. She yanked on the knob and left the door standing open, then hurried to the kitchen utility closet. If she had to speak right now, she'd never manage a whisper. The scent of pine cleaner and dust enveloped her as she stepped inside with Hope and hunkered down behind the closed door. She quietly listened.

Footsteps paused by the hall. "The attic," a male voice said quietly. "Angel, you check the bedrooms. Niguel, come with me. Find the woman and kid."

She pressed her forehead against the wood. Hope's tight grip on her hand was painful, but Gracie squeezed her daughter's fingers reassuringly. She waited until footsteps went past the kitchen and down the hall. Holding her breath, she stepped into the kitchen. The coast was clear, but it wouldn't be for long. She and Hope rushed to the back door.

She put her hand on the knob. What if there was someone else from the van outside too? Biting her lip, she eased open the back door and peered outside. The yard was empty.

She tugged on her daughter's hand. "Shh," she said.

Staying as close to the old brick building as possible, she led Hope down the alley to where it exited onto the street. A quick glance up and down the crumbling sidewalk dissuaded her from stepping out. Teenagers with tattoos stood smoking in groups. They could be part of the neighborhood gang. It wouldn't be safe to ask them for help.

She ducked back into the alley. Across the lane stood an old church, one she'd attended a few times with Hope. As far as she knew, its doors were rarely locked, even though it had been vandalized several times. The pastor had told her if someone needed what the church had that badly, they could have it.

"Let's see if we can get into the church," she whispered to Hope. The two of them dashed across the alley to the side door, which opened to her tug.

They stepped into a cool darkness that smelled of old wood and dust. The familiarity of the odor took her back to her childhood. She crept along with her hand on the wall until she reached the entry. The place had a deserted air, so she didn't think the pastor was here. Stepping to the front door, she opened it and peered outside. The morning sun hid behind clouds, and she heard a train whistle a few blocks over.

She ducked back inside. An ancient black phone sat on the table by the door to the sanctuary. Her hand hovered over the receiver, then she snatched it away. She'd seen articles in the papers of what the cartels did to informers. Their tongues were cut out before they were executed. She had to get away, find a place to hide where they'd never find her.

The train whistle blew again. *The train.* She still had the tickets to Alpine that she'd bought a few weeks ago, before Cid talked her out of leaving. If she and Hope could get to the train, they could escape.

The teenagers ignored them as she and Hope ran across the street to the intersection. They hurried down busy Taylor Street. A few men whistled at her through their open windows, and she knew her wedding dress was an attention getter she didn't need. The train platform was just ahead. The strong smell of diesel fuel burned her nose, but the odor signaled her escape. Passengers stared down at her from inside the train as she hurried to the steps.

She dug through her purse past the wallet, lipstick, and gum to find the train tickets. With the tickets in her hand, she and Hope boarded the train. Her wedding dress raised a few eyebrows as she walked by the other passengers, but no one spoke. She pushed toward the back, where she could hide Hope if the men came looking. Two seats together were a welcome haven, and she sank onto the upholstery before her legs could give way.

Safe, at least for now.

Her little girl's eyes were huge in her white face. "Are the bad men coming?" she asked.

Gracie embraced her and kissed the top of her head. "It will be okay," she whispered. She licked dry lips and watched through the window across the aisle. Her muscles trembled, and she knew if she'd been standing, her legs wouldn't have supported her.

The conductor shut the door. They were leaving. A sigh eased from her lungs. The train lurched, then pulled away from the platform as a man came running down Taylor Street. He glanced up and down the street but didn't look at the train.

Her last glimpse of him silhouetted in front of the platform showed the butt of a gun jutting from his jeans' waistband. The train picked up speed, and she settled back against the seat. Though lulled by the clack of the wheels on the tracks, she knew the danger was far from over. They'd think about the train eventually.

I could go home instead of to Bluebird Crossing.

"No," she whispered. "I can never go home."

Hope burrowed her head into Gracie's lap. Her long lashes fluttered, and Gracie smoothed her daughter's delicate brows. "Sleep, little one," she whispered.

Night was coming, and there would be many stops along the way in the next day and a half. She glanced at her wallet. How much money did she have? She opened it and stared at the single five-dollar bill inside. They could drink water at the stops, and maybe she could buy a couple of apples for Hope. But then what? When the money was gone, how would she feed her daughter until she found out if she could get a job in Bluebird Crossing? Where could they live until she received a paycheck? She had a bit of money in her bank account, but the minute she touched it, they'd find her.

Her cell phone was in her purse as well, but she had no one to call for help. Her throat thickened, and she swallowed hard. Blinking fiercely, she told herself not to cry.

THE FIERCE SOUTHWEST TEXAS SUN BEAT DOWN ON LIEUTENANT MICHAEL Wayne's face as he disembarked at the Alpine platform. Whoever invented train travel should be lined up in front of a firing squad. It had to be a hundred degrees out here, but he should be used to it after his stint in Iraq. He dropped his duffel bag at his feet and scanned the scant crowd for Rick Bailey's face. Wonder of wonders, the train from El Paso had arrived a little early. At least he hadn't had to ride the thing long. And he'd had a front seat.

The elderly gentleman, Zeke, disembarked and shook Michael's hand. "It's been good talking to you, Lieutenant. If I were you, I'd find a wife to help you raise those kids."

"Easier said than done, sir." The man's statement heightened Michael's sense of ineptitude. He was ill equipped for the task ahead of him. What did he know about raising kids—especially a daughter? He grew up without a mother and knew how hard it was. He'd never dreamed his kids would have to endure it too.

Zeke released Michael's hand. "Thank you for your service, son."

"You're welcome, sir." Michael marveled at the fellow's strong grip. Zeke looked like he was at least eighty.

His back erect, the gentleman grabbed his backpack and walked away with a spry step. More people followed him as the train emptied. As Michael turned to watch for Rick again, he noticed a young woman who held a little girl of about five by the hand. What caught his attention more than the fragile beauty of her fine-boned face and full lips was the wedding gown she wore. It was creased and spotted as though she'd worn it several days. Her dark-blond hair hung in wisps around her cheeks where it had fallen from a shiny clip.

The little girl glanced up with an appeal in her brown eyes. Her pink dress was all ruffles. A layer of dust dulled the shine on her patent leather shoes. "Mommy, I'm hungry," she said.

"I know, Hope," the woman said, her voice full of defeat. "I'm out of money." She blinked rapidly, but a tear escaped and trickled down her pale cheek. She turned to a woman beside her. "Would you be going to Bluebird Crossing? My daughter and I need a ride."

"No, dear, I'm sorry. I live here in Alpine. There's my husband." The woman waved at a craggy-faced man in a cowboy hat and walked away.

The young woman's face took on more determination, and she turned toward the next person exiting the train. Michael started toward them, his hand going to the pocket that held his money clip. The woman swayed as her knees began to buckle. What little color remained in her face leached out. He sprang forward in time to catch her before she crumpled to the walk. As he lifted her in his arms and carried her to a nearby bench, he noticed how slight she was.

"Mommy, Mommy!" The little girl ran after them with tears streaming down her face.

"It's okay," Michael said, pitching his voice to a low, soothing murmur. He laid the woman on the bench, then pressed his fingers to the thin skin of her wrist. Her pulse jumped erratically beneath his fingertips.

"Hope," the woman muttered, her lids still closed.

He glanced at the little girl hovering beside her mother. "Hope, has your mommy had anything to eat?"

Hope shook her head. "She only had five dollars when we ran away. She bought some apples, but she said she wasn't hungry and I could eat them."

"How long ago was this?"

Hope wrinkled her forehead. "We rode the train all day yesterday and slept on it last night."

It was middle of the afternoon now, so Michael assumed the woman hadn't eaten in two days. He wanted to ask why Hope's mommy had run away from her wedding, but it wasn't his business. "What's your mommy's name?" he asked Hope as he took out his water bottle.

"Gracie. I'm Hope. Hope Lister," she said.

Gracie Lister. The name fit the delicate woman on the bench. Her nose had a dusting of freckles. Translucent eyelids fluttered, then opened wide, revealing eyes as blue as the cheery storefront behind them. A tiny scar gleamed on her forehead.

She started to sit up, but he pressed her back. "Easy. Here, have a sip of water." He held the bottle to her lips, and she swallowed a mouthful. "A little more," he instructed.

She nodded and took another drink. "Thank you so much," she said. "I don't know what came over me. The heat maybe."

He helped her sit, then pushed her gently forward until her head was down. "Sit up when your head clears. Take deep breaths."

After a few inhalations, she straightened. "I feel much better," she said.

"Hope says you haven't eaten in two days."

A delicate bloom of color stained her cheeks. "I'm fine."

"I don't think so, ma'am. I heard you tell Hope you had no more money. Where's your luggage?"

Her hands twisted together in her lap. "I . . . I had to leave it behind."

He saw the fear in her eyes, the way she couldn't hold his gaze. Was she running from an abusive fiancé? A distasteful marriage arranged by her family? Her left hand was bare, so apparently she'd escaped before the marriage happened.

"Do you live here?" she asked, glancing around. Her pupils dilated as she watched the crowd moving past. The muscles in her throat convulsed, and she shrank back against the bench when a tall man came toward her. Her breath eased from between her lips when the man passed without another glance at her.

"No, I'm heading to Bluebird Crossing."

Her head came up. "Could we catch a ride with you?"

"Why are you going to Bluebird?"

She wet her lips, and her gaze darted away. "I'm looking for a job."

"In *Bluebird*? Ma'am, you're not likely to find much there."

"I—I have a contact there," she said. "Someone to help me."

While he knew the folks in his tiny burg were neighborly, he couldn't see her finding any real job there. "I can give you a ride when mine gets here." He glanced at the parking lot. "I don't think he'll be here for another half hour, though."

"I'd be so grateful," she said, more color coming to her face.

"How about we get something to eat?" He held up his hand when objection gathered in her eyes. "My treat. Hope is hungry."

The rebellion in her eyes disappeared, and she nodded. "Thank you."

He nodded across the street. "A sub sandwich sounds good to me. How about you?"

"Hope loves turkey sandwiches," Gracie said.

He took Gracie's hand and helped her stand. "You okay? Dizzy or anything?"

"I'm fine," she said.

As he led her across the street, he noticed the way she glanced over her shoulder and the tension in her muscles. What was she running from?

2

GRACIE FORCED HERSELF TO NIBBLE IN A LADYLIKE MANNER INSTEAD OF taking the huge bite she wanted. Food this good should have a luxury tax on it. The aroma of fresh-baked bread added to her ravenous hunger.

Hope had already gulped down half her turkey melt. "Can I have more milk?" she asked.

"Sure, kiddo," Michael said. He left his own sandwich untouched and went to the counter for another carton of milk. He pulled out his cell phone as he waited in line with his black beret tucked under his arm.

Gracie watched him as he stood with his shoulders squared in his army dress blues. The sun shone through the window onto his tanned face. She guessed him to be in his early thirties. Soldiers inspired an innate sense of trust in her, probably from having grown up near a military base. His voice looked like ocean waves, blue with whitecaps that rolled to the shore. What would he say if she told him that? She rarely spoke of her synesthesia.

She turned her attention back to her sandwich when she saw the stares of the other patrons. She knew how she must look to them: *loser* should be tattooed on her forehead. The bedraggled wedding gown announced how pathetic she really was. Every time someone came in, she tensed, though she knew her stalkers couldn't have tracked her here already. At least she didn't think so.

"Want me to open your applesauce?" she asked Hope.

"Yes, please," Hope mumbled, her cheeks bulging with the last of her sandwich.

Gracie tugged off the foil top and slid the container to her daughter. Her appetite left her when she saw Michael approach. His expression was hard to read with his blue eyes hooded and his lips in a firm line.

He opened the milk and set it in front of Hope before sliding into his seat. Perching his hat on his knee, he picked up his sandwich. "Who do you know in Bluebird? Maybe I could call them for you."

She nibbled on her sandwich to delay her answer. Would he try to dissuade her again? She had nowhere else to go. "Edna Haskell. I designed her living room in California before she left to go back to Bluebird."

"Edna Haskell. That's Dan's mother."

"She said if I ever needed a job to come see her. She runs a day care there, and I've done that kind of work in the past." No need to mention it was far in the past.

"You have her number?"

She nodded and dug a slip of paper out of her purse. "I talked to her a month ago, and she knew I was thinking about coming."

"Your marriage must have been kind of sudden, then."

Gracie bit down on her lip nearly hard enough to draw blood. "It was." What did he know of the desperation that had forced her to try to build a better life for her daughter?

Michael dug out his cell phone and punched in the number. Gracie's nails bit into her palms as she waited.

"Dan, hi. This is Michael Wayne. Yeah, I figured you'd heard I was heading home. That kind of news travels fast in Bluebird. Listen, could I talk to your mom a second?" His face sobered. "I'm sorry. I hadn't heard. What about her day care?"

Gracie's stomach clenched, and she thought she might throw up. Something bad had happened. She could see it on the handsome soldier's face. Lifting her bottle of water, she took a gulp of it and nearly choked.

"Talk to you soon, Dan. I'm sure sorry." Michael closed his phone. "Edna had a stroke two weeks ago. She's in a nursing home and not expected to recover."

"Oh no!" Gracie had looked up to the older woman as a safe haven. Her eyes burned. What was she going to do?

"The day care has been turned over to one of her employees, who just hired her sister to help with the workload. I don't think you're going to find a job there."

She swallowed hard. "I see," she said, her voice quivering.

Michael's kind eyes studied her face. "You've worked with kids awhile?"

She nodded. "I love kids." She hesitated. "I should tell you it's been about two years. I thought Edna would give me a chance, though."

He chewed on his lip, picked up his soda, then put it down without taking a sip. She noticed there was no ring on his left hand. "My ex-wife died two weeks ago, and I've got two kids to raise," he said. "I'm going to need to hire a nanny or something."

"I could do that," she said quickly. "I know you don't really know me, but I have excellent references, both in my current job and at the day care where I worked."

He nodded. "For tonight, let's get to Bluebird. I'll call your references tomorrow, and we'll decide if the idea will work out. I gotta warn you, though, I live in the wilds of the Big Bend area. No city life."

"I'm okay with that," she said. At least Hope would have a bed to sleep in.

He nodded. "I'd better explain a few things. I'm renting a house, sight unseen, outside Bluebird. You've never been to the area before, have you?"

"No, but Edna told me about it."

"We're near the Rio Grande and very isolated. Big Bend National Park is a few miles away, but don't let that fool you. You'll likely see more tarantulas than people."

She suppressed a shudder and hoped he didn't notice. "I-I can handle that."

"I'll be working for the Border Patrol, and I'll be gone a lot."

Border Patrol, just like Cid. She'd landed right in another hornet's nest. Her initial trust of this man faded. "We'll be living in your house?"

He nodded. "I'm told the place is big but rundown. I'll do the best I can to fix up an apartment for you and Hope, though. The owners have said I can do anything I want there. If you had a car, I suppose you could rent a place in town, but I doubt you'll find much available."

Every instinct shouted for her to run. But where could she run to with no money? Hope would be hungry again in a few hours, and Gracie couldn't even buy her another apple. Without this offer, she'd have to seek out a shelter to provide a bed for Hope tonight.

She tipped her chin up. "Would I have a lock on our door?"

His blue eyes widened, but he nodded. "Sure, if that will make you feel safer. I'm a pretty decent fellow, though."

"Tell me about your children."

His smile came, full of pride. "I've got one of each. Jordan is eight, and Evan is six."

Gracie smiled. "You must have missed them terribly." She squeezed her daughter's hand. "I'd be lost without my Hope."

"I haven't seen them in four months, but I talk to them on the phone every week."

"I'm sure they waited for your calls."

"I made arrangements to get back from Iraq as fast as I could when their mother died."

"When did you say that was?"

"Two weeks ago."

"You didn't waste any time. Was it hard to get leave?"

He shook his head. "I'm on a special task force to aid the Border Patrol for the next couple of months, then I'll need to go for training before starting a permanent job with them."

"How long will your training be?" she asked, calculating things in her head. This job might work out for longer than she dared to hope.

"Fifty days. The kids aren't allowed to go with me, so I'll need someone dependable to care for them full-time."

She studied his expression and saw the concern for his children in his eyes. It did much to endear him to her. "Who has cared for the children since their mother died?"

"A neighbor, Allie Bailey, has taken charge of them. I've met Rick but not Allie."

"They live close by?"

He nodded. "They own Bluebird Youth Ranch. They rescue horses and match them up with inner-city kids who have been abused."

Gracie leaned forward. "How wonderful! I'd like to see that."

"They're the next ranch over. The folks are neighborly, so you'll see lots of them, I'm sure. If we decide you can handle the job, that is." His tone warned her to assume nothing.

If. She had to get the job. "I promise to take very good care of your children."

"Just love them and make them mind," he said. "I don't think they got much love or discipline from Kate." He put emphasis on *discipline*.

"I can handle them."

A muscle bulged in his jaw. "I suspect they'll be a handful."

"How long were you divorced?" Not her business. She wished she could have called back the words.

"Three years." He pushed back from the table. "We'd best be going. Rick is probably out there looking for me."

"You didn't eat your sandwich," Gracie said.

"I'm not hungry." He scooped the debris from the table and deposited it into the trash bin.

Gracie winced at the waste. Taking Hope's hand, she followed him outside. The bright sunlight made her blink, and she coughed at the hot scent of asphalt. Her throat was raw and sore. She couldn't afford to get sick and started to fish in her purse for some zinc drops until she remembered she didn't have any. And no money to buy more. She and Hope had nothing but the clothes on their backs.

Michael glanced at her. "I think you need something else to wear.

The last thing we need is the gossip that's sure to follow you if you arrive in that getup."

"I-I don't have money to buy anything."

"A pair of jeans and a T-shirt will hardly break me." He nodded to a women's shop. "Pick out what you need."

Warmth spread through Gracie's chest. "I'll pay you back," she promised.

"Jordan will have something to fit Hope, I think," he said. He glanced at his watch. "Get a move on. Rick will be here any minute." He handed her a credit card.

The plastic was still warm from his body. Just like his soul. She'd never met such a generous man. "I'll be right back."

The clerk eyed her but said nothing as she and Hope browsed the racks. It took Gracie no time to find an inexpensive pair of jeans, a pink T-shirt, and a dollar pair of flip-flops. She slipped into the dressing room. She tore the soiled dress from her body and kicked it away. The stains on the wedding dress matched the ones on her soul. The dress held too many reminders of the shambles she'd made of her life. If she had scissors, she'd cut it up.

The clothes fit fine. She removed the tags and carried them out to the clerk and handed over the credit card. She stuffed the dress in the garbage on the way out.

THE STRAINS OF THE OLD SONS OF THE PIONEERS SONG "COOL WATER" played on the radio. Gracie rode along the nearly empty ribbon of I-10 in the backseat of the big crew cab truck. The sound waves carried music to her ears and the scent of seawater to her nose. She wasn't thirsty, but the thought of a shower was more appealing than she ever would have imagined. She longed for crisp, white sheets smelling of soap and sunshine, and a pillow deep enough to bury her worries.

Hope had fallen asleep an hour ago, and Gracie's shoulder cramped from the weight of her child's head. She didn't dare move. Her daughter might awaken and sense her mother's thoughts that maybe, just maybe, she'd made the wrong decision. Alpine was about an hour and a half from Bluebird Crossing, Michael had said, so they should be there soon. The sun crept closer to the horizon with every minute, and it would be dark soon with only the stars for light. No street lamps out here. No people to call to for help either. No shelters, no government agencies. Just endless cactus and mesquite trees.

At least they were safe in this vast area, and Cid would have trouble finding her. At least that's what she told herself as she rested her hot forehead against the cool glass of her window. The rumble of the men's voices could lull her to sleep if she let them. She'd immediately been drawn to the stocky man with the voice that looked like red rocks. Michael had introduced him as Rick Bailey, then the two men talked about ranching and horses for the duration of the trip. The subject left her with nothing to say.

"How much farther?" she asked, glancing at her watch. Nearly seven.

Michael twisted in the passenger seat to glance at her. "Another fifteen minutes or so. Need a break?"

"No, I'm fine." Though her bladder felt as though it might burst, she wasn't desperate enough to search out the nearest cactus. She didn't want to be a bother to anyone. Craning her neck, she stared out at the same landscape she'd been staring at for hours: blue mountains rising in the distance, arid sand, and a bowl of sky that made her feel insignificant.

And alone.

"Having second thoughts?" Michael asked, facing forward again.

She spared a glance at the back of his head. His brown hair was as clipped as his speech. Neat, regimented, and conveying high expectations. She'd earn every penny she received from this man. Her glance went to her daughter's soft curls. Gracie didn't have the luxury of pride. Not anymore.

"I'm not having second thoughts," she said, struggling to control the slight tremble in her voice.

"So that vibration back there wasn't panic?"

She saw the grin when he turned to face her again. Maybe he wasn't as uptight as he seemed. "Maybe a little. When you said we'd be out in the boonies, you weren't kidding. You're sure there's a town out here somewhere?"

"If you can call Bluebird Crossing a town," Rick said. "I'd call it a wide spot in the road."

"Not even a Wal-Mart?"

Michael hooted. "Not even a convenience store. Just a two-pump gas station, a general store that sells groceries along with hardware, and a couple of cafés. Blink and you'll miss it."

She thought she saw the dim glow of lights in the distance. "Is that it?"

"That's my place, Bluebird Youth Ranch," Rick said. "We're not stopping there, though. Allie has Michael's house ready. She's waiting there with the kids."

"I can't wait to see my kids," Michael said, his voice eager.

"Allie wanted to tell them you were coming, but she knew they'd want to come with me, and we didn't want to subject them to the three-hour trip, plus the wait."

"Evan isn't the most patient kid either," Michael said.

"There's that," Rick agreed.

A handful, Gracie decided. "What about Jordan?" she asked.

"She collects insects," Michael said. "And snakes."

"Aren't there poisonous ones around here?"

"Yep, so be prepared." Michael's grin flashed again. The truck slowed, then passed the driveway. A wooden sign hanging over the entrance proclaimed the ranch to be Bluebird Youth Ranch.

"So you rescue horses?" Gracie asked. She spotted a swaybacked reddish horse on the other side of the fence.

"Yeah," Rick said.

The truck accelerated along the dark road. As they left the security lights of the Bluebird Ranch behind them, darkness hid the hills again. Something howled, and she hugged herself. It had been years since she'd heard a coyote. The blackness sent a deeper chill through her, and she wished she had a sweater.

A wink of light grew brighter in the distance. "There's your place," Rick said. "Shannon MacGowan owns it."

"Jack's wife owns it, not him?" Michael asked.

"Her uncle left it to her, and Jack oversees it, but it's still in her name. She's the vet in town. You'll likely meet her soon. I'm warning you now, it needs work."

"Which is why it's so cheap," Michael said. "Jack said they'd take any work I did off the rent."

"And he'll stand behind that."

"Just how rough are we talking here?" Michael asked.

Rick didn't have to answer. The security light on the barn revealed the weathered paint on the house and the sagging porch steps. Gracie had seen worse, but she noticed the way Michael studied the bleak house. Not even a shrub softened the harshness of the sandy plane on which it sat.

She opened her door and eased out from under Hope's head. "It's not so bad. A little paint and it will be fine." She stretched her legs.

The porch light flipped on. "Daddy!" Two children tumbled through the screen door.

Michael sprang from the truck to greet them. He squatted, and they leaped into his arms. His hug was awkward. The wash of light from the truck illuminated the rapt faces of his children. Evan was a miniature Michael with light-brown hair and an eager smile. A pink ribbon held Jordan's dark hair off her face. She wore jeans, a pink T-shirt, and pink sneakers. Definitely a girlie-girl, even if she did collect snakes and insects.

"Did you bring me a snake from Iraq?" she demanded.

"Sorry, kiddo. No snake."

Her lower lip pouched. "I wanted a baby cobra!"

He hoisted her in is arms. "Over my dead body. Baby girl, you'll be the death of me."

Evan stepped away from his father, stuffed his small hands in the pockets of his jeans, then glared at his father. "What took you so long?"

Michael ruffled Evan's hair. "I hurried, buddy."

A woman stepped onto the porch. "I told them you were coming just a half hour ago," she said. The beautiful Hispanic woman's smile encompassed Gracie with a warm welcome. Her voice lit Gracie's vision with soft yellow. She held a toddler boy in her arms.

Michael stood and took his children's hands. He glanced at the woman. "You must be Allie."

Her smile widened, and she came down the creaking porch steps.

"I could have picked you out as Evan's daddy from a mile away." Her gaze flickered to Gracie.

Michael's smile faltered, and he glanced at Gracie too. Was he the one having second thoughts? Gracie lifted her chin and extended her hand. "I'm Gracie Lister. I'll be caring for the kids." She could have added the *for now* she saw on Michael's lips but didn't.

Allie's eyes widened. "Wonderful! It will much better for them to adjust to their own home."

One advocate. Maybe.

"Mommy?" Hope's voice came from the truck.

Gracie glanced behind her as her daughter popped her head out of the open door. "Hi, sweetie. Mommy is right here." She helped her daughter from the truck, and Hope stood rubbing her eyes.

"This is your daughter?" Allie asked.

"Yes, this is Hope. She's five."

Allie smiled down at the child. "My daughter, Betsy, will love to have a new friend. She's six. She's at Jack and Shannon's for the night, but I'll bring her over tomorrow." Then, looking back at Michael, she said, "Come on in, and I'll show you around."

Gracie sensed Michael's gaze on her as she followed the little brunette inside. He might be having second thoughts, but she'd prove herself to him. She had to—for Hope.

3

Fresh paint. The smell reassured Michael that at least some work had been done on the house. He glanced around at the tan walls. The wood floors were clean, though scarred. "You did a lot of work here, Allie."

"Actually, Shannon hired someone to paint and clean it up," Allie said, transferring her son to Rick. The toddler giggled and grabbed hold of Rick's ear. "She also brought an exterminator in to kill all the spiders in the attic. The place was infested with black widows and brown recluse. No one's really lived here in ages. Shannon spent a few weeks here before she married Jack, but she didn't get any real repairs done."

Michael tightened his grip on his children's hands. There was so much to catch up on with them. Too much. "How many bedrooms?"

COLLEEN COBLE

"Six. Plus a huge attic if you need more space," Allie said. "I've got chili on the stove. We should get Matthew home to bed. Three beds are all made up, and there's more bedding in a chest in the master bedroom at the top of the stairs. I can stay and do that if you like."

"No, no, I can handle that," Gracie said. Her voice was soft and hesitant, and she knelt and lifted Hope into her arms.

Michael watched her a moment. She was like a feral cat afraid of having something thrown at her. He realized Allie was still speaking and forced his attention back to her.

Allie pointed up the stairs. "There's a suite at the end of the hallway—two rooms with a connecting door and a shared bathroom. That might work for you and Hope," Allie said. "I didn't make it up because it's so far from Michael's room, and I thought he'd want the kids close to him."

"I do," he said. Evan began to run around the room. "Don't run inside the house, Evan," he said. The boy ignored him. On his next pass, Michael grabbed him. Evan fought him and began to cry.

Gracie took his son's hand. "Evan, did you have supper yet? Are you hungry?"

"They wouldn't eat until their dad got here," Allie said, her tone apologetic. "I'm sure he's tired and hungry."

Michael frowned. These kids needed discipline, not coddling. Gracie might have been a mistake. He remembered the other problem he needed to solve. "You're about Gracie's size, Allie. Would you have some clothes she can borrow? She came away without any belongings."

Allie's eyes widened. "Of course." She glanced at Gracie. "You need . . . everything?"

Gracie's cheeks reddened, and she nodded. "I'm sorry."

"Don't be sorry! I'll be glad to share. You're what, a 6?"

Gracie looked down. "Yes. Anything will do. Maybe a few things you were going to give to the Salvation Army? I'll buy some things as . . . as soon as I get my first paycheck." She bit her lip. "And anything your daughter has outgrown would be even more appreciated. Hope wears a 5."

"I have some of Betsy's things packed away. We have tons of things in that size," Allie said. "I'll get them out as soon as I get home."

"Some of Jordan's things might fit her." Michael nearly reached for his checkbook, then didn't. He wasn't sure yet if she would work out, and he suspected she'd take offense at an offer of charity. "Thanks for everything you've done," he said, walking Rick and Allie to the door.

"I'll run some things over for Gracie and Hope yet tonight," Rick told him before they slipped out. "Tomorrow morning I'll come by and take you to buy a truck."

"Thanks." Michael shut the door behind them.

"Would you mind if I found our room and washed up? Hope and I are both filthy," Gracie asked.

"Go right ahead. Help yourself to some of Jordan's pajamas for Hope. You need me to come with you?"

"No, I can find it. Thanks," She went up the stairs with her daughter in tow.

He smiled at his children. "How about some supper?" His stomach rumbled at the smell of chili. With the children tagging along, he found his way to the kitchen.

The old white cabinets, the stained sink, and the cracked linoleum made him pause in the doorway. He'd hoped for better than this for his kids, even though he knew rentals in this area were hard to come by. He'd get some work done on this place first thing. He ladled up soup for the three of them. Gracie still hadn't reappeared by the time they were done eating, and he wondered if she was hiding out in the bathroom.

"Daddy, will you read us a story?" Evan asked, tugging on his hand.

"A story, a story," Jordan chanted, pulling him toward the living room.

Michael allowed the children to lead him to the brown sofa. He sat on the upholstery, worn slick by years of use. A crusty old bachelor used to own this house, and Michael dimly recalled the guy's niece, Shannon. A lifetime ago. "What do you want me to read?" he asked.

"*If I Ran the Circus*," Evan said, thrusting the Dr. Seuss book into his hand.

"No, read *The Cat in the Hat!*" Jordan said, running to grab the book from the bookcase.

"Evan has his book already. We'll read yours next," Michael said. He lifted her onto his lap when her face puckered. In five minutes he'd made her cry. He'd forgotten how much the kids argued. Kate had coddled them too much.

He sensed Gracie before he saw her. The air thickened and became charged with electricity. She stepped into the room with her daughter by the hand. The pajamas Hope wore dragged on the floor.

Michael lifted Evan onto his other knee. "There's room for Hope if she wants to listen to the story," he said.

"Oh no, you need time with your kids," Gracie said. "We don't want to be in your way."

"We'll have lots of time." He smiled when Hope tugged her hand from her mother's and went to him shyly. Jordan scowled but scooted over to make room for the other little girl. Hope's hair was damp, and the scent of soap wafted to his nose.

He hesitated. "There's chili in the kitchen."

"We'll eat after your story. Hope loves stories." Gracie stepped into the room and sidled to the armchair. She sat and folded her hands across her knee.

Michael opened the book. "'In all the whole world . . .'" he began. In moments, the three children were engrossed in the story. He should have been too, but he was more conscious of the way Gracie rested her chin on her hand and watched her daughter with softness in her blue eyes.

Did he have a right to ask why she'd fled in her wedding dress with no luggage? She claimed to have good references, so he'd call them first thing in the morning, but if they didn't check out, she was out of here. He wouldn't entrust his children to just anyone.

Life had beaten her down, but whatever she'd gone through had not smothered the spark of determination in her eyes to care for her daughter. That was an attitude he admired.

MICHAEL HAD A NICE READING VOICE. SHE CLOSED HER EYES AND WATCHED the blue waves of his sound wash over the insides of her eyelids. He finished up the final page of *The Cat in the Hat*. If not for him, she would be trying to keep Hope warm on a park bench somewhere in Alpine.

But men always had a hidden agenda, and she didn't know what his was yet. Once the children were in bed, she'd try to find out more about the soldier. He was too good to be true. He might have rescued them, but he'd want payment of some kind. She dreaded knowing what that might be.

Michael closed the book. "Bedtime, kiddos."

"No, Daddy!" Jordan threw her arms around his neck and hung on. "You just got here."

He hugged her. "And I'll be here tomorrow and the next day and the day after that."

Her brows lowered. "You're not going back to fight?"

"Nope. I've got a job right close by. You and me and Evan are going to live here."

"Forever?"

"Well, maybe not forever. I might buy us our own place when I find something we like. But we're staying here in the desert."

"You've still got your uniform on," she pointed out.

"I'll still be a soldier for a few more months while I'm on a special assignment. When that's done, I'll take some training and join the Border Patrol."

Hope slid off his lap and ran to her mother. Gracie lifted her daughter onto her knees. The child's weight anchored her as she rested her chin on Hope's head. For Hope's sake, she would find a way out of the mess Cid had created for them.

"Want some dinner?" she whispered against her daughter's hair. Hope shook her head and leaned against Gracie. Her eyes began to close. Gracie wasn't hungry either. Too much excitement.

"Baths, then bed." Michael glanced at Gracie.

"I'll bathe them," she offered quickly. Though every muscle ached, she wanted to carry her weight and make him glad he'd hired her.

Jordan thrust out her lower lip. "I want Daddy!"

"Me too!" Evan flopped on the floor and drummed his heels. "I want Daddy!" he wailed.

"They're overtired," Gracie murmured.

"I'll do it," Michael said to her. Then to the kids: "Enough of the tears. I'm tempted to let Miss Gracie handle you two after this kind of display. I'm not going to tolerate disrespect. Got it?"

The kids sobered. Evan stood and slipped his hand into his father's. "Can I sleep with you, Daddy?"

"No, you have your own bed. Time for you to be a little man. Let's get a bath."

His stern voice made Gracie wince. "I think there's a bathroom outside Jordan's room."

"One way to find out." He carried the children up the steps.

Gracie put Hope down and followed. The house smelled of pine cleaner and lemon wax. Someone had gone to a lot of trouble to make it as nice as possible, though even cleaning couldn't mask the worn tread on the steps and the battered woodwork. Still, the cheery red hall rug was new and bright, and the paint was fresh. She itched to put a little design into the living room.

Michael stopped at the first doorway and peered in. "A bedroom," he said.

"The bathroom is there." Evan pointed to the next doorway. "And there's another one in your room."

Gracie walked past them and stepped into the bathroom. The large room held another claw-foot tub. A shower curtain on an oval rod surrounded it. The wall and floor tile was white and looked old, but it was in good shape. She knelt and plugged the drain with a rubber stopper, then turned on the water. The forceful stream held a tinge of rust, and she grimaced.

"I want bubble bath," Jordan announced. She squirmed to be let down, and when her father deposited her on the tile, she went to the vanity and began to rummage through it. "There's no bubble bath." Her brows drew together, and she folded her arms across her chest. "Mommy always put bubble bath in our water."

"We'll get some tomorrow. I don't have any bubble bath, but I've got some vanilla-scented lotion in my purse. It will make you smell nice and pretty. I'll get it in a few minutes."

"Okay." Jordan began to strip off her clothes.

"I'll borrow some pajamas for Hope while you bathe the kids," Gracie said, backing out of the bathroom with Hope by the hand. She listened to Michael tell the children how to wash while she went to Jordan's bedroom. The man had a lot to learn about children. He couldn't treat them like soldiers.

All the clothes were neatly folded in the dresser, and she lifted out a pair of pajamas for Jordan. A picture caught her eye, and she picked it up. A young woman with brown hair and eyes held Jordan and Evan on her lap. Their mother, Kate? Jordan had her eyes and hair color. The three of them sat on a swing on a brick patio surrounded by flowers and vines. Hadn't Michael said they'd lived in San Antonio? Bluebird would be an adjustment for the children.

Gracie stepped to the next room and found pajamas for Evan. She got the lotion from her purse and handed everything through the door to Michael. While they waited, she and Hope explored the other rooms of the upstairs. Every plain, beige bedroom held utilitarian furniture. Gracie longed to do something with Jordan's room, make it more girlish and sweet.

The bathroom door squeaked, and Michael stepped into the hallway with both kids in his arms. Their hair was still wet, and damp patches showed on his white T-shirt and dress slacks. "I can't guarantee I washed everything, but they're cleaner than they were."

"Jordan's room is right beside yours, and Evan's is beside that. Let me show you."

He glanced around. "Place is kind of plain," he said.

"But it's clean. And there's lots of room."

"Are your rooms okay?" he asked.

She laced her fingers together. "Yes, they're fine. I made the beds. I hope that's all right."

"Of course it is. I want you and Hope to be comfortable. Is there a lock on the door?" His smile was gentle.

"No, but I can put a chair under the knob for tonight."

He chuckled, a warm sound that soothed the goose bumps on Gracie's arms. "I'll put Hope to bed," she said, taking her daughter's hand.

"I want to talk a minute. Can you come down to the living room when you're done?"

Uh-oh. She massaged the tired muscles in her neck and nodded. Hope was nearly asleep before Gracie pulled the sheet up and placed a kiss on her daughter's cheek. Her knees shook as she stepped into the hallway and went down the steps. Was he having second thoughts? She wouldn't blame him if he was.

She found him in the living room. Standing in the doorway with her hands clasped in front of her, she waited for the ax to fall.

"Sit down." Michael said, perching on the sofa armrest. "I'd like to learn more of your philosophy on child rearing."

She cautiously sank onto the worn cushion of an armchair. "I'll care for your kids like they're my own." She winced at the desperation in her voice. A calm, confident tone would have been better.

"I'm sure you will." His blue eyes studied her face. "I want the kids taught some discipline. Are you up to that job?"

"Kids need love *and* discipline," she said. "I'll follow your wishes, of course."

"Kate always let them run wild," he said in a heavy voice. "I expect we'll have our hands full correcting that."

"They've just lost their mother. They're going to need a lot of cuddling and reassurance."

He frowned. "Are you the type to give in to every demand?"

"Of course not! But I hope to help you find the right balance."

His frown deepened. "When I tell them to do something, I expect obedience."

A wave of heat enveloped her face, and she dropped her gaze. "Of course," she said. "I'll do all I can to mold them into well-behaved children. They're very sweet."

"And willful," he said.

She studied the flowers on the carpet until she had the courage to lock eyes with him. "They aren't small soldiers, you know. They're children."

"Children who need to be taught how to behave."

"At eight, Jordan is just discovering how to handle structured rules and learning about self-discipline. At six, Evan has been dependent on his mother. A mother who's been ripped away. He's likely going to be fearful and uncertain about the future. Both children will be dealing with serious issues."

He hunched his shoulders. "All kids have trauma of some kind."

"This is the worst kind."

"You sound like you've studied child development."

"I have." She didn't shrink under his stare. "Please, just be gentle with them. They need your love right now more than anything."

"Of course I love them."

"Don't be afraid to show it. They're good kids."

"They're unruly," he said.

She nodded. "Give them time to grieve. We'll steer them the right way."

His eyes narrowed. "Are we going to be on the same page, Gracie?"

"Maybe we'll bring some good balance between us," she said, forcing a laugh.

He grinned then. "I'm glad we met. I think the kids will love you."

She held his gaze. "I'll never forget what you've done for me, Michael. Never."

He colored and broke the bond of their locked stare. "Anyone would have done the same."

"No," she said softly. "No, they wouldn't. You were our guardian angel today."

"I've never been accused of being an angel," he said, smiling.

"This is coming home for you, isn't it?" She glanced around the room. "When did you last live here?"

"I grew up in Bluebird but haven't lived here since college. Kate and I went to Alpine to school, then I joined the army. She followed me from base to base except when I was sent out of the country." He grimaced. "Which was too much to her liking. She divorced me."

"I'm sorry."

He shrugged. "It was a long time ago. I was sorry she died though. She was a good mother."

She heard the pain in his voice. "It's hard on the kids."

"Yeah, I hate that." His eyes took in his surroundings. "Kind of grim here. But it will do for now." He rubbed his head. "I sure miss Caesar."

"Caesar?"

"My dog. He and I worked together for three years. I had to leave him behind in Iraq."

"You've had a lot of changes lately."

He shifted where he sat. "How are you—really? You obviously ran away from your wedding. Is there anything I can do?"

His tone washed over her with the soothing sensation of blue waves. His sympathy clogged her nose with tears. She hadn't cried, not yet. It was a luxury she hadn't afforded herself. There hadn't been time. Her eyes filled too. Her throat closed, and she struggled to keep the tears from falling. She despised women who used tears to manipulate a man, and she wasn't going to be one of them.

She sprang to her feet. "If there's nothing else, can I go to bed?"

He rose. "Of course. I'm sorry about your problems, Gracie."

"Thanks," she said through her thick throat.

"I'll check your references tomorrow." He nodded toward a garbage sack by her chair. "Rick brought some clothes over. Things will look better in the morning."

"I'll be all right." She grabbed the bag, then rushed from the room and ran up the stairs.

Her eyes burned as tears poured from them, but at least he could not see them. She grabbed a pair of pajamas and stepped into the bathroom she shared with Hope, then ran water hot enough to scald her. As she slid into the hot water, she choked off sobs. Crying never solved anything.

She scrubbed the contamination of her old life from her skin until it was pink and stinging. She and Hope had a chance for a new life here. She couldn't blow it. If ever she needed wisdom, it was now. The lessons of her past mistakes should show her a new path, and she intended to take it and be smarter.

When she was dressed in the soft cotton pajamas, she grabbed her purse from the floor and went to the connecting bedroom. She took out her cell phone and charger and plugged it in. Almost immediately it beeped, telling her that she had a message. The bed squeaked when she sat on the edge with the phone to her ear and her hands shaking.

Cid's voice shocked her. "Gracie, where are you? Are you all right? Call me."

She dropped the phone. He was alive! She put her hand to her mouth. Maybe she'd run too soon. But no. Getting away from him had shown her how completely she'd deluded herself about her reasons for marrying him. Security wasn't enough to base a relationship on. The marriage would have been a huge mistake. And she doubted Cid could protect her from those men, even if he wasn't involved—though she suspected he was.

She listened to the message again and tried to ignore the urgency in Cid's voice, a voice that had always made her see orange clouds. She'd thought that meant excitement.

Gracie jabbed the key to delete the message. Her pulse yammered in her chest, and nausea roiled in her stomach. She was safe here. Of course she was. If she could, she'd toss the cell phone so he couldn't contact her again. But if she did, her father would never call. Not that she was likely to hear from him, but her hope refused to die.

4

GRACIE'S EYES BURNED LIKE SHE'D LIVED THROUGH A SANDSTORM, BUT IT was lack of sleep that plagued her. She'd propped a chair under the doorknob in her room and in Hope's, but the early morning light washed away her fears.

In the kitchen, she tugged at the fabric of her borrowed jeans, but it glommed right back onto her skin. It wasn't that they were the wrong size, but she rarely wore anything that accentuated her figure. She would have worn the new ones she bought, but she'd worn them yesterday over her filthy body and wanted to wash them first.

"You look pretty, Mommy," Hope said. She slurped down the rest of the milk from her cereal and wiped her mouth with the back of her hand.

Michael's eyes flickered. "You need some different jeans? You're tugging on them."

Gracie rinsed her hands at the sink to delay her answer. If she told him the truth, it would appear she wanted an advance for more clothes. Or a handout. "I'm just not used to stretch jeans," she said.

She went to the table and began to clear it of the dirty dishes. Cartoons blared from the TV in the living room where Jordan and Evan were.

When Hope scampered off to join the other kids, he leaned forward. "Sit down and tell me about your past jobs. I need to call your references."

She pulled out a chair and sat down, then poured cereal and milk into her bowl. "Not much to tell. I've done several things since I've been out on my own—maid service, waitressing. When Hope came along, I wanted to be with her, so I found a job in a day care."

"You said you hadn't done that for two years."

She nodded. "When the director decided to redecorate, I had some ideas, so she turned me loose. Parents loved it, and I got my first job decorating bedrooms. Before I knew it, I had the beginnings of a business."

"Home decorating?"

"And home staging. It's been hard making ends meet, but it was work I loved. And I thought I was building a new life."

"You didn't have any training?"

"Only what I read in books and magazines."

"Wow." He gestured toward the dingy cabinets. "This house is a dump. I hate the thought of my kids living here."

"It's got potential."

"What would you do with it?" he asked.

"What's your favorite music?" she asked.

His brows raised. "What's music got to do with it?"

Heat flooded her cheeks. This was always the worst part of explaining how she worked. "I find a client's tastes in music help me figure out what they'll like."

"Explain that."

Usually a client took her claim at face value. She'd rarely delved into the full story. "I have something called synesthesia. Have you ever heard of it? The word means 'joined sensation.'"

He shook his head, but he took on a more alert expression. "Is it a disability?"

"No, no, nothing like that. I consider it an asset. It's another layer of senses. Studies show many babies and children have the ability to taste or see sounds."

"You're kidding! What does sound taste like?"

She decided not to get into specifics. "It might be how some metaphors came into being. Such as the night being like black velvet. The simile combines sight and touch."

"So what do you see and taste?"

"All of us are different. I see shapes and colors when I hear music. And I sometimes taste sounds." *And voices*, she could have added, but she didn't want to go there. "So hearing your favorite music helps me picture a design that would be pleasing to you."

"My favorite music artist is Alan Jackson."

"Do you have a CD in the house? I haven't actually listened to any of his music."

"I have it on my iPod." He fished a small Shuffle out of his pocket and handed it to her. "It's all Jackson."

She hated seeing music for the first time with someone watching.

If only she'd figured out a way to get the information without telling him. She held the earbuds close to her ears and played the first song. "Gone Country" blared into her ears. Flashes of color exploded in her vision. Terracotta and periwinkle flowers erupted on a gray-green background. Lowering the earbuds, she handed the iPod back to Michael.

"You know just what to do now?" His eyes held sharp interest.

She nodded. "I think so. For the living room, I'd—"

He held up his hand. "No, don't tell me. I'm just going to let you do it. I want to see what you come up with."

"But what if you hate it?"

"Has anyone ever hated it?"

"No."

"Then I won't either. It's in your hands."

"That's scary."

He grinned. "Rick knows a neighbor with a crew cab truck for sale. I'm going to go buy it this morning."

"I'll jot down some ideas."

"When I get back this afternoon, let's take the kids to town for ice cream. I'll drop you at the hardware store and you can get paint. There's a small furniture store right next door. Get what you need."

She managed to maintain her composure, though inside she was dancing. The house was like a tomb. No color, no life. But that was about to change. "Budget?"

"I've got five thousand dollars saved. Will that do it?"

"I can stretch that to do the whole house."

His eyes widened. "No kidding?"

She nodded and glanced around. "I can make curtains, and slipcovers for the sofa. Same with bedding for the kids' rooms. I can paint those old beds and dressers. Paint is cheap."

"What about this lousy floor?"

She glanced around the kitchen. "This will take more money than anything else. A new floor and counter will cost, but I can tile it for much less than buying something prefab."

He studied her face. "You changed the minute we started talking about this. Five minutes ago you were a frightened mouse. Now your color is up, and your eyes are sparkling."

She laced her fingers together. "It's something I know."

"Sounds like it." He pulled out his phone. "I need to call your references now. Can you give me a couple?"

She nodded and dug out her cell phone, then jotted down two numbers on an old envelope. "This is the day-care director's number. And the next number is my last client's. Please don't tell them where I am, though. Just in case Cid—" She shut up at her own mention of Cid's name. Michael was smart enough to make a note of it.

She fixed herself some cereal while he stepped into the other room and made the calls. Her references would be stellar, at least. She was a good employee. She'd work her fingers off for her daughter. Laziness had never been Gracie's failing. Instead, she failed Hope by consistently making the wrong choices.

With ferocious energy, she scrubbed at the spots on the counter. Every time she thought they'd found a place to settle, something went wrong. This last episode with Cid was just the latest of many. Hope deserved better than this vagabond life, and Gracie clung to a desperate hope that this time things would change.

The spot refused to budge, and she attacked it with renewed force. Though this kitchen was grungy and old, it could be a home for her, for Hope. They could make fond memories here. In Gracie's mind's eye, she could see a white picket fence in the backyard, and Hope walking to the podium to accept her high-school diploma. Michael might have given them the key to a decent future.

Michael entered the kitchen again. "They love you. The day-care director couldn't stop singing your praises. So you're hired. The kids go back to school in a couple of weeks. I don't need to report to work until Monday, so I can help you here with the hard stuff."

She put down the sponge and scouring powder. "I thought you didn't want to know what I was doing," she said.

He studied her. "You're doing it again. The minute we start talking about the house, you change. Your eyes are sparkling again, and your voice is even louder. You must love it."

"I do." But more than that, when she worked with color, she could lose herself in it and forget all she'd done.

BY FOUR O'CLOCK THE NEXT DAY, THE HOUSE REEKED OF PAINT, AND Michael's muscles ached. Work on Monday would be a reprieve. Who would have guessed painting could wear a guy out? The color Gracie picked out for the living room was a gray-green that calmed him. She'd painted his bedroom the same color. The girls' rooms were a pale lavender he liked as well, and Evan's room was a dark blue that matched his Dallas Cowboys memorabilia.

Michael watched Gracie from the doorway to Jordan's room. Kate would never have let the kids help paint, but Gracie put down plastic and showed the kids how to use a paintbrush. Jordan and Evan were working on the headboard of the bed, and not doing a bad job.

Gracie glanced up, and their gazes locked. A pink ponytail holder corralled her blond hair, though an escaped lock brushed her right cheek. "You like the color?" she asked.

"Yeah. But more important, Jordan does."

"I *love* it, Daddy," Jordan proclaimed. She wiped white paint on her jeans.

"I might have to buy her new clothes," he said, grinning.

"It's worth it. Learning these things now will give her confidence."

He couldn't argue with that. "I thought I might check out the attic and see if there's anything worth using up there. You want to join me?"

"Sure." She wrapped her roller in a bread sack and laid it on the plastic. "Kids, keep working on the bed. I'll be back to help you touch it up in a few minutes."

"Okay, Miss Gracie," Evan said. "We're good painters, right?"

"You certainly are," she agreed with a smile. She stepped past the three children to join Michael in the doorway. "Do you know how to get up there?"

"I found the stairway. It's at the other end of the hall." He led her to a door. "Right here." He'd left the light on, and the glow from the third floor illuminated the stairs. "I'll go first. Just in case the exterminator didn't get all the spiders."

She shuddered. "Be my guest."

"I want to keep Jordan out of here until I know for sure. She'll be catching them."

The stairs were steeper and narrower than normal stairs. They rose quickly to the attic. His head poked into the space, and he glanced around before emerging into the room. "All clear. They've vacuumed and cleaned up here too. It's nice." He reached down and helped her up the last few steps.

"That'll give you a workout," she said, gasping as she joined him on the attic floor.

A jumble of boxes, tables, chairs, rolled-up rugs, lamps, and pictures was stacked in nearly every corner, though it was clear every-thing had been moved, cleaned, then put back. "Where do we start?" he asked, glancing at Gracie.

Her eyes seemed to drink in the jumble of junk. "Oh look!" She darted forward and hauled out a table.

The finish was cracked and stained. "That's good?" he asked, rais-ing his brows. "Looks like trash to me."

Her finger traced the outline of the piece. "You have to look at the lines. This is Arts and Crafts. It's simple with great lines and will fit beautifully into the design." She dragged it over to the top of the stairs.

"If you say so. Maybe we should just buy new stuff. This all looks like junk to me."

"Oh no, this is a treasure trove!" Her muffled voice came from under the eaves. She dragged out a rug, then struggled to unroll it.

"Here, let me help you." He grabbed an end of the rug and yanked. An Oriental rug lay revealed in the dim light.

Gracie knelt and examined the underside. "It's a real Persian rug," she gasped. "It has Iranian knots." She ran her hand over the brilliant colors. "I don't think it's even been on the floor." She glanced up at him. "We should ask the owners before we use this. It's probably worth some money."

"They're on vacation another week. Allie told me Shannon said she'd seen everything in the attic, and we can use whatever we want. So this is good? I kind of like the colors."

"It fits my plan perfectly."

A cell phone rang. It wasn't his. He glanced at Gracie. She pulled out her phone and glanced at the screen. The color drained from her face, and her smile went missing. "Aren't you going to answer that?"

She shook her head. "I don't recognize the number." Animation disappeared from her voice like a switch had been thrown. No trace of her confidence remained.

"Are you afraid of something, Gracie? You want me to answer it?"

She wet her lips. "It's better to ignore it." Her voice quavered.

"I believe in meeting a challenge head-on."

"Sometimes avoidance is better."

"That just lets the problem escalate. Nip it in the bud."

The cell phone stopped. She began to roll the rug up. "This can't be nipped."

"So why did you run from your wedding? You never said." Her head was down, and he couldn't see her face. "Gracie? You can talk to me. I'd like to help if you're in any trouble."

She rose and went to the other corner of the attic. "There are some lamps I'd like to use over here."

He followed her, stopping her flight with his hand on her arm. "I think we need to talk about this."

"I don't," she said, her voice low. "I want it to go away." She still hadn't looked up at him.

"Have you ever known a problem to just vanish on its own?" he asked. Was she shaking? When she clamped her lips together and turned away, he realized it would take more than a casual question to get her to open up.

GRACIE RUSHED DOWN THE STEPS TO GET AWAY FROM MICHAEL'S QUES-tions. She gasped when she saw the spill of paint on the wooden floor in Jordan's bedroom. "Let me grab a wet towel."

"Don't move, Evan," Michael ordered his son, who stood in the middle of the puddle. "Who did this?"

Gracie rushed down the steps and grabbed a roll of paper towels, then ran back upstairs. Michael was still questioning the children, and all three were in tears when she stepped into the bedroom. She knelt and began to mop up the liquid.

"If no one confesses, you'll all have to take the punishment," Michael said in full military tribunal mode.

Gracie gritted her teeth and kept on mopping. Challenging him in front of the children would be the wrong thing to do. "Raise your foot, Evan," she said quietly. When the child lifted his sneaker, she wiped it clean. "Go wash your hands now." The boy shot a fear-filled glance at his father, then bolted for the door. "You girls get washed up too. We'll discuss this in a few minutes."

As soon as the girls were out the door, Michael folded his arms over his chest. "They needed to admit who did it."

Gracie sat back on her haunches. "It was clearly an *accident,* Michael. None of them did it on purpose. Punishment should be given for defiance, not for spilling something." He blinked, and his mouth sagged. He said nothing, but she could see the wheels turning in his head.

"My dad sent me to my room whenever I spilled my milk," he said, frowning.

"Children who are shamed for things they can't control grow up resentful and uncertain," she said. "If you'd told them not to lift the can and they did it anyway, then spilled it, it would be a different story."

"Maybe they did."

She shook her head. "The can was in the same place. One of them accidentally kicked it over. It wasn't deliberate."

"I don't really get it," he said. "They should've been more careful."

"They're children. Children make mistakes. Would you want to be punished for a mistake?"

"No," he admitted. "But I think we should own up to it when we make a mistake and not try to hide it."

"I see what you're saying. A good compromise would be to tell them no one will be punished, but you want to know what happened."

His expression softened. "You're good for me, Gracie. And for them. You can tell I know more about soldiering than I do about raising kids."

Warmth spread through her veins, and she couldn't look away from his gaze. Had she ever felt such an instant connection to a man? Even the colors of his voice made her think of safety. And family. She remembered her father's military bearing. He'd been in the service when he and her mother met and had never lost the posture. Maybe that was why she was so drawn to Michael.

Glancing around the room, she realized Jordan's bedroom was the exact shade of the room where Gracie grew up. And the gray-green of the living room matched her father's den at home. There was danger in trying to re-create a lost life, but staring into Michael's blue eyes, she wished she could.

5

ACTIVITY BUZZED AROUND MICHAEL. PRINTERS HUMMED, AND OTHER library patrons talked in low voices. The kids were at story hour, but he'd promised them a canoe ride and picnic afterward. After two days of painting, he was ready for some R & R.

He only had a few minutes before Gracie returned and he collected the kids. She was out getting the food together. She'd been different toward him after their talk in the attic yesterday, and he meant to find out why. He tuned out the dim babble and launched a Web browser. He typed in "Gracie Lister wedding" and hit enter. The first link was to a newspaper in San Diego. Gracie's face smiled at Michael from the computer screen. He studied the face of the man next to her. The engagement announcement identified him as Cid Ortega. A Border Patrol agent. Michael raised his brows.

He pulled out his phone, then dropped it back into his pocket. It wasn't his place to find the guy's number and call him. Gracie had her reasons for running. A man might be a saint at his job and a devil to his family. Michael had seen it plenty of times. Her personal life was none of his business.

A movement beside him made him look up. "I've got our lunch ready."

He quickly closed the browser and prayed she hadn't seen what he was looking up. "Ready to go?" When he leaped to his feet, he nearly knocked over his chair.

She fell into step beside him. "I got sub sandwiches, chips, fruit, and juice. And pie."

"Sounds like a feast."

"What's our plan?"

"We'll head to the river and put in at the Santa Elena trailhead, then paddle to Fern Canyon and have our picnic there. I thought the kids would enjoy looking for rocks. Maybe Jordan can find some insects." He pretended not to see Gracie shudder. At least there was no suspicion in her face. The angle must have been wrong for her to see the screen.

He collected the kids and ushered them out to the truck. A trailer bearing the canoe was hitched behind it. Driving along the Ross Maxwell Scenic Drive, he stole an occasional glimpse of Gracie's rapt face. The road wound through switchbacks, then descended toward the Rio Grande. The towering cliff walls left him speechless every time he saw them.

When they reached the river, he parked. The kids piled out of the back and ran toward the water. "Wait for us," he called. "And watch where you step. There might be rattlers. And don't get in the water yet," he called sternly.

Jordan's voice floated back to him, then the kids turned and stood where they were. "We're not babies, Dad."

"We'll only be a minute." He began to loosen the restraints on the canoe. "You want to help me with this?" he asked Gracie. He lifted the expedition canoe overhead, his hands on either side.

Gracie did the same, but she stumbled as she helped him carry it to the water. The kids ran just ahead of them. "Stop right there," he called when they neared the water. The kids groaned but waited until he and Gracie reached the river.

He stared at the placid surface. "Let's flip it into the river. On the count of three." He counted it off, and they heaved the canoe into the water. It bobbed in the gentle current. "I'm going to need your help maneuvering the canoe. The kids are too young to help." He noticed her wince. "Are you limping?"

"I had a rock in my flip-flop." She stood back from the shore the minute they tipped the boat into the river. "It looks deep."

He studied her averted face. Her cheeks had lost their color. "I think I hear fear in your voice. You're afraid of drowning?"

"No, but I'm worried about the kids," she said, never taking her eyes off of them.

"You ever go canoeing?"

"No." A flush colored her pale skin. "It looks easy to tip."

"The water is low right now. It's not more than chest high in any spot we'll go through. This is a good place for them to learn to canoe."

Her gaze went to the children. "They're awfully young."

"I'll teach them all about it. It's not hard."

Her smile was forced. "I hope you have life jackets."

"Of course. They're in the back of the truck."

"I'll get them." She rushed back to the truck and returned a few moments later with the cooler and a cloth bag, which she held by the drawstring. She set down the cooler and called the kids to her, then began to smear sunscreen on them.

When all three children were greasy, she stood and approached him. "You're next," she said.

"I don't like to be greasy. Besides, I've been in Iraq. I don't need sunscreen."

"Yes, you do." She squeezed a generous amount into her hand and slapped it on the skin of his upper back exposed by his tank top. "You're not even tanned here."

The touch of her hand on his overheated back was cool, but a jolt he couldn't explain went through him. He couldn't remember the last time a woman had touched him, even impersonally. All his objections left his tongue, and he stood mutely as she applied the lotion.

"Now me," she said. She handed him the lotion and turned her back to him.

He stared at the bottle, then at the smooth skin on the exposed portion of her back. He poured a liberal amount in his palm and rubbed his hands together, then spread it across the top of her back and shoulders. The warmth of her skin heated his palms, and the scent of vanilla wafted up from her smooth back. He nearly dropped the bottle in his haste to hand it back to her and step away.

"Thanks." She spread more over her legs, arms, and chest.

He found it nearly impossible not to watch. "Let's go," he said.

The kids squealed and dashed through the shallow water to the canoe. "Wait for me," he called. "You'll tip it. Life jackets."

He grabbed up the life jackets and paddles. Jordan and Hope had claimed the middle seat. Evan was on the seat in the bow. Michael sloshed through the water in his tennis shoes. The water was warmer than he'd expected. He cinched the kids into their gear, then directed Evan and Hope onto the floor to balance the weight.

"On the way back, you can sit on the seat," he promised Hope. He motioned to Gracie, who stood on the bank. She waded out to meet him. "Here's your life vest," he said, helping her slip it on.

She eyed the swaying boat. "How do I get in without tipping it?"

He led her to the stern. "I'll help you." He steadied the canoe with one hand and assisted her into her seat with the other. The kids shrieked with excitement when the canoe rocked as she awkwardly clambered onto the seat. "This will be the easiest place for you to ride. All I need you to do is use your paddle as a rudder. I'll do the paddling, and when I say left or right, that's the direction I want you to steer us." He showed her how to drag her paddle in the water to make the boat turn. "We'll practice."

She glanced at the children. "What if I make us tip over?"

"You won't. And even if we tip, all we have to do is stand up. The water won't be over any of our heads." He found he was relishing a day spent in her company.

EVERY TIME THE CANOE ROCKED, GRACIE WAS SURE THEY'D END UP IN THE water, but Michael handled the canoe with expertise. The kids sat quietly and watched the towering walls of Santa Elena Canyon glide by. The pink, blue-gray, and tan walls stretched from the river to the heavens. It was a place one could almost hear the whispers of God.

Gracie shook off the thought. Over five years ago, she'd come to grips with the realization that God was through with her, so why was she dwelling on him again? The problem was this solitude. She missed the hustle and bustle of the city and the demands of her job to keep her regrets at bay.

Hope leaned her head against Gracie's knee. "I have to potty," she whispered.

Jordan turned around to look, and the canoe rocked. "Me too."

"Try to sit still, girls." Gracie grabbed at her daughter when the boat rocked again. "How much farther?" she called to Michael.

"Almost there. Just around the bend." He bent to paddle faster.

A few minutes later, he called for her to turn in to the tributary. The limestone pebbles covering the bed of the river shimmered in the sunlight. Ferns grew along the boulders. "Here we are. Time for lunch and a swim." He leaped from the canoe and steadied it. "All ashore."

"Me first!" Jordan stood and the canoe nearly capsized.

"Steady," Michael warned. He grabbed his daughter around the waist and lifted her from the vessel, then did the same to the other children. "Your turn," he said to Gracie.

Gracie was sure she'd tip the boat and make a fool of herself. Their lunch would end up soaked and it would be her fault. The hard bench bit into the backs of her thighs, and she gripped the sides of the canoe so tightly, she couldn't feel her fingers anymore. "I'll capsize it."

He swished through the water and leaned in close. "I'll lift you out."

At least he wasn't mocking her. His blue eyes held a confident smile. The canoe rocked a bit in the current, and she wanted out of the boat in the worst way. "Don't drop me."

"I wouldn't think of it." His grave gaze held hers. He held out his hands. "Come on, honey. There's nothing to it. And if we tip the boat, it's no big deal."

Hearing an endearment like that on his lips touched her in a way she couldn't explain. She knew he didn't mean anything by it, but a warm sensation spread from her chest. The boat rocked violently when she stood, but he scooped her from the canoe and carried her to the shore. Not even her feet got wet.

He set her down on the rocks. "Better now?"

"Thank you." She watched him beach the boat. Once her pulse slowed, she went to help him. "I'll take the bag," she said. It held swimsuits, dry clothes in a plastic bag, suntan lotion, and first-aid supplies.

"Hey, Daddy, there's a pool," Evan called.

Small rocks slid away beneath Gracie's flip-flops as she followed Michael up a trail to the pool at the base of the cliffs. She led the children to a discreet place to potty, then used the small shovel she brought to cover the area. She helped the children change into their suits, then stretched herself out on a rock while they splashed in the shallow pool.

She glanced up to find Michael's blue eyes focused on her. "I feel like a lizard in the sun," she told him.

"Prettiest lizard I ever saw," he said, smiling. "You're doing a great job with the kids, Gracie. With the household. Everything runs like a jackrabbit across the desert. Finding you at the depot is the best thing that ever happened to me and the kids."

Warmth spread up her neck. Hopefully he'd think the heat on her face was from the sun. "It's been good for me and Hope too. We'd be sleeping on a park bench if not for you, Michael. I can never repay you for what you've done for us."

"It's a win-win situation," he said, grinning. "I'm going to change into my trunks and join the kids." He grabbed his suit from the bag and disappeared into the designated dressing area.

Jordan came dripping out of the pond. She flung herself down beside Gracie, then flopped onto her back and threw her left arm over her eyes. "I want to go home," she said, her voice breaking on a sob.

Gracie rubbed the little girl's arm. "I thought you were having fun, honey," she said. "Are you hungry? We can eat anytime."

Jordan shook her head. "The last time we were here, Mommy was with us. She used goggles and tickled my legs underwater. She braided my hair with ferns. I miss her." Tears leaked from under her arm and rolled down her cheek.

Gracie scooted up beside Jordan so she could cuddle the little girl, spoon-fashion. "I'm sorry, Jordan. I know your mommy wishes she were here. She didn't want to leave you."

"Yes, she did," Jordan said in a desolate voice. "She wanted to go to the movies with Daniel. She wouldn't let me go with her, and I cried. She cried too. Maybe she didn't see the truck coming. It was my fault." She rolled away from Gracie and began to sob.

Gracie hugged the little girl's back tight against her chest and kissed the wet cheeks. "It's okay to cry, honey," she whispered. "I know it hurts to lose your mommy." Her throat swelled and memories slammed into her. Visions of her own mother lying in a pool of blood. "It's not your fault though, Jordan."

Gracie wished she could say the same about her own mother's death.

6

MOONLIGHT BRIGHT ENOUGH TO CAST SHADOWS STREAMED THROUGH Gracie's window. Every muscle ached, and she stretched her legs out to enjoy the cool touch of the cotton. Downstairs, the TV rumbled. How could Michael stay awake after a day of canoeing? After the weekend he would start work. She'd be on her own here. She was going to miss him. Getting close to him so fast was a mistake she recognized but was unable to abort.

She should be sleepy, but the day had brought back too many memories. Maybe she should read. She flipped on the light and grabbed the novel on her bed table. She flipped to the dog-eared page, but before she read the first sentence, her cell phone jangled beside her. Fumbling to turn it off before the noise woke the kids, she realized it was a multimedia text message, not a call, from a number she didn't recognize.

She flipped it open and called up the message. A picture filled the screen. It was of her and Hope at the park last summer. They both wore happy grins. The message attached to it read, "Come home, Gracie. I miss you so much. We belong together."

She deleted it. Though maybe she owed Cid an explanation, his calls gave her the creeps. Her inability to read motives had nearly led her to a mistake that would have impacted Hope in terrible ways. Her daughter was all that mattered.

A rap sounded on her door. "Come in," she called, dropping the phone onto the bed.

Michael's form filled the doorway. "I thought I heard your phone. Is everything okay?"

"Just fine," she said with a smile. The air thickened between them. The day had been so good, and she hated the suspicion that simmered like water about to boil. "Thanks for making the day so fun."

He smiled then, and the fog lifted. She pointed to the chair. "Sit down a minute. I need to talk to you about something." When he nodded, she realized he thought she wanted to unburden herself about the phone call. "It's not about me," she said. "It's Jordan. And Evan too, though he's hiding it better."

He settled on the chair in the corner, then she kicked her way out of the covers and perched on the edge of the bed. "Jordan is taking her mother's death hard. They argued the night Kate died, and Jordan's worried the upset caused the accident. Guilt like that is hard to get past."

"She'd never mentioned it to me," he said.

"Swimming today reminded her of her mother. The last time they were there, Kate was with them."

"I remember that day," he said. "It wasn't as idyllic as Jordan remembers."

"I tried to comfort her, but you might do a better job. You're her daddy. A little girl needs her daddy. No one is as big and strong as you in her eyes." She choked over the words and cursed her weakness. This wasn't about her—it was about Jordan.

"I know so little about raising kids," he said. "I'm used to commanding men."

"Kids are these little creatures packed with emotion. You never know if they're going to laugh or cry."

"Maybe that's it."

Questions hovered on her tongue, but none of them was any of her business. He was her employer, nothing more. "You're a good father and always try to do the right thing by them."

He smiled then, but just barely. "What is the right thing? It's hard to know. I want them to be good citizens."

"You love them too," she said. She didn't doubt it. "It's not just your responsibilities that drive you to rear them right."

"Kate always said I kissed her like it was one more thing to check off my list." He shook his head. "Sorry, that was out of line. You're not interested in my personal issues."

She found she was more than interested. And it needed to stop. "I'm sorry." She forced an air of finality into her voice. Maybe he'd take the hint and leave.

He leaned forward. "I can talk to you, Gracie. Why is that? I've wondered about that all day."

"I'm nothing special," she whispered.

"You are. Maybe it's the way you listen so intently. You take in everything around you."

"I like listening to your voice," she said, unable to hold the words back.

He looked down at his hands. "This might anger you, but I looked you up on the Internet today."

It would all come out now. The whole sordid mess. She should have expected this. Yesterday she'd avoided his questions. He wasn't one to let a puzzle go unsolved. That gaze of his was too keen and penetrating.

"And did you find out enough to send me packing?" she asked in a choked voice.

"All I found out was that your ex-fiancé is a Border Patrol agent. You came back before I saw anything more. Is there anything else you want to tell me?"

"N-no," she whispered, fighting the despair rising in her chest. He'd find out everything the very next time he looked her up. Then she and Hope would be on the streets.

"I've known of plenty seemingly good men who smack around their wives or girlfriends. I'm not judging you for running, but did you even explain to your fiancé why?"

She shook her head and clamped her trembling lips together.

He leaned forward. "Who are you really, Gracie? You're like shale. For every layer that slides off, there's another one under it."

"I'm just me. A single mom who wants the best for her daughter."

He shrugged. "You've been here a week, and the only thing I know about you is that you are good with kids, you see colors in sound, and you know how to decorate rooms."

She forced a smile. "Isn't that enough weirdness to last a lifetime?"

He shook his head. "I have no idea where you grew up or if your parents are still alive. I don't know how you came to have Hope or how you've managed to raise her alone. I don't know what made you run off on the day of your wedding without any of your belongings. It's all a blank."

"A dull and boring story you've likely heard a million times."

"Most women talk all the time, but you sit and watch more than you speak."

She couldn't take the intensity in his eyes and glanced down at her feet dangling from the edge of the bed. "I'm your employee. We're hardly friends."

"I'd like to think we could be friends and still maintain a professional relationship. There's no servant-master hierarchy here in West Texas. A man or woman is judged by character."

Please, please leave me alone. No more questions. "I thought the West had the reputation for not probing," she whispered. "For letting people be who they are now rather than who they used to be."

"Is that what you want? A clean slate?"

"Yes," she said, finally holding his gaze.

He rose from the chair. "Fair enough. If you ever want to talk, I'll listen. But no more questions."

He might not question her, but she knew he'd keep digging. And she'd have to confess it all.

ON MONDAY, THE LAST THING MICHAEL WANTED WAS TO LEAVE HIS WAIL-ing children on the front porch with Gracie, but he was already late for his first meeting with the Border Patrol. Dressed in his camouflage uniform, he hugged the kids and promised to be back, then rushed to the truck and drove to headquarters in Presidio.

The sleepy town hadn't changed in the years he'd been away. He parked outside the small stucco building and trod the boardwalk to the open front door. The temperature already hovered near a hundred on this sunny August day.

A man in a Border Patrol uniform picked desultorily through a filing cabinet and barely looked up when Michael stepped in. "Good morning. I'm here to see Chief Patrol Officer Lanny Pickens," Michael told him.

The portly man straightened and turned to face him. Blue eyes looked out from under shaggy white hair and brows, though his face bore no lines of advanced age. "That'd be me, soldier."

Only then did Michael see the two stars on the man's collar. Numerous awards decorated his uniform as well. "Sorry." He saluted. "Lieutenant Wayne with the army reporting, sir."

The man swept a thatch of white hair from his forehead. "Welcome to the circus, Lieutenant. Your unit is set over just north of Terlingua. If you decide to join them."

"Why wouldn't I? I want to be here."

"If I were you, I might hightail it back to civilization. Or Iraq."

"Is there a problem?"

"If having a price on your head is a problem, then yeah, there's a problem." He pulled out his desk chair and settled into it. "Have a seat. Coffee?"

Michael had tasted enough stale office coffee over the years. "No thanks. What's happening?"

Pickens flipped a pencil around in his fingers. "When it got out that you were returning home, we heard rumblings of a price on your head. Vargas has offered to pay twenty thousand dollars to the man who kills you."

"Vargas. As in the man who killed my brother?"

Pickens nodded. "He's a snake. Kills without compunction."

A flash of his children's faces gave Michael pause. What would happen to them if he was killed? There was no family left to look out for them. "Why would he want to kill me? I haven't been back here in years. Does he think I'll seek revenge for Phil's death?"

"It was Phil's fault his two brothers were killed, so to Vargas it's justice to take out Phil's brother."

Michael blocked the familiar pain. Phil had died six months ago in a car accident. Prior to that, he had stopped a large shipment of arms from passing through to Mexico. In the fracas, several men were killed, including the brothers of the kingpin, Lazaro Vargas. Vargas himself was still behind bars.

He marshaled this thoughts. "Phil's dead. Isn't that enough for Vargas?"

"Not to that madman. You'll need to watch your back."

"I always do. What's happening in the field right now?"

Pickens stepped to a large map of the Big Bend area and stabbed a meaty finger at the Rio Grande. "Normally we deal with illegals crossing the river for jobs, or smuggling marijuana. But this is bigger. We thought they were coming across right by El Paso, then an agent saw two men on horseback cross here."

"Drugs?" Michael asked.

Pickens stabbed a point farther to the west. "We're pretty sure last time they brought in over ten million in cocaine. Your unit is here." He pointed to a spot by the river. "They've got an observation post set up."

Michael whistled softly. "I was told they might be bribing someone on this side."

Pickens shrugged. "I'm not convinced about that, but we do know this is likely only a part of what's coming through. It's our job to jam the pipeline."

"Where do you want me?"

"With your knowledge of the area, I've asked for you to be on mounted sentry duty. You'll need a horse. Bailey out at Bluebird Ranch has offered to let you pick any of his rehabilitated stock. Take a gander at them and get one with stamina. You'll need one by next week."

Michael nodded. "Good of Rick to offer."

His boss studied Michael's face. "Let's get something clear, Lieutenant. I heard you requested this duty, and that you're planning on taking Border Patrol training and staying here permanently. If you've come back to the area to avenge your brother's death, you can turn around and leave. I'll not have a vigilante on my team."

Michael kept his face stiff. "I'm not out for revenge."

"You're sure?"

Michael's muscles tensed. "Look, sir, this is my job, nothing more. I'm here to bring criminals to justice."

Pickens's large mustache twitched. "Your brother had a lot of passion for his work and believed in the importance of protecting our borders. You don't share that passion?"

Did he? Michael hadn't thought of it in those terms. "I believe in following orders. In doing my duty."

"Without emotion?"

"Emotion can keep me from thinking clearly, so I never let it get in the way." Michael shrugged. "It's what I'm trained to do. If my commander tells me to apprehend terrorists who are strapping bombs to kids in Baghdad, that's what I'll do. If you need me to stop drug traffic, I'll be Johnny-on-the-spot."

"Good. I thought it best to clear the air. Finding your brother's killer is not your job. It's mine." Pickens's teeth showed briefly in a smile under his mustache.

Michael kept any expression from his face. "Of course."

"With that out of the way, I'll be glad to have you on my team after your training. Oh, and I've got a surprise for you."

Michael rose from his chair and stood at attention. Maybe a superior officer was in the building. Pickens entered a door behind them and returned a few moments later with a leash. Michael gasped when he glanced from his boss's hand to the pooch trotting behind him. "Caesar!"

The black lab's head came up, and he lunged toward Michael. Pickens dropped the leash and let the dog go. Michael fell to his knees as the dog leaped against his chest and showered him with wet kisses. He hugged Caesar and inhaled the good scent of clean dog. Caesar's coat was like fine silk under his fingers.

"I didn't think I'd ever see you again, buddy. Last time I saw you was under a date palm tree in Iraq," he muttered. Leaving his dog had been harder than he'd expected. The two of them had been a team for three years. He roughed up Caesar's ears and the dog whined with pleasure.

"I thought you'd be pleased," Pickens said.

Michael glanced up to find Pickens wearing a grin nearly as big as the one stretching his own lips. "How'd this happen?"

Pickens shrugged. "If we're going to bust this drug ring, we need a good sniffer. Your commanding officer said this guy was the best and the two of you work like one. He arranged to send him over and had him wait here for you."

Michael kept his hand on the dog's head. "He's lost weight."

"He wouldn't eat much after you left. Your commander says he's yours."

"Mine?" Michael's smile widened.

"He's no good to the regiment without you. I hear that all he did was lie on the floor after you left. Wouldn't work with anyone else."

Michael had been nearly as inconsolable. "Thank you, sir," he managed to choke out.

"Don't thank me. Thank your commanding officer." Pickens glanced at his watch. "If we go now, I can introduce you to Phil's old partner. He'll take you out to your unit. Ready to get to work?"

"That's why I'm here." Michael followed him to the green SUV parked outside. He put the dog in the backseat, then hopped in beside Pickens. "Where we headed?"

"We located a crossing west of town. The last storm created a sandbar across the Rio Grande, and the coyotes found it."

"You have someone watching it?"

Pickens nodded. "Hector Estevez. He was Phil's partner. He's assessing how many have come through there so far and is going to give direction to your unit's watch station."

Michael watched the desert landscape zip past the window. He'd never thought to be living here again. They rolled through Bluebird Crossing, and it was like going through a time warp. The place hadn't changed at all, but he had. He was older and wiser, he hoped, the only one of his original family left now that Philip was gone. As they drove, he caught a glimpse of the old house on the outskirts of town where he'd grown up. It wasn't possible that his little brother was dead.

Pickens pulled off into the desert behind a parked SUV with the Border Patrol logo on the door. The other vehicle's front tires nearly touched the muddy water running past. A stocky man in his twenties squatted beside tire tracks. Another man in his forties stood watching.

"I'll leave you here," Pickens said. "I've got an important call coming in."

Michael nodded and got his dog out, then joined the men. Estevez glanced up when Michael joined him and asked, "You're Estevez? What'd you find?"

"Three trucks through here so far," Estevez said. "Loaded." He stood and looked Michael over. "You're Lieutenant Wayne? You have the look of Phil. I'm Special Operations Patrol Agent Estevez."

The guy was making sure Michael knew his rank. "I hear you were my brother's partner." He glanced at the other man, then extended his hand. "Lieutenant Wayne."

The man took it. "Senior Patrol Agent George Parker."

Estevez put his hands on his hips. "Let's get one thing straight right up front: I know you've got more decorations than a Christmas tree, but I'm the expert here. You need to listen twice as much as you talk for a while. This isn't Iraq. And you're on my turf. You National Guards are here in a supplementary position only. You're to do what I say when I say it."

Cocky kid. Michael could have him on the ground in two seconds. "Of course."

Estevez's lips tightened. "I just want to be clear who's in charge."

"We're clear," Michael said. He was used to taking orders, but this kid was still wet behind the ears. His irritation faded when he saw Caesar's ears go up. A low growl emanated from the dog's throat. "Someone's out there," he said. "Hit the ground!" Some sixth sense made him grab the kid and yank him down behind the SUV.

Estevez tried to shake off Michael's grip, but the first bullet pinged against the bumper. Both border agents drew their guns and returned fire as a volley of shells hit the vehicle. Michael pulled his revolver. He saw a flash of green and aimed at the movement, then fired. A man fell. He heard a shot, then the sound of an engine. Dust billowed from the tires of an old pickup that sped away.

A heavily accented male voice floated out the window. "Señor Wayne, you are a dead man."

He rose from his crouched position and followed Caesar to the fallen man, who lay behind an agave plant. He was dressed as a Mexican national, in his forties, and his sightless eyes stared at the glaring sun.

Vargas was wasting no time in trying to kill him.

7

A PACK OF COYOTES HOWLED IN THE DISTANCE. ANOTHER PACK ON THE other side of the canyon replied. Michael sat in the living room with his Bible in his hand. Only one light pushed back the night. The clock on the mantel read 11:00. After tossing and turning for half an hour, he'd finally gotten up and come downstairs. The nightmares that haunted him had little to do with the unseen faces of his enemies and much more to do with concrete fears.

He'd done the right thing all his life, and to the best of his ability. God should have honored his faithfulness, yet here he was with two motherless kids, an experience he'd sworn he'd never allow his children to go through. He leaned his head against the worn headrest on the chair. Once upon a time he'd thought serving his country and his

God would result in fulfillment and contentment. Then why did this ache still keep him awake?

The last four days on sentry duty had confirmed he stood directly in the line of fire. The man he'd shot and killed his first day out was part of the cartel that had killed his brother. Michael wasn't a man to second-guess his decisions, but he did now. What would happen to his kids if he died? At Michael's feet, Caesar raised his head. The floorboard creaked.

Gracie stood in the doorway. Her blond hair spilled onto the white robe she wore. She clutched the top of it closed at her neck. Her eyes were wide, and they went from him to the Bible in his hand, then back to his face. "I thought you were down here."

He put down the Bible. "Couldn't sleep either?"

She stepped into the room. "No."

"Problems with the kids this week with me gone?"

"No, they've been very good." She wet her lips and took another step. "I-I've got a problem."

He motioned to the sofa. "Sit down." At least she was going to share it with him. He hadn't figured her out yet. He liked her. She was great with the kids. But she held so much of herself back that he hadn't been able to get a handle on who she really was. When she walked past him, he caught a whiff of vanilla. The clean, light scent was like the mask she'd shown him so far. A plain, blank canvas. But he knew there was more underneath.

She arranged herself on the sofa so the oversized robe covered her fully. Her toes peeked out under the hem. Pale-pink polish adorned them. When Michael realized he was staring, he averted his gaze from her tiny feet, then tugged at the collar of his shirt.

"So what's the problem?" he asked.

She clasped her hands together in her lap. "We're enrolling the kids in school tomorrow, but I was thinking about homeschooling Hope. Do you suppose I could get an advance for books? I've been saving as much of my wages as I can, but with so many things to replace, it's not quite enough."

He frowned. "Why would you want to homeschool? The school in Bluebird is small and intimate. She'll get plenty of attention and can interact with other kids."

She looked down at her hands. "I-I just think it might be best."

"Best for her? Or for you? You don't have any experience teaching, do you?"

She cupped her face in her hands and sighed. "I can't enroll her in school. It's the records."

"Ah." He nodded. "I get it. Your fiancé might track her here. Is he that bad?"

She pleated the robe with her fingers. "It would ruin my life if he found me. I don't know what to do." Her voice cracked, and she cleared her throat before looking up at him. "What can I do to keep our whereabouts secret, Michael?"

His name on her lips shouldn't have made a blip in his pulse. The move, the reunion with his kids, and events on the job must have been more wearing than he'd expected. "Change her name maybe? I know the town lawyer. You could change both your names."

"But that will take a long time. What about school in the meantime?"

He rubbed his forehead. "I don't know. Let me talk to the principal in the morning. I have to enroll my two hoodlums too. You don't even have a birth certificate for her, do you?"

She shook her head. "It's not something I typically carry with me."

He grinned. "Stupid question, huh? If we can transfer her records from the old school, they'll have a copy of her birth certificate."

"But we have the same problem with tracking us here if the records are transferred."

He nodded before she finished. "Maybe homeschooling would be best for a week or so."

"A week or so? What will that gain me?"

"Then you could say you've been homeschooling her and could start from scratch. They'd have to test her, but we might be able to skate on the identity thing for a while. What books do you need? I'll get you some."

"If it's only for a short time, it's not worth buying them. I could get some books at the library in town."

"They could get whatever you need on interlibrary loan."

A smile, one that looked genuine, curved her lips. "Thanks. I'll leave you alone to your reading."

He wanted to tell her not to go—that he didn't want to be alone—but he kept his mouth shut and watched her rise and pad from the room in her bare feet. He should be used to his own company and that of other men. His stint in Iraq had taught him about self-sufficiency and the depth of his internal reserves, but there was something about a woman's presence that brought calm to a room. Not that he'd ever had much of it. He had no real memories of his mother, and his marriage had lasted only long enough to produce the kids. Kate wanted excitement and the constant stimulation of parties. He'd craved the peace found only at home with his family.

His thoughts went back to his dilemma. Who would care for the kids if the cartel was successful? A way out came to mind, but he wasn't sure he was that desperate.

THE SQUEALS OF CHILDREN AWAKENED GRACIE. THINKING SHE'D OVER-
slept, she bolted upright, then realized it was only seven. The kids were
up early. She stepped to the adjoining room and glanced at Hope's empty
cot, then grabbed her robe and threw open the door. The scent of cinnamon wafted on the air. Waffles? Rolls? Whatever it was, the aroma made
her tummy rumble. She'd only picked at her supper last night.

She followed the fragrance and found Michael in the kitchen with
all three children and the dog. Flour dusted their pajamas and their
hair. And the counter and the floor. Caesar's black fur had a dusting of
white. Even Michael had a swipe of it on his left cheek. Hope sprinkled
powdered sugar on waffles, and Jordan followed it up with cinnamon.
In heavy doses. No wonder Gracie could smell it from upstairs.

She rescued the waffles from the girls. "Smells good."

Jordan made a grab for the plate. "It needs more cinnamon."

"I think the next one needs it more." She slid another plate of waffles in front of her, then turned in time to stop Evan before he over-
flowed the glasses with orange juice.

"Thanks." Michael swiped at his forehead with the back of his
arm. "I thought this would be easier with the kids' help."

She smiled. "Maybe not easier, but more fun." It took a special sort
of guy to let kids play with sugar and cinnamon. Something more than
military discipline lurked beneath that close-cropped haircut. She had
the kitchen to rights in a few minutes, and the kids sat down to eat.

"Ew," Evan said. "It tastes funny." He spit the bite back onto his plate.

"Evan, that's rude," Michael said. He grabbed a paper towel and
scooped away the partially eaten bit. "You probably got one with too
much cinnamon."

"It's not my fault," Jordan said, raising her voice. "I put just enough
on it. He's being mean."

"Kids, your dad worked hard on breakfast. The least you could do is be grateful," Gracie said. She settled beside Hope.

Hope leaned over. "Mommy, it tastes funny. Salty."

Salty? Gracie cut a piece with her fork and tasted it. She nearly choked. "Um, Michael, did you use baking powder or baking soda?"

He shrugged. "I don't know. It's all the same, isn't it?"

"No." She laughed and went to the cupboard and pulled down the yellow box of baking soda. "Was it this you used?"

"Yeah, that's it. Baking soda. I had Evan help me and he got a little much in there, but I figured it would just help them rise more. Is something wrong?" He lifted a bite to his lips and tasted it, then grimaced before manfully swallowing it. "It's gross."

Jordan tasted it and spit it out. "Can I have cereal?"

Michael stood and began dumping the waffles. "Yeah. You need help?"

"Dad, I'm eight. I can fix my own cereal."

Gracie hid her smile behind her hand, but a giggle escaped that swelled when Michael glowered at her. He was pretty cute in that apron, but she wasn't about to say so.

"At least you let the kids help," she said. "How about an omelet?"

"Kick a man when he's down," he muttered, but he was smiling. "I was trying to save you work."

"And I appreciate it." She glanced at her watch. "We need to hurry if we want to get there before the line starts."

"I get to go to school," Hope chanted.

Gracie hadn't explained anything to her daughter yet. The tears would flow when Hope found out. She loved school. She exchanged a glance with Michael.

"I'll talk to the principal," he mouthed.

He stared at her for a long moment, and she wondered what that was all about. It was as if he'd seen her clearly for the first time. She couldn't quite make out his expression. Speculation? Distrust? She wished she had the courage to ask him.

"I'll fix the toast," Jordan offered.

"That would be great. Hope, you get out the jam and butter," Gracie said when she saw the frown gathering on her daughter's face. Hope wasn't used to having to share her mother's attention. "We can all help."

By the time they were ready to go to town an hour later, Gracie was limp from Jordan's tears over not being able to wear the shirt she wanted (in the laundry) and Evan's proclamation that his sneakers were too small. She'd managed to find him a pair that fit, but Jordan had to endure wearing a pink shirt she claimed she hated.

Once at the school, Michael disappeared to the principal's office with his two while Gracie took Hope to a bench outside to explain she couldn't go with the other kids yet.

"It's just for a little while," she told Hope. "We have to get some records transferred. We had to leave without them, remember?"

Tears rushed to Hope's eyes. "I want to go to kindergarten," she wailed. She hid her face in Gracie's lap. Caesar whined and licked Hope's cheek.

Gracie smoothed her daughter's soft curls. "I know, sweetheart. Maybe you and I can have some special time."

"Can we go see Betsy every day?"

"Betsy will be in school too."

Hope's face crumpled again, and Gracie wanted to cry herself. She hugged her daughter and promised they could bake cookies together and go for field trips to see the birds.

Michael exited the school with Evan and Jordan in tow. "Let's go to the library," Michael said. "We'll get you some books, Hope. Then your mommy can teach you at home for a little while."

"I want to go with the other kids." She hid her face against Gracie's leg.

Gracie exchanged a helpless glance with Michael. "How did it go?"

"We'll talk later. Come with me."

"What about Caesar?"

"I'll let him wait in the back of the truck. It's in the shade." He called the dog to him and told Caesar to stay in the truck.

The library was across the street from the school. The low-slung concrete-block building, its windows coated with reflecting film, hunkered on the rocky lot. She and the children followed his stiff shoulders up the walk and into the coolness of the building.

"What did the principal say?" she asked when she caught up with him outside the front door.

"I'm working on it."

There was something going on that she didn't understand. Michael's shoulders were tense under his camo. He stared at her as if he was trying to read her mind. Standing there with the sun heating her skin, she wanted to bolt. It wasn't that there was an air of menace between them. But what emotion hooded his eyes and tightened his mouth?

"Let's go," he said after a long moment of silence.

He walked toward the bank of computers along an inside wall. She took the kids to the children's section where story hour was going on, then wandered to a computer. After having been cut off from the world for two weeks, she longed to know what the papers had said about the agents' deaths. Michael wasn't at a computer like she'd expected. He was in a corner with a big guy in a cowboy hat, and the two huddled together in conversation.

She launched the browser and surfed to the *San Diego Union-Tribune*. There was nothing about the shooting on today's news, so she searched for Cid's name. Two articles appeared, and a sheen of perspiration broke out on her forehead. Her hand shook as her finger hovered over the mouse. Did she even want to read about him? She wet her lips and clicked the mouse to launch the article.

"Fiancée sought for information in shooting deaths," the headline proclaimed.

Gracie gasped, and Michael glanced over at her. She managed a smile, but she wanted to burst into tears. The Feds couldn't think she had anything to do with the murders. She quickly scanned the article. The dead agents had been found outside her home, and she had been seen fleeing the site in a wedding dress. The Feds were looking for her and Cid. She wanted to lean her head against the keyboard and wail.

Should she call the police in San Diego? If she did, they might be able to track her phone signal. Maybe she could write them a letter and send it to one of her clients to post for her in San Diego. She rubbed her forehead. This was more than she could deal with.

Would she and Hope have to flee this haven too?

8

THE FAN ABOVE MICHAEL'S HEAD BLEW WARM AIR INSTEAD OF COLD.
Wally Tatum's face grew more somber as Michael explained what was happening in his life.

The attorney scratched his chin. "So if the unthinkable happens and you're killed in the line of duty, the kids would be parceled out to foster care."

Michael nodded. "I don't even like hearing you say that."

"Anyone else you could ask to be their guardians?"

"There is no one," he said. "I've got friends, but you don't saddle friends with two kids to raise." Rick and Allie were busy helping disadvantaged kids, and they had their hands full. He couldn't ask this of them, not when he'd been out of touch with Rick until recently. And Allie was a new acquaintance.

"Army buddies?"

He shook his head. "They all have their own lives."

"I get it. You're someone who doesn't like to ask for help," he said. "Maybe you'd better be finding a wife."

Wally had brought it up first, not him. "I grew up motherless myself. I sure don't want that for my kids. What if I remarried and my wife adopted the kids?" Gracie's sweet smile flashed through his mind.

Wally grinned. "You holding out on me, son? Who's the lucky woman?"

"Hardly lucky," Michael said. "What if that happened? What about a new wife adopting them?"

"Then she'd be their legal mother. The state wouldn't take them either."

Just as he'd thought when the crazy idea first occurred to him last night. "The best thing for me to do is stay alive," he said with a grin.

"Might be easier said than done. You mentioned a price on your head."

"I'm careful."

"No matter how careful you are, it could happen. I always tell my clients to plan for the unthinkable."

"Yeah, I guess I'd better do that. Thanks, Wally. Send me your bill."

"Consider it a welcome-home gift." Wally clapped him on the shoulder, then strolled to the exit.

Michael glanced at Gracie. She sat hunched in front of the computer. He watched her chew her lip and study the screen as though it held the answer to all her problems.

He walked toward her, and she glanced up. "Ready?" he asked.

She nodded and jumped to her feet. The screen was still up on her computer as he neared. She reached down to close the window, but he saw the San Diego newspaper logo before it blinked off. She was looking up news back in San Diego, maybe checking on old friends. He took her elbow and she jumped. His fingers tightened, and he steered her toward the children's department. The kids were still listening to the story.

"How much longer?" he asked a library aide.

She glanced up at the big clock on the wall. "Another half an hour unless you want to take them."

"We'll let them stay." It would give him time to talk to Gracie alone. "I need to talk to you."

He guided her out the door. The creosote bushes by the front door gave off a pungent odor, and he saw her wrinkle her nose. He inhaled and let the aroma fill his lungs. The Chihuahuan Desert had a beauty found no other place.

Caesar greeted him with a woof and a concerned stare. The dog always knew when he was upset. Michael opened the truck door for her, then went around to his side. This probably wasn't going to go well.

The sun had already turned the cab into an oven, and he turned the air-conditioning to full blast. He swiped his forehead but knew the perspiration beading there had little to do with the heat.

"Everything okay?" Gracie's blue eyes held his gaze.

He liked looking at her. In spite of her problems, the stillness she pulled around herself calmed him. What he was about to suggest would help her, too, and that made it easier to bring up. "I've got a problem. I need your help."

Her smile came, a sweet curve. "Michael, you saved my life. There's nothing I wouldn't do for you."

He swallowed hard. "It's a lot to ask, Gracie."

"Tell me."

"I had a brother. Philip was two years younger than me. The Border Patrol was his life. He lived, ate, and slept his job."

"Sounds like someone else I know."

He shrugged. "Maybe. But I'm just doing my duty. Philip let his emotions get the best of him. He never could think things through dispassionately."

"He sounds like someone I'd like."

"He was a great guy." His eyes misted.

Gracie touched his hand. "Was?"

"He busted a big movement of drugs coming into the country. In the confrontation, two men in the drug cartel were killed. Both were brothers of the kingpin, who swore revenge on Phil. One night when he was on his way home, someone ran him off a curve up on King Mountain. He went over the edge and into the canyon. His truck burst into flames. There was no body left to recover."

He coughed at the lump that formed in his throat. Most days he never let himself imagine what Phil's final moments must have been like, knowing he was hurtling toward certain death. Clearing his throat, he forced himself back to the present. "It was a revenge killing."

She put her hand over his. "I'm so sorry, Michael." Her fingers tightened. "I know it hurts."

Had he ever felt a hand so soft? Or seen eyes such a clear shade of blue? And why did she draw him so strongly? She was nearly a stranger. No, not nearly. She *was* a stranger. "I shouldn't trust you, Gracie, but I do. Why is that?"

Moisture glistened in her eyes, and she withdrew her hand. "I'm nothing special," she muttered.

"Yes, you are." He reached over and took her hand again. "I think we can help each other."

Her eyes grew more tender. "I'd do anything I can to help you and your children, Michael. You rescued me when I had nowhere else to turn. I owe you."

"It's okay if you say no to what I'm about to ask." His voice faded away to nothing. Could he even choke out the words?

Her fingers tightened around his. "Ask me. I'll do anything."

"Vargas isn't content to have killed my brother. He's put a price on my head as well."

Her eyes dilated, and her lips parted. "Your kids have gone through so much. They can't lose you too. You should move far away where he can't find you."

"I don't run from trouble," he said.

"Maybe you should start!" The color leached from her cheeks, and her eyes seemed to fill her face.

"The thing is—if I die, my kids have no one. They'd go to foster care."

"No!" she muttered fiercely. "I'd care for them, Michael. I wouldn't let that happen."

It was the kind of reaction he'd hoped for. "Protective Services wouldn't let you without being approved."

She bit her lip. "I see. I could seek approval."

"I don't think it would be that easy, Gracie. You're trying to hide your identity." He knew he'd scored a hit when she bit her lip and withdrew her hand.

"What can I do, then?"

"We can help each other. You need a new name for Hope. I need a mother for my kids. I don't want them to grow up motherless. I hated coming home to an empty house."

Her hand crept to her mouth. "Wh-what are you saying?"

"I'm suggesting we marry." He took her hand again. "Separate bedrooms. I know we don't love each other, but I like you, Gracie."

Her fingers squeezed his. "I like you, Michael. More than I should."

He barely heard that last sentence, but it made him feel warm inside. "You're kind to the kids, and I think you will love them. I can love Hope too."

"I love Jordan and Evan already," she whispered.

"It's a good solution to our mutual problems. I can adopt Hope, and you can adopt my kids."

"You'd adopt her? Legally? Why would you do that, Michael? Take on responsibility for us that way?"

"It's a risk for you too," he reminded her. "You're taking on the care of two more kids, and not just temporarily."

"This would be . . . permanent?"

"Well, yeah, isn't marriage usually permanent?" He tried to smile and failed. "I'll be good to you and Hope, Gracie."

"I don't doubt that. It's just . . . I don't know what to do."

He forced enthusiasm into his voice. "You and Hope can start a brand-new life."

"We can enroll Hope as Hope Wayne instead of Lister. Get a different birth certificate," she said.

"It's a good solution, I think."

She quit trying to pull her hand away, but her eyes had widened. "It seems . . . extreme."

"It is. But the circumstances we're in are extreme too."

Her brows wrinkled. "I don't know, Michael."

"Think about it. But think fast. We don't have a lot of time if we want to hide that you're both here. And I have to be at work every day. Something could happen to me at any time."

"Why don't you quit, then? Get a different job. You don't have to be in the military or the Border Patrol."

"The military is all I know."

"You're smart. You could do anything."

Her words bolstered his hope. "My dad was a major in the Air Force, and he raised us to serve our country. Besides, Vargas's men can find me no matter where I go."

"But why? You've done nothing."

"He wants revenge. It's that simple."

"Why me?" she whispered. "You don't really know me."

"I can see your good heart, Gracie."

Those long lashes of hers fluttered fiercely. "I'm not what you think."

"No," he agreed. "You're more. We make a good team."

Her smile peeked out. "We do make a good team."

"I hate to ask anyone for anything, but you need me as much as I need you."

"Cid would never find us," she said.

He nodded. "It's mutually beneficial, and that's something I can live with." Better than a real marriage. He'd tried that once and failed. This seemed . . . safer somehow.

He saw the light come on in her expression, and she nodded. "Separate bedrooms?"

"Absolutely."

"Okay."

"I'll make the arrangements. I think we can do it today. The waiting period can be waived for me." There was no good explanation for the warmth that started in his belly and spread up to his heart. At least no reason that he'd admit to.

TWO WEEKS AGO, GRACIE WAS ABOUT TO MARRY ANOTHER MAN. NOW, HERE she was in jeans and a white blouse, about to say, "I do," to a man she barely knew. She must be crazy. No, not crazy. Desperate.

They'd dropped the kids off at Rick and Allie's. Michael thought it best to explain to them tonight when there would be time to deal with the questions. Her flip-flops slapped against the tile floor. The sound rose and bounced against the walls in a crescendo that brought a burst of red and gold to her vision.

Who ever heard of getting married in jeans and flip-flops? She glanced at Michael. Or jeans and a T-shirt? She wished for a nice summer dress and sandals at least. Michael strode along beside her with his shoulders squared like a man heading to the gallows with courage. Was that how he felt?

Michael's confident stride faltered as they neared the judge's chambers. "You're sure you're ready to do this?"

"I'd be lying if I said yes," she whispered. "But I think it's the best thing for our kids. I'm just scared."

"I'd rather face a sniper in the Iraqi desert," he said, grinning. "I know we're not starting in a normal way, Gracie, but I'll be good to you."

"You've already done more for me than any man I've met."

"I'm not a stingy man, and anything I have is yours. Just love my kids, that's all I ask."

"I already do," she said, searching his face. "I won't spend your money recklessly."

"Our money," he corrected. "You'll have a checkbook and ATM card. Money means nothing to me. All that matters is my family."

She could learn to love him. The realization made her knees sag. They could have it all—the family she'd always dreamed of. No, she didn't love him yet, but if she let herself . . .

He caught her by the hand. "You okay?"

"Ye-yes, I'm fine. Scared, like I said." She would *not* allow her emotions to get tangled up. She'd been that route before. Love made her vulnerable. This was an arrangement to help them both. They would be friends, but nothing more. That's all he wanted. And all she wanted, too, of course.

"Let's do it, then." He held open the door for her.

She entered into a cavernous room that smelled like it had been in existence for a hundred years. The ancient odor left the taste of something like tea on her tongue. The late-afternoon sun slanted through the window and touched the old but solid wood furniture. The black and white tile dated from another century. Faint music played. The delicate Chopin made her see pink crystals dancing in the air. A good sign maybe?

She'd never put much stock in her sixth sense, but maybe she should let herself believe.

A woman sat behind the desk. The bailiff stood nearby, pen in hand to sign as witness. The judge's shrewd gaze from behind steel-rimmed glasses caused Gracie to look away.

"Good to see you, Judge Thompson," Michael said. "It's been a long time."

"The last time you were in this courtroom, you'd been out tipping cows," the judge said, her voice severe. "At least you're a law-abiding citizen now."

Tipping cows? Not the Michael Gracie knew. What had happened to his life that stripped him of his fun-loving side?

The woman turned her attention to Gracie. "I'm Judge Julia Thompson. And you're the bride. Gracie Lister, is that right?"

"Yes, ma'am. Er, Judge."

"Are you both entering this agreement of your own free will?"

Gracie glanced at Michael. "Yes," she said.

"You bet," Michael said.

"Good." The judge turned to Michael first. "Michael, will you have this woman to be your wedded wife, to love her, comfort her, honor and keep her, and forsaking all others, keep you only unto her, for so long as you both shall live?"

Gracie hadn't been to a wedding in a long time. She'd forgotten what the couple promised. Oh, to be comforted and loved for her lifetime! That was only a dream, wasn't it? How could Michael even promise something like that?

"I will," he said in a steady voice.

"Gracie, will you have this man to be your wedded husband, to love him, comfort him, honor and keep him, and forsaking all others, keep you only unto him, so long as you both shall live?"

A knot lodged in her throat. What did she know about honoring this kind of sacred vow? She opened her mouth, but nothing came out.

"Gracie?" Michael asked in a whisper.

"I will," she said in a firm voice.

"Soldier, take your bride's hand."

Gracie clutched his hand like a life raft. Heart palpitations filled her chest. Maybe this was a mistake.

The judge's no-nonsense tone droned on. "Repeat after me: I, Michael, take you, Gracie, to be my wedded wife, to have and to hold, for better for worse, for richer for poorer, to love and to cherish, from this day forward."

Michael repeated the words, his voice steady.

Cherish. Had there ever been such a lovely word? Gracie's parents had cherished her once. Once upon a time, she thought God did too—until she couldn't think of him without shame. Until she didn't deserve anything from him.

She realized the judge was waiting for her to repeat the vows as well. "Sorry." Gracie managed to get through the vows by clinging to Michael's warm hand.

"Do you have a ring for the bride?"

Michael nodded and dug a plain gold band out of his pocket. He slipped it on her finger, and she thought she might suffocate. She had no ring for him. Nothing to give him. She was a pauper who would be on the street if not for him.

The cold band encased her finger, and she stared at it. The vows she'd just spoken mocked her. What did she know about any of this? She'd been running for years without taking time to develop real relationships. She was a poor judge of character—look at how Cid had blinded her.

"Do you have a ring for the groom?"

Gracie started to shake her head, but Michael slipped another ring into her hand. "Yes," she said, closing her fingers around it for a moment before she slipped it onto his finger. So that's where he'd gone right after lunch. To get rings.

"Inasmuch as Michael and Gracie have consented together in wedlock and have witnessed the same before this company, and pledged their vows to each other, by the authority vested in me by the State of Texas, I now pronounce you husband and wife." The judge smiled. "You may now kiss your bride."

Gracie looked up at her tall, handsome husband. Her gaze went to his firm lips, and her own parted. Michael took advantage of her unspoken invitation and leaned down. His warm breath touched her face, and she inhaled the scent of him, a scent that had attracted her from the moment she met him. His warm lips probed hers.

She wasn't quite certain about the sequence of events that followed. One second she was returning a chaste kiss, and the next she had pressed her lips to his in an ardent embrace and had her arms wrapped around his neck. The kiss heated the pit of her stomach and made her gasp for air. If she didn't know better, she would have said Michael was kissing her like he meant it.

She tore herself out of his arms. Heat flamed in her cheeks, and she didn't dare look at him. What must he think of her?

9

MICHAEL'S WEDDING RING CLUNKED AGAINST THE STEERING WHEEL OF HIS truck. He'd either made the biggest mistake of his life or . . . He couldn't finish the thought. His gaze slid to his bride, who sat pressed against the opposite door of the truck as if she might jump from the truck any minute.

"I . . . I'm sorry," he said.

She turned her head from the passing yucca and prickly pear cactus. "Sorry?"

"For the kiss." He cleared his throat. "I had no right to kiss you like that. You don't have to be afraid."

She straightened. "I'm not afraid."

He raised one brow at her. "So that's why you're about to bolt out the door?"

A slight chuckle escaped her lips. "I . . . I'm just not sure about what we did."

"It's a little late now," he said, his tone sharpening. "The marriage is legal and we've signed the papers to apply for adoption of the kids."

"I know." Her head fell back against the headrest. Caesar took advantage of her proximity and swiped his tongue across her cheek. She sat back up. "What's next?"

"We wait for Wally to call. The papers are signed, and he thought he could rush it through."

"How long?"

"Maybe just a couple of weeks. Judge Thompson will work with him."

"So you have to stay alive until then."

"Something like that. Would you be sorry if I died?" Her lips parted, and her eyes widened. "Scratch that," he said. "Stupid question."

"Yes, it was." She grabbed her purse and began to rummage through it with jerky movements. "I wouldn't have married you if I didn't think we could at least be friends, Michael. I'm not some kind of mercenary who marries for money or security. I thought this was going to be a partnership."

"I'm sorry," he said for the second time in two minutes. The kiss had changed everything. He'd thought he was doing this for clear, logical reasons. The way his memory kept returning to the softness of her lips had nothing to do with logic, though.

Her cell phone rang. She glanced at Michael, then laced her fingers together and looked away.

"Aren't you going to answer that?"

"No."

"Who has your number?"

"Just Cid and his family. One or two others."

"No friends?"

She shook her head. "I don't have many friends." The cell phone quit ringing.

"Hiding your head in the sand doesn't work. Isn't it better to know what he wants?"

"I'd rather not worry."

"How can you not worry if you have no idea what he might say? It's illogical."

"So I'm illogical. My life changed today. I've got enough to worry about without adding more."

"At least check your caller ID and see who it was."

"I'm sure it was Cid. And I don't want to talk to him. Not today."

He pressed his lips together and turned into the driveway that led back to the Bluebird Youth Ranch. Horses grazed on the other side of the fence. A particularly bony one caught his eye. "Looks like they've rescued a new horse," he said. The bay had sores on his rump and a long cut, probably from barbed wire, on his chest.

Gracie glanced at the horse, then looked away. "The poor thing."

"You don't like horses."

She fingered a scar on her forehead. "I haven't been on one since I was thrown at twenty."

"You shouldn't let fear rule you."

Her hands trembled, and she clenched them together. "I . . . I'm not a child, Michael. I've been running my own life without suggestions from you for quite a few years." She inhaled quickly. "I'm sorry. I shouldn't have raised my voice."

Did she really think she was doing a great job of running her life? Had she forgotten he found her fainting from lack of food? He knew he should back off, but the words wouldn't stay locked behind his teeth.

"Is that why you were on the run with no money to your name and no way to care for your daughter?"

Her head came up. Her cheeks colored. "I guess I deserved that."

He rubbed his head. "No. No, you didn't. Strike that remark. I have no room to throw stones. Not with my track record of failure in my first marriage."

"You sound like you have regrets."

He gave her a wry glance. "I guess it was hard on her—my being deployed so long."

The wariness in her eyes ebbed. "It was no less hard for you."

"We were so young." He raked his hand through his hair. "I'm not sure she knew what being a soldier's wife meant. It seemed adventurous at the time."

"Then reality set in. For both of you."

"Exactly."

"Did you fight a lot?"

"Yeah." He shrugged. "She knew I loved her, but she didn't respect the sacrifices I was making—for our country, for the kids, for her."

"Did you think of her sacrifices? I'm sure she wanted to be with you. You were her partner, the man she loved."

He scowled at her. "I gave her everything to make up for that, Gracie. I was the one in the line of fire every day. She didn't respect that."

Gracie nodded. "She had an affair, didn't she?"

"Yep," he said hoarsely. "I don't like to think about it."

Her gaze held his. "I won't do that, Michael."

He wished he could read the intensity in her eyes. "I never thought you would."

Her eyes darkened, and she opened the door without saying more. Had he offended her in some way? Michael sat behind the wheel, breathing heavily. He'd blamed Kate for three years, but what role had his job played in the failure of his marriage? Surely he'd done everything he could to make her happy. If he was out of town, he sent flowers on her birthday and their anniversary. He wrote to her every day when he was stationed overseas. He called at every opportunity. When duty called, he made sure he answered. Wasn't that what a man was supposed to do?

Now, he wasn't so sure.

GRACIE STOPPED TO EMPTY HER FLIP-FLOPS OF SAND. FOR JUST A MINUTE, she'd allowed herself to hope they might be a real family, but she wasn't sure Michael understood what being a husband was all about. Didn't he know a woman needed the man she loved to put her first? Not his job, not his country, but her. And to say he didn't think she'd have an affair—was it because he found her unattractive and thought other men would too?

She sighed. Hope was safe now. That was all that mattered.

Allie met her at the front porch. Dressed in jeans and a red shirt, Allie turned a fresh face toward Gracie. Her smile faltered. "What's wrong?" She watched Michael walk toward the paddock.

"Men are unfathomable."

"I was about to take feed to the horses. Come along and tell me about it."

Gracie fell into step beside her. "Where are the kids?"

"Rick took them with him to the back pasture. He was going to let them rope some particularly dangerous stumps."

Gracie smiled. "Are you always this calm?"

Allie smiled. "I can rant and rave with the best of them. So what did Michael do?"

Gracie paused to shake a rock from under her arch. "He dispenses advice like Pez candy. He's hardly led the perfect life himself. According to him, his divorce is all his ex-wife's fault. You'd think he'd at least admit he wasn't there for her."

"Rick said she ran off with a neighbor in El Paso when they were living there. The neighbor had a wife and son."

"I'm not condoning what she did, but no marriage breakup is solely one person's fault. I'd go crazy too if my husband was always off somewhere. It's clear to me that he put his job above his marriage."

They reached the barn door, and Allie paused. "I don't know him well. But I can see where Michael might tend toward being a crusader. That's something to appreciate about him, though. Not many men would have gone as far as he did to help you."

Gracie's ire began to ebb. "I'm grateful for that," she said. "I'm an adult. I have a brain."

Allie swung open the barn door. "So tell me about the wedding. And congratulations! I didn't get a chance to tell you I'm happy for you."

Gracie laughed. "You think I'm overreacting from wedding jitters, don't you?"

"I wouldn't judge that," Allie said primly, but she slid a sly glance Gracie's way, and both women laughed.

Gracie followed her into the barn. The strong scent of hay and horses took her back to the home where she'd grown up. The big two-story stucco house in the high desert outside Pecos, Texas, bloomed strong in her memory again, as vivid in her mind as this big barn. She stopped inside the doorway and watched the dust motes dance in the sunlight through the windows. Tack hung on the walls, and rough wooden paddocks divided the interior.

Her mother would be lying dead in the stall right there.

"I don't think I can go in," she managed to say before she backed away, then turned and bolted outside.

Allie followed her. "Gracie, what's wrong?"

Gracie ran from the barnyard out across the desert, her flip-flops kicking up sand behind her. She ran until she couldn't hear Allie calling anymore. She ran until her lungs caught fire, but she couldn't outrun the memories. Tears blurred her vision, and she didn't see the rock in her path. Her big toe struck it, then she was falling. She put out her hands to catch herself, and her left hand drove into a prickly pear cactus. The fiery sensation that enveloped her palm brought her to her senses.

She snatched her hand out of the cactus and rolled onto her back. Bright sunlight nearly blinded her, and the pungent scent of the creosote bush beside her helped anchor her even more. Tears rolled down her cheeks, and she cradled her left hand with her right. Everything hurt. A trickle of blood ran down her right leg, and her left knee ached.

Rocks crunched to her right, and she squinted up to see Michael running toward her. Just what she needed. Another lecture on how stupid she was. She choked back the sobs lodging in her throat and swiped the wetness from her cheeks with the back of her right hand.

Michael knelt beside her. "Let me see." His warm fingers closed over the wrist of her left hand. "You've got a ton of needles in here. I need to get you back to the house. Can you walk?"

"I think so." She allowed him to help her up. Her breath hitched in her chest with the need to cry.

He slipped his arm around her waist and helped her hobble back. "Did the horse scare you?"

"No. I . . . I just couldn't go in the barn. The last time . . ."

"The last time you were in a barn?"

She drew a deep breath. He'd opened up to her. Could she do less? "The horse that threw me killed my mother. I couldn't take the smell of the hay."

"I'm sorry. That's why you didn't want to talk about it before. You feel responsible?"

Her throat dammed a torrent of words. She couldn't swallow them down. Her gaze locked with Michael's, and she nodded miserably. "I knew Diablo was dangerous," she whispered. "I don't know why I climbed on him. It was stupid."

"You were a kid. Kids do stupid things."

"When Mom saw him bucking me, she ran to help. H-he trampled her." A boulder formed in her throat.

His hand tightened around her waist. "It wasn't your fault, Gracie. You were a scared kid."

She was still scared. That word pretty much summed up how she'd felt about her life ever since. All these years, and all she'd managed to do was keep putting one foot in front of the other. And what did she have to show for it? A life stuck in poverty and dependence on other people. On Michael.

GRACIE'S PALM STILL BURNED, THOUGH MICHAEL HAD REMOVED THE needles with duct tape. "Duct tape works for everything," he'd joked. His light banter kept her from thinking about how she told him what she'd never revealed to anyone else. What was there about her new husband that got under her skin and made her open up?

His big hand circled her calf as he cleaned her abrasions. Caesar pressed his warm body against her other leg. The heat of Michael's fingers should have relaxed her, but she sat on the edge of her seat and wished Allie were here instead of in the barn. She didn't want to be alone with her new husband.

She looked down on the top of his head. His short brown hair was thick with a slight wave. She wondered how it would feel. Coarse or fine? Like she'd ever know.

"There, all disinfected," he said, rising from the floor. "Does it still hurt?"

"I'll be fine." She kept her left palm turned up. The reddened skin throbbed, and she wished she could slow her pulse. If he'd step away from her, it might return to normal on its own. He stepped back, and she hastily rose. "I think I'll go outside and see if the kids are coming."

"I'll go with you."

Great. Couldn't he let her be for a while? He filled her head with cotton. Out on the porch, she inhaled the desert breeze, a mixture of sunshine, dust, and desert vegetation. The scent looked as green as new grass.

A pickup pulling a trailer caught her eye. Dust spewed from the truck's tires and from the trailer it pulled. She shaded her eyes and stared. The man behind the wheel wasn't familiar. The truck rolled to a stop, and the burly man inside got out. Caesar growled and lunged toward him.

"Easy boy," Michael said, grabbing the dog's collar. He exchanged a puzzled glance with Gracie.

The man strode to the trailer without speaking. A clang followed as he lowered the ramp and went inside. Moments later he reappeared, pulling the lead of a horse that looked like its next stop should be the pet food factory. The horse's hair was sorrel, though skin showed through in more places than she could count. Its head drooped and the bones of its back showed under the hide. The poor thing wobbled on its spindly legs.

Tugging on the lead, the man stalked toward the porch. He tied the lead to the porch rail. "Here's another horse for you. Bailey didn't want me to shoot it, so it's all yours." He spun on his heel and got back in his truck.

Gracie coughed at the dust the truck stirred up. She exchanged a glance with Michael. "Is that what people do? Just drop off horses that are nearly dead?"

"So I hear." Michael rubbed the blaze on the horse's face. "This poor boy hasn't had enough to eat for a long time."

Gracie took a step nearer. This horse looked enough like Diablo to be his son. Same white blaze, same black socks. If she dared to stroke him, he'd most likely bite off her fingers. The horse raised his head, and his dark eyes met hers. The misery in his eyes made her gasp.

"You poor thing," she whispered. This wasn't Diablo. This was an animal as mistreated as any she'd ever seen. She believed he knew as much about misery as she did. She wanted to take him home with her and help him. When she glanced at Michael, she found him glaring at the last trace of dust left by the truck.

"That guy should be prosecuted," he muttered. "This was a nice horse once. Good lines. Sweet temperament." He stroked the gelding's neck. "Easy, boy."

Gracie wished she had the courage to draw closer to the creature. "He might make a good horse for the kids," she said.

"And for you," Michael said. A slight smile lifted his lips. "How long since you've touched a horse? Since the one threw you?"

"Yes," she admitted.

"He's yours," Michael said.

She retreated a few feet. "I don't want a horse."

"It will be good for you."

"Rick might want him."

"Rick will just want him in a good home."

It took all her courage to hold his intent stare. Was he remembering the way he'd kissed her? She'd been able to think of little else. His gaze dropped to her lips, and she dropped her hand from the horse's neck.

"I . . . I'm afraid, Michael."

"I'll help you get over it. Would you deny the kids a horse?"

He always managed to back her into a corner. "They'll have to care for him."

"That's fine."

"I . . . I'll be right back," she said. "I'd better get my purse so we can load him up and get out of here."

She fled to the house. She wasn't up to the task of picking her way through this minefield of emotion. Her purse was in the kitchen. She splashed cold water on her face, then grabbed a paper towel and patted it dry. The shock of cold cleared her head. She stared out the window at Michael, still patting the horse. How could she go from total frustration with him to feeling she'd die on the spot if she didn't step into his embrace? She knew about physical attraction—that's what had gotten her into trouble in the first place. What she felt now was more, something deeper she didn't understand.

A beep sounded behind her, and she realized it was her cell phone indicating a message. Turning from the sink, she rooted through her purse and pulled out her cell phone. It was probably Cid again. She called up her voice mail. There were two messages.

At first she didn't recognize the voice, then it clicked. Sam Wheeler, Jason's dad. And Hope's grandpa. She hadn't heard from the family since Jason's death. How on earth did Sam get her number? She was so taken aback that she missed most of what he said, so she replayed the message.

"I know you're surprised to hear from me, Gracie, but I need to talk to you about Jason's estate. Please call me." He gave the number, then hung up.

Jason's estate? As far as she knew, the only money he had was what he'd spent of hers. His parents lived in an exclusive subdivision of Scottsdale on ten-plus acres. Her finger hovered over the keypad. If Hope had an inheritance coming, Gracie should call and find out about it. She shook her head. That family had only brought her heartache.

She called up the other message. "Miss Lister, this is Special Agent Adams. I need to talk to you about the murder of two federal agents that occurred outside your home. Please call me back." He rattled off the number and the message ended.

Gracie forced oxygen into her lungs. Should she call him back or keep trying to hide? She'd deal with it tomorrow, she decided.

"Everything okay?"

She turned to see Michael in the doorway. Her smile had to be forced, but it was the best she could offer. "I was just checking my messages. That phone call earlier? It was from Hope's grandfather."

"It's unusual to hear from him?"

"He's never even acknowledged her existence. I didn't think he knew about her. I'm not sure why he's calling now."

"What did the message say?"

She told him. "I don't want to get involved with that family again. Or let them influence Hope."

"I'll check him out."

Michael was one of those people who had to try to fix everything. She let herself hope he could fix her life too. Her right fingers twisted the ring on her left hand. Maybe he had already begun.

10

THE SCENTS OF SWEDISH MEATBALLS, SOME KIND OF MUSTARD-CRUSTED potato casserole, and limpa bread filled the worn kitchen. Michael hadn't been able to find lingonberry jam in the small grocery store, so Gracie settled for strawberry. The delicious aroma made him more ashamed of his abominable waffles this morning.

The kids were outside watching every move of the horse they'd named King, though Michael had never seen a horse more unworthy of the title. He'd warned them not to go on the other side of the fence, and though he trusted them, he kept an eye on their three small bodies through the window on the door. Evan especially could scramble under the fence in a heartbeat, and he feared nothing.

"What can I do to help?" Michael asked Gracie.

"You could get out the green beans and snap them," she said. "We'll be ready to eat in about half an hour."

"My least favorite job," he muttered.

A dimple flashed in her cheek. "You asked."

He smiled back. "And I'll do it. But I don't have to like it." With the microwavable bag in front of him, he sat at the kitchen table and began to snap the beans and put them in the bag. "Where'd you learn to cook like this?"

"My mom. She had all these great Swedish recipes. I used to think someday I'd open a café and serve all Swedish dishes. I found out that even in California, people like variety. But this is all I know how to cook. She never taught me how to make pot roast or fried chicken."

"I make a mean fried-chicken dish," he said. "I'll make it one night. You shouldn't have to do all the cooking."

"I like to cook. Maybe I'll buy a cookbook and figure out how to make something besides Swedish food," she said with her back to him.

What would she do if he stepped up behind her and pressed a kiss on the back of her neck? He rolled his eyes. Obviously, he'd been without a woman too long. It was crazy the direction his thoughts had taken ever since she put that ring on his finger. Somehow, he regarded her as *his*. No, strike that. It wasn't the ring. It was the kiss. He'd suddenly begun to see her as a woman. A very desirable woman. Testosterone—that's all it was. Any woman living here in his house would cause the same reaction.

Who was he kidding? Not even Kate had been able to draw his thoughts away from work for long. Now it would be a struggle to work on research after dinner, when he'd much rather sit and examine Gracie's thoughts.

"You okay with the name the kids gave your horse?" he asked.

She turned to face him. "King is cute." Her lips curved into a smile.

He stepped next to her and stuck out a thumb. "Lick," he said. Her eyes widened, and she gently touched her tongue to his thumb. He rubbed it against the sticky mark on her cheek. "Jam," he said. "I could have licked it off, but I thought you might slap me."

The smile lit her eyes. "I might have."

All he'd have to do was take one step, and she'd be in his arms. He forced himself to step back. She'd made her feelings pretty clear. "I can set the table," he said, working for an impersonal tone.

"Fine."

He glanced up at the bite in her voice. Her lips were in a firm line and she was stirring the sauce with a vengeance. What did he say? He gave a mental shrug. "We should redo this kitchen. I used to be pretty handy with a hammer. We could get the cabinets from Lowe's and install them one weekend."

"I think a kitchen redo will take more than a weekend." Her voice was still clipped.

"Are you mad about something?"

"I'm fine." She beat the sauce harder.

He put down the last plate and grabbed a handful of forks. Women. He might as well save his breath. "Should I call the kids?"

"I'll do it." She stepped past the table to the back door. "Kids, supper!" she called.

He watched her as she stood on the stoop and waited for them. The dying sun lit her hair and outlined her slim figure. Maybe she'd caught on that he was attracted to her and it had made her mad. It was going to be a long night.

The kids came barreling into the kitchen with Caesar on their heels. He pointed out the chairs for Evan and Jordan. Gracie and Hope sat across from them and he took the head of the table. Gracie brought the food.

"Ew, what's that?" Evan asked, wrinkling his nose. "It looks gross."

"Swedish meatballs!" Hope said. "You'll like it. It's my favorite."

"I wanted a hamburger," Evan said, folding his arms across his chest.

"You have to at least try it," Gracie said. She ladled up one meatball and a spoonful of the potato casserole.

"You're not the boss of me," he said. "I don't have to eat it, do I, Daddy?"

He nearly told the boy he would have to eat two as punishment for the back talk, but he saw the trepidation on Gracie's face. The kids had to know the truth. "Gracie *is* the boss of you, young man. Just as much as me. She worked hard on fixing a meal she thought you'd like."

"If I eat it, will you play Chutes and Ladders afterward?" Jordan put in.

He exchanged a long look with Gracie. "Kids, Gracie and I have something we need to talk to you about. It's a big surprise. When you're through eating, we'll tell you about it."

"Is it another horse?" Evan scooted his chair closer to the table and stuck a fork in the meatball. He licked it. "Hey, it's sweet." He took a tiny bite, then finished it off. "Can I have another one?"

Gracie's smile widened. "Sure. How many?"

"Three!" He pushed his plate to the bowl, then dug into the meatballs when she put them on his plate.

"Tell us the surprise, Daddy," Jordan begged. "Are we getting a puppy? You said we could have a puppy."

"I brought you Caesar. What more do you want?" He grinned when his dog flicked his ears at the mention of his name.

"I love Caesar, but he needs a son. Don't you, Caesar?" Jordan asked. The dog barked and pressed his muzzle against her leg.

"Eat your supper." At least the announcement defused the controversy over the food. He dived into his own plate of food. "This is really good," he mumbled past a mouthful.

"Thanks," she said, not looking at him.

When they were finished eating, the kids waited impatiently for Michael and Gracie to finish. He wasn't sure how to begin. They'd just lost their mother. Now he was going to tell them they had a new mother. That was the main gist of the message. Not that he had a new wife, but he'd just replaced their mother. He hadn't thought that through. Maybe they should wait awhile. He nearly told them the surprise was a trip to town for ice cream, but he knew only the truth would do. They were bound to hear it. This was a small town. A guy couldn't get married and not have the whole town know.

He scooped Evan onto his lap. "I want to tell you what Gracie and I did in town today."

"You got a puppy!" Jordan said, scooting off her chair. "Where is it?"

"No, not a puppy, honey. I've been worried about you kids. It's important for kids to have a mommy and a daddy."

"Our mommy died," Evan said in a tragic voice.

Michael hugged him. "Not on purpose, son. She didn't want to go. She loved you both very much. She would want you to be happy." He glanced at Gracie, who was sitting on the edge of her chair. Had she suspected it would be this hard?

"Where's the puppy?" Jordan demanded again.

"There's no puppy, honey. At least not yet. We'll get one soon. This is better than a puppy. Gracie and I were married today. She's going to adopt you kids and I'm going to adopt Hope. We're one family now. You have a new sister, and Hope has a brother and a sister."

The mouths of all three kids gaped. When the wailing began, he wanted to bolt from the room, but he forced himself to try to explain. No one was listening.

JORDAN DIDN'T LOOK UP WHEN MICHAEL ENTERED HER BEDROOM. SHE SAT cross-legged on the floor with a doll in her arms. Caesar lay beside her with his head on her knee. Her tearstained face turned away when he spoke her name. He knelt on the floor beside her. "You're acting like a baby, Jordan. I want you to stop this behavior."

Her face crumpled, and tears rolled down her cheeks. "I want *my* mommy. Not a pretend mommy."

"You like Miss Gracie. And you have a new sister."

Jordan rocked back and forth. "Mommy used to sing to me at night before I went to sleep. She always smelled so pretty. Like sunshine." Caesar whined and nudged her arm with his nose. She flung her arms around the dog's neck and wept harder.

He nearly told her to buck up, then closed his mouth. How would Gracie handle this? He softened his tone. "I'm sorry, sweetheart. If I could bring your mommy back, I would."

"You're glad she's dead!" She wailed even louder. "You don't love us. You always loved your job more than you loved us."

She'd heard those words from Kate. He squeezed his lids shut, then sighed and stared at his small daughter. "I love you more than anything, Jordan."

"Then why are you gone all the time?"

"Dads have to work so their kids have money for food. For your dolls and clothes. I can't just stay home or we wouldn't have a house to live in." He ran his hand along her hair. It was as soft as a kitten's coat.

She raised her head from Caesar's fur, then crawled onto Michael's lap. "Are you ever going to go away again, Daddy?" she asked, her voice forlorn.

He hugged her tight. "No, honey. I got a job here so I could come home to you every night. I married Gracie so you'd have a mommy to wash your clothes and braid your hair. Everything I do is for you."

"Promise?"

"Promise." He rocked her in his arms. Maybe it hadn't been true in the past, but he wanted it to be that way. He'd been too careless of how his children felt about his absence. Too worried about living up to his dad's expectations. His dad was gone now. Michael kissed her cheek. The salty taste of her tears pierced him with failure. It was possible to do better. Change his focus.

Gracie had helped him see that.

He rose with his daughter in his arms and carried her to bed. After tucking her under the sheet, he knelt by her bed and held her hand.

"You haven't prayed with us since we got here, Daddy. You used to."

"I'm slipping, aren't I?' Though he smiled down at her, a steel band encased his ribs. What a hypocrite he was. Trying to do right by everyone but his kids. "Is there anything special I should pray for?"

She nodded. "Pray for it not to hurt so much. And for Jesus to take care of Mommy." She clutched his hand.

If the band got any tighter, he wouldn't be able to pull in any oxygen. In a choked voice, he prayed for little Jordan and for Evan. For

Hope, too, and for him and Gracie to be the parents the children needed.

GRACIE TUCKED HER NOSE INTO HOPE'S SWEET-SMELLING NECK AND kissed the soft skin. She pulled away just enough to stare into her daughter's sleepy eyes. "Love you, punkin."

Her daughter twirled her fingers in Gracie's hair. "More than Jordan and Evan?" she asked.

Gracie tickled her neck with more kisses. "More than life itself. More than chocolate. More than peanut M&M's."

Hope giggled. "More than peanut-butter fudge?"

"More than a Dairy Queen Peanut Buster Parfait. You'll always be my special girl."

A contented smile hovered on Hope's lips. "I like having a brother and sister, but you're *my* mommy first."

"That's right. But we can all be a family. Loving them doesn't mean I love you less. Okay?"

"Okay," Hope said, her eyes beginning to drift shut.

Gracie tiptoed out of Hope's room and started toward hers, but she wasn't sleepy. The events of the day needed too much pondering. She went down the steps and slipped on her flip-flops. They were already crumbling from the rough stones. She would get more shoes when she got her next check. She gasped when she remembered Michael had said his money was hers, that she could just write a check for what she and Hope needed.

Not that she had the courage to do it. She was still very much the interloper here, no matter what Michael said.

Making sure the screen didn't slam behind her, she stepped onto the porch. On her way down the steps, she saw an animal lumber from under the structure and nearly screamed, but it was just an armadillo.

A whinny from the barn drew her across the yard. King nickered from the paddock as though he recognized her. She drew close to the fence, and he came to meet her. In the glare of the security light, she saw the sores on his back clearly.

"Did someone beat you, King?" She put her trembling hands behind her back, then reconsidered and stretched out a hand.

When he nuzzled her palm, she forced herself not to flinch. This poor baby wouldn't hurt her. Her scars weren't visible like his, but they existed nonetheless. She leaned on the fence and lifted her face to the breeze, fragrant with sage. A dog barked behind her, and she whirled to see Michael approaching with Caesar at his side.

"Hey, Gracie," he said when he reached her.

A weary droop to his shoulders made her step closer. "What's wrong?"

He propped a boot on the lowest rung of the fence. "Just realizing I've not been the man I'd hoped for my kids."

"Are we ever the parents we hope to be?"

"You don't have any trouble. I see you running to anticipate what they need before they ask. You never get ruffled or irritated with their questions. Or with Evan's boundless energy."

"It's all a front."

He raised his brows. "Really?"

She nodded. "It's like a coat I slip on. I act patient when I want to yell at them or be cheery when I want to cry."

He grinned. "I get it. Courage isn't being fearless. It's stepping out when I want to retreat."

"Half the time I'm terrified I'll say something that will warp them for life."

"You inspire me, though. I wanted to tell Jordan to grow up when she was sulking, but then I wondered what you'd do. It changed things."

Heat rushed to her cheeks. "You actually wondered what I'd do?"

A smile tugged at his lips. "Yep."

"I'm hardly a role model," she whispered, averting her gaze. If she didn't, she'd take two steps into his arms.

"You are to me."

The pleasure that flooded her chest was disproportionate to his words. She rubbed the gelding's nose again. Her fear was ebbing, at least her fear of this horse. "You fed King already, didn't you?"

"Yeah, but it wouldn't hurt to give him a bit more. I'm taking it slow with him."

She glanced back at the wounded animal. "Poor horse. He's been so mistreated."

"I don't understand a man who would treat a horse like this."

"That's because you are honorable," she said. She felt his quick glance but kept her attention focused on the horse. "You're all bound up in always doing the right thing. Do you ever want to let it all go and do what *you* want?"

"All I've ever wanted was to be a soldier."

"Why? What drew you to the military?"

He rubbed King's ears. "My dad, I guess. When I was growing up, he talked about the glory of serving your country."

"Men die that way."

"All men die eventually, but dying in the service of others—that's a death worth experiencing."

She shook her head. "Why chase death?"

"I don't. But when it comes, I want to know I made a difference. Dad said facing the knowledge he could be shot anytime made him appreciate every day all the more."

She clasped her arms around herself. "Seems a little wacky to me."

He turned his head and stared into her face. "Tonight I realized I hadn't talked to you about the most important thing I should have before we married. Jordan asked me to pray with her, and I never even asked if you're a Christian."

Heat burned its way up her neck and scorched her cheeks. "That's pretty personal, Michael."

He held up his hand with the wedding ring. "We just tied our lives together, even if it's in name only. I want my kids, including Hope, to know God loves them. Have you thought about faith at all?"

A mountain of memories lodged in her throat. "I grew up in the church," she managed to say.

"But not now?"

"Not in over five years."

"What happened?"

She tried to smile and failed. "Life. If you ask whether I believe in God—whether I'm a Christian—I'd say yes. But it's hard for me to pray after all I've done."

"You're talking about your mother now. That wasn't your fault."

She turned on him. "It *was* my fault! I see her face every time I look into Hope's eyes. She's the spitting image of my mom."

"I don't understand why you blame yourself so much."

"Mom would have loved her. She never got the chance to kiss Hope's cheeks or be called Grandma. I deprived her of that."

"It was an accident." He studied her face. "So why *did* you get on that horse?"

She closed her eyes. "I don't even remember."

His voice pushed her. "Or don't want to? What was happening in your life right then?"

"Too much." She clamped her jaw shut so tight it hurt. He didn't need to know. "Since then, God has blocked me from enjoying any happiness. Every time I think I've found a spot to settle, he closes the door."

"Maybe he's trying to tell you something."

"That I'm a failure? I already know that."

"What about your dad? Is he still alive?"

Hot tears blurred her vision. "As far as I know."

"Does he know what happened the day your mom died?"

She nodded. "I couldn't bear the condemnation on his face. I ran away that night."

"You haven't seen him since? Or talked to him?"

"No. Can we talk about something else?"

"You could go see him, Gracie. Air it all out."

"I can't," she whispered. "He hates me. I know it."

"Can you honestly say Hope could do anything to make you hate her?"

"That's different," she protested.

"I don't think so." His warm fingers closed around her arm. "You need to find some peace."

"It doesn't exist in my world." She turned and ran for the house, even though he called after her.

Easy enough for him to spout the platitudes. He'd done everything right. A coyote howled in the distance, and the sound brought a wave of red balls across her vision. Red was the color of guilt.

11

Grit coated Gracie's eyes. The weekend had been full of strife. It was nearly eleven before they got the children settled down last night. Then she'd spent another hour writing a letter to the FBI. She slid it inside an envelope addressed to her former boss at the day care, then put it in the mailbox by the road.

The bus had already come and gone with Jordan and Evan, who had little to say to her. Even the normally sunny Hope had picked at her breakfast until Gracie gave her the assignment of writing a page of her ABC's. Today should be better with the older kids in school and Michael at work. She had a list of things she wanted to do that would keep her mind busy. When Hope's lesson was over, Gracie was going to give this house a good scrubbing.

Hat in hand, Michael stepped into the doorway. "I need to pay the rent. Want to come along and meet the folks who own the house? I hear they have two girls about Hope's age. Might make good playmates."

Gracie glanced up. He hadn't slept any more than she had. "I thought I might clean house today."

He snapped a leash on Caesar. "I was planning to drop by Rick's afterward. He's giving me a horse and I thought you might help me pick it out. You know horses. Then I can drop you back here before I go to work."

She smiled. "Is this a ploy to help me face my fear?"

"Maybe I just like your company."

She laughed. "Now I know you're up to something."

He grinned. "It's been a rough weekend. There's strength in numbers."

Hope sprang to her feet. "I'll come!" She shoved her bare feet into small pink flip-flops that matched her shirt.

"Okay, we can finish your schoolwork later," Gracie said. She followed him and Hope to the front door, where she paused to slide into her flip-flops. Her knee was still sore from the fall, but the exercise would do her good.

"Where are we going, Daddy?" Hope asked.

Gracie saw Michael's eyes widen when Hope called him Daddy. They exchanged a smile.

"We're going to visit the people who own this house. They raise horses."

"Like they do at Bluebird Ranch?" Hope asked.

"Not exactly. These folks raise racehorses."

"Ooo." Hope clapped her hands.

The hot desert wind drove needles of sand against her bare legs.

The murky sky to the west hinted of a sandstorm. Gracie buckled Hope into the backseat, then popped a DVD into the player for her before getting in the front with Michael.

Her lips were chapped, and she rooted in her purse for her lip gloss. When she couldn't find it, she dumped the contents on the seat beside her. Ah, there it was. She glided on a coating of mint gloss, then began to put everything back in.

"What's that?" Michael asked, glancing at the small brown leather book in her hand.

Her fingers tightened around the worn binding. "My dad's New Testament." Storing it in her purse had battered it even more than her father's usage had. "He was a pastor." She unsnapped the testament, and it fell open to Luke 15.

He glanced down again. "The Prodigal Son a favorite of yours?"

She fingered the fine paper. "It was my dad's favorite passage of Scripture."

"We're all prodigals, really."

She studied his square jaw. "Not you. You're the good son who stayed home. Did his duty."

He winced. "That guy wasn't exactly the hero of the story, you know."

"Sure he was. He didn't hurt his dad." She swallowed past the rock in her throat. "I'm the real prodigal, I guess. But there's no home-coming for me." She laughed, then realized how bitter she sounded.

"You sound flippant about that."

"Not flippant, just resigned."

"There's always God. He's always there waiting."

She held up her hand. "Please, no sermon. I grew up sitting on the right side of the sanctuary in the second pew from the front. I've heard it all." Caesar whined and pressed his wet nose against her neck. She nearly leaped from her seat at the shock of cold. When she patted the dog, he whined in her ear, then lurched back to fall across Hope's lap.

"Let's change the subject." As she closed the testament, her gaze fell on the phrase "not worthy to be called your son." That summed up the sense of inadequacy she struggled with most days. *Not worthy.*

She had no problem seeing herself in the prodigal son, but she could never go back home. All the regret in the world wouldn't change how she'd broken her parents' hearts, or how her pride had killed her mother.

FOR THE REST OF THE TRIP, GRACIE DIDN'T SPEAK A WORD TO HIM. Michael glanced at her set jaw. Was she remembering her dad, or was she thinking of something else? "This is it," he said. The truck rolled through the gate.

Gracie gasped when they stopped. "Wow," she said.

Michael glanced over at her. "A little overwhelming, huh?" he said. "Jack's a nice guy, even if he is filthy rich." He couldn't remember much about Shannon, though he vaguely recalled a quiet blond girl with vivid blue eyes. He parked the truck in front of the circular driveway that swept past the grand porch columns.

"I think I'll wait here," Gracie said.

"I want you to meet them," he said. "And Hope will want to meet the girls."

"They'll be in school," she reminded him.

"Oh, right. Well, I still want to introduce you."

Before she could answer him, a woman stepped through the

front door and waved. Her blond hair just touched her shoulders, and she wore a smile that welcomed them in. She came down the steps toward the truck, and Gracie ran her window down as she approached.

"You must be Michael and Gracie," she said. "I'm Shannon MacGowan. Come on in. I've got fresh coffee all ready."

Gracie's smile emerged, and gazing around the grounds, she got out of the truck. "You've got some beautiful horses."

"Jack raises them. Aren't they gorgeous?"

Michael was looking at a particularly handsome black horse with white socks. "That's a real beauty. I'm on my way to Rick's to find one. I need one for my job."

Shannon smiled. "For Border Patrol? You don't need to go to Rick's. Take your pick. Jack would be glad to donate one to you."

Michael gaped. "We could pay you something for him. I'm not sure what the government budget is, but I can find out."

Shannon waved her hand. "Jack would want you to have him. That's Fabio."

Gracie laughed, and Michael realized he'd never heard her giggle before. She'd never let loose with full-on mirth. He didn't get what was so funny. "Fabio. Weird name." Both women burst into gales of laughter. "What's the joke?"

"Remind me to show you on Amazon who Fabio is," Gracie said. Her cheeks held pink now, and her blue eyes sparkled.

"I'm not sure I want to know."

"He won't answer to another name. Jack tried when he found out, uh, the truth." Shannon laughed again. "I named him because he's so gorgeous. He's a spoiled thing. Be prepared with lots of carrots."

Michael followed the women into the house. Hope stayed out to throw Caesar's Frisbee to the dog. Travertine tiles stretched down the hall. The place was a palace. "Nice digs," he said.

"No thanks to me. It was like this when I moved in a year ago." Shannon led them to the living room, which was furnished with comfortable sofas and chairs in warm colors. "Let me get you some coffee."

"I'll help." Gracie followed her.

Michael glanced around the room and saw pictures of two smiling girls. They were the spitting image of Shannon.

"Cute, aren't they?" Jack MacGowan stood in the doorway. Dressed in boots and jeans, he was the quintessential cowboy. Someone just meeting him would never suspect he controlled thousands of acres of ranch land and had more money in the bank than most people on Wall Street.

Michael rose and shook his hand. "Hey, Jack. Looks like marriage is treating you well."

Jack patted his stomach. "I'm not hurting for good food, though that's because we've got a great cook." He advanced into the room. "Shannon sent me in here to tell you that you can have Fabio. But forget about changing his name. He'll look the other way and ignore you."

"What's with the name thing? The girls were giggling about it like they were still in high school."

Jack's grin widened. "I'll show you. Follow me." He led them to the kitchen, where they found a Hispanic woman rolling out tortillas. Gracie and Shannon stood talking by the coffeepot.

"Enrica, I'd like to show our guest who Fabio is named for," Jack said.

The cook sniffed. "Mr. Jack, it is not that funny." She reached into the voluminous pocket of her apron and withdrew a paperback book. She handed it to Jack.

He grinned and flashed the front cover toward Michael. The male model on the front had a bare chest and long, flowing hair. "That's Fabio."

Michael nearly choked. "You mean I have to call that horse Fabio in front of my coworkers?"

"Yep. You still want him?"

"Of course. Thanks, Jack. Maybe we can get him to answer to something else."

"You won't get it done. Fabio knows his own mind."

"That's right," Shannon said. She carried the loaded tray past them. "He knows he's beautiful and he won't let you forget it."

"Don't smirk," Michael told Gracie as she walked by with amusement lighting her eyes. He and Jack followed the women back to the living room. He settled in an overstuffed armchair as they passed around trays of coffee cups and cookies.

"I'll trailer Fabio over for you this morning," Jack said.

"Are you sure? I can come get him." Michael accepted a cup of coffee from Gracie.

"I have an errand to run, so it's no trouble."

"Thanks!" He glanced at Gracie. "Have you met Jack?" he asked her.

"In the kitchen, before you came to see the real Fabio's picture." She cupped her coffee in her hands and sat on the sofa beside Shannon.

He quirked an eyebrow their way. "You were going to throw me under the bus at work and just let those guys tease me. At least now I know what to expect."

Gracie laughed. "I think you look a little like Fabio," she said. "They'll think you named the horse after yourself."

Shannon and Jack burst into hoots of laughter. "That's love for you," Jack said. "Only a wife would think you looked like a hunk."

Gracie's face colored, and she stared into her coffee cup. Did she really think he was good-looking? Michael didn't know where to look—at her flaming face or into the knowing grins of his host and hostess. If they only knew the real situation.

"You're just jealous Shannon didn't compare you to Fabio," he finally got out.

"You're right. I think I should be offended," Jack said, directing a grin at his wife, who stuck her tongue out at him. "Didn't take long for you to grab her up."

"When I first laid eyes on Gracie, I knew she'd make the perfect bride," Michael said with a smirk he knew would infuriate her.

Their gazes locked. A smile tugged at her lips and his grin widened at the bewilderment on the faces of their hosts.

Jack's laugh was uneasy. "You're a lucky man."

"More than you know." Michael glanced at his watch, then swallowed a gulp of coffee. "I hate to run, but I'm going to be later than I expected to work." He drained his coffee and glanced at Gracie. "Ready?"

"Leave her here, and we'll run her home," Shannon said. "I haven't had a girlfriend in for a while, and I need to talk about something other than horses."

"Run for your life," Jack advised Gracie. "She'll talk your ear off." He got up, kissed Shannon, then followed Michael to the door.

Michael wondered if he should have followed that advice himself. Getting attached to his new wife might be the most dangerous thing he'd ever do.

GRACIE SIPPED AT HER NEARLY COLD COFFEE. MAYBE SHE SHOULD ASK TO be taken home. Shannon kept glancing at her watch. They'd had a pleasant visit while Hope played with some of Shannon's girls' toys, but Gracie feared she might be wearing out her welcome.

Shannon leaped to her feet. "Sounds like someone is here. Just a second." She rushed out of the room.

Gracie put down her empty cup. A cacophony of voices echoed in the hallway. It sounded like several women. Her visit here might get prolonged, and she had a dozen things she wanted to accomplish yet today. The voices grew nearer, and she looked expectantly toward the doorway.

A host of women—at least ten—came smiling into the room. Allie led the pack. They carried packages and gift bags.

"Surprise!" Allie said. "This is all for you. A little wedding shower."

Shannon ushered the last of the women into the room. "I could see her fidgeting and was beginning to worry she'd demand to be taken home," Shannon said. "Allie pulled this all together last night."

Fighting the moisture in her eyes, Gracie stood and put her hands to her hot cheeks. "I can't believe it."

"We have no idea what you need, so we just got things we'd like to have in our own homes," one woman said. A pretty brunette, she had a toddler by the hand. She was introduced as Janet Pickens, wife of Michael's boss, Lanny. The toddler was their grandchild.

There were so many names, Gracie had a hard time keeping them straight. Everyone insisted she open her gifts right away. Most were kitchen gifts or decorative items.

"The house is pretty spare," Shannon said. "I bet you're still trying to find enough tableware."

"Michael finally bought some," Gracie said. "I love these plates you bought. Blue is my favorite color." The blue and white Pfaltzgraff had been something she'd wanted for a long time.

Allie's smile was a bit wicked. "Wait until you see what I got you." She handed Gracie a pink bag.

It weighed practically nothing. Gracie pasted on her smile. She suspected whatever the gift was would make her blush. Removing the tissue paper, she peeked inside the bag. Something white and lacy lay at the bottom. Heat rose up her neck, but she pulled out the lingerie and held it up. A delicate teddy dangled from her fingers. "I . . . I love it," she said.

For just a moment she let herself imagine the expression on Michael's face if he ever saw her in it. She needed to quit thinking about him in that way. This thing was going to go in the bottom of her dresser. She stuffed it back into the bag as the women laughed.

"It's okay, you're married," one woman said. "No need to be embarrassed."

"Thanks," Gracie mumbled to Allie. "It's really beautiful."

"I'm sure Michael will be knocked on his patootie when he sees you in it," Allie said. "It's got to be tough to find time for romance with three kids in the house. And you're newlyweds. I wish you'd let us throw you a real wedding instead of the quick one in the judge's chambers."

"We didn't want a fuss," Gracie said softly.

Shannon's smile widened. "The other part of the gift is that we're going to watch the kids for you while you honeymoon. We're sending you to the Chisos Mountains Lodge. You can save the teddy for that." Her eyes twinkled.

"A . . . a honeymoon?" How on earth would she get out of this?

"Jack called and said he told Michael when he took the horse over. Michael was speechless!" Shannon's smile was triumphant.

"The lodge is so nice," Allie said. "You'll love it. The elevation makes it cooler, so you can have a fire in the fireplace even though it's the middle of August. So romantic!"

That wasn't the word Gracie would have chosen. "Thank you," she said. "It's too much."

"Everyone needs a honeymoon," Allie said. "A chance to bond and talk without the distractions of caring for the kids."

"I rather like distractions," Gracie said. She managed a smile when the women all laughed.

"Michael will be a better distraction," Janet said. "Lanny says Michael is going to be a great asset to the Border Patrol."

"Think he'll even be able to get off work?" Gracie asked.

"Don't sound so hopeful," Shannon said, laughing. "You'll make us think you don't want to be alone with your new husband."

"I . . . I was just worried. I didn't want to get my hopes up if it's not going to happen." She could feel beads of perspiration break out on her forehead.

"I'll make sure Lanny doesn't throw a wrench in the works," Janet said. "Start thinking about what you'll take."

"I'm not sure about leaving the kids. Hope is still adjusting."

"She loves Betsy. She'll be happy to stay with us," Allie said.

"And I'll take Evan and Jordan," Shannon said. "We'll keep them busy with the horses. Don't worry. It's all going to be fine. It will be a weekend you'll always remember."

In more ways than the women could even imagine. Gracie wished she could have seen Michael's face when Jack told him what they had planned. Had he tried to wiggle out of it as hard as she was? Probably harder, she decided. Maybe she could get sick. Or maybe one of the kids would have a school function they couldn't miss. There had to be something she could do to avoid being with Michael alone. If she had the courage, she'd tell these friendly women the truth, but she couldn't bear to see their fallen faces. She would just have to grin and bear it.

12

MICHAEL HAD NEVER RIDDEN A HORSE WITH SUCH A SMOOTH GAIT. THE intelligence in the gelding's eyes pleased him, too, and in the three hours he'd owned the horse, the two bonded. The horse seemed to anticipate Michael's thoughts and desires. Caesar loped alongside them with his ears up and his nose down. Michael hoped the dog was on a scent that would yield something worthwhile.

He needed all the help he could get to keep his thoughts from straying to the bombshell Jack had dropped. A honeymoon with Gracie. That news had probably filled her blue eyes with panic. If he was honest with himself, he'd admit his pulse had kicked the minute Jack mentioned it. He was way too attracted to his new wife. But was that so wrong? He'd known her long enough to see the kind of woman she was. Pursuing these emotions to see where they led might be—interesting.

Caesar broke into a run. Michael dug his heels into Fabio's flank and took out across the desert after the dog. Caesar was in full hunt mode. Michael scanned the rolling blue hills and peered past soft green vegetation for any hint of movement. Moments later, the dog paused at a paloverde tree and began to paw at the sand. Michael reined in his horse and dismounted. He looped the lead over a tree branch and knelt to see what the dog had discovered.

"What'd you find, boy?" he asked. The dog whined and continued to dig. Michael went to his saddlebag and dug out a small shovel. "Stand back," he commanded.

The dog fell back, and Michael thrust the shovel into the dirt. It was soft here, probably from being disturbed recently. He lifted out three shovelfuls, then the blade struck something. He scooped faster until a large metal box lay revealed. Leaving it in the hole, he called in his find to army headquarters, who promised to notify Border Patrol. They'd want to recover any forensic evidence from the area. Caesar's reaction told him drugs were inside. He didn't need the confirmation of seeing them.

He put his shovel away and waited. The sun beat down hot on his head, and a trickle of perspiration ran down his face. He wiped the sweat away with his forearm. Caesar growled low in his throat, and Michael immediately hunkered down. A whine ran past his head, and he realized it was a bullet. He threw himself to the hard ground, then rolled as he pulled out his revolver. Fabio reared, and his rein loosened. Moments later he galloped away.

A shadow moved by a pile of rocks partway up the hillside. Two men, both Mexicans. And both armed. He needed cover. He crab-crawled to the tree and lay on his stomach. Spitting the sand from his mouth, he peered toward the rocks. Caesar took off toward the men, and Michael called the dog back. They'd shoot him for sure. Taking out his phone, he called the incident in. The officer on the other end of the line told him to wait for backup, but he glanced up toward the rocks again. The men were still there, gesturing with their guns. No doubt they wanted the drugs they'd hidden, but they'd have to go through him to get them.

"Mr. Wayne," one called, "we want only our property. Take the box out and put it on the rock over here. We will not shoot, and you will be free to go."

Probably a lie, he decided. If he got that close to them, he'd be able to identify them. A shot through the head, and their worries would be over. He squinted at the gaping hole. Was there something more than the typical stash of marijuana or cocaine? He should have peeked inside, but he hadn't wanted to disturb any forensic evidence.

What really concerned him was that they'd called him by name. How did they know who he was? He stared at the figures moving around the rocks. They could be after the bounty on his head. Regardless, he wasn't about to hand over the box. Reinforcements would be here soon. All he had to do was wait them out.

Almost before the thought formed, a flurry of bullets flew his way. The men began scrambling down the rocks. He could return fire, but once his ammo was exhausted, he'd be helpless. The rest of his ammo was in his saddlebag. With Fabio, who was out of sight.

They were looking away as they maneuvered on the rocks. Michael crawled from the tree to a rock. He patted his leg, and Caesar joined him. When the men reached the desert floor and began to advance toward his position, he aimed at the feet of the closest one.

He squeezed off a shot, and the bullet kicked up sand where it struck by the man's toe. Both men dived for the rocks again. While they were positioning, Michael dashed for another tree. If he could keep them off center until help arrived, he might survive this.

He crouched in his new spot and waited. One man cursed, then Michael heard the other say in Spanish, "He's as tough as his brother." Did these men kill his brother? A red haze filled his vision. He started to stand and shout at them, but common sense took over. He needed to stay alive for his kids. But once reinforcements arrived, he would interrogate these men.

The *whop-whop* of chopper blades overhead drew another shout from the men. They scrambled up the path through the rocks. Michael stood and shouted for them to stop, but they didn't look back. He lunged toward the hillside. One was almost in reach. With a leap, he tackled the youngest man bringing up the rear.

Pain encased his kneecap, then radiated in all directions, but he hung on as the man wrestled out of his grip. Michael made another grab for the guy's ankle and missed. When Michael tried to get up, his leg buckled under him. Helpless, he watched the men disappear around the curve in the path.

When the chopper landed, Lanny and two other Border Patrol agents alighted. They loaded him on a stretcher, but he refused to let them put him on the helicopter until Lanny opened the box.

"What's in it?" Michael asked as his boss bent over the container.

Lanny straightened. "AK-47s. And a little pot. Good work."

"Not good enough. I think they killed Philip." He'd promised Lanny there would be no vendetta, but Michael found he was going to have trouble keeping his word about that. He curled his fingers into fists. He would find those men.

"Look here," one of the agents said. He handed a letter-sized poster to Michael.

Michael's fingers spasmed. "Get me home." He stuffed the paper in his pocket. "I need to check on my family."

GRACIE WAS ON HER HANDS AND KNEES, SCRUBBING THE CRACKED LINOLEUM in the kitchen, when she heard a vehicle crunch on the driveway gravel. She popped her head up and glanced out the window to see a big SUV park by the porch. Michael's truck and trailer rolled to a stop behind the SUV, but two strangers got out of it. A man exited the SUV and approached the front door. He wore a green Border Patrol uniform.

She dried her hands. "Wait here, Hope," she told her daughter, who was copying letters onto lined paper. She went to answer the firm rap on the screen door. She stared through the screen at the man on the other side. He was in his thirties with brown eyes and skin weathered by the sun and wind.

"Howdy, ma'am. You're Mrs. Wayne?" he asked.

"Yes."

"I'm Israel Fishman with Border Patrol. We've got your husband in the SUV, and I wanted to make sure the door was unlocked to bring him in."

She gasped and put her hand to her throat. "He's hurt?"

"Rapped his knee trying to catch a shooter. The doctor said to keep ice on it and keep it elevated. He's not supposed to put any weight on it for a couple of days. We'll bring him in." The man tipped his hat, then went back down the wooden steps. "And we'll put the horse in the barn and feed him so you don't have to worry about more than a grouchy husband." He grinned.

The two men from Michael's truck approached the SUV's front passenger door, which swung open. Gracie didn't like how white Michael's face was or how he grimaced when the men helped him out. The men made a sling with their arms and carried him across the yard and up the steps. Caesar watched as if to make sure they were doing it right.

"Where do you want him?" Fishman asked.

Michael answered for her. "In the living room."

She shook her head. "In his bedroom. He won't be able to get up the steps."

He glared at her. "I'll sleep on the sofa. I'm not spending two days looking at four walls."

Uh-oh. She'd always heard it said a sick man was worse than a kid. She was going to have her hands full taking care of him. She shrugged. "In the living room, then."

Puffing, the men carried Michael down the hall to the sofa and deposited him on it. She scooted over a footrest, then lifted his injured leg onto it.

He winced. "Appreciate the help, guys."

"Anything for Phil's brother," Fishman said.

Michael rose onto his elbow. "You knew Phil?"

Fishman nodded. "Good man. Pickens has me investigating his death."

"What have you found out?"

"Nothing you don't know. Not yet, at least. But I'll track down Vargas's henchmen." He went toward the hall.

"Thanks," Gracie told the men, following them to the door.

"He's been grousing since we got him," Fishman said. "You might want to put on your boxing gloves."

"I think I can handle him," she said. "You seem a little tense. How did he take that fall?"

"Running after arms smugglers."

"Did he catch them?"

He shook his head. "I'm just thankful he didn't get shot. There was gunfire." He glanced away. "Sorry. I'll be in trouble for telling you that, I'm sure."

In her mind's eye, she saw Michael lying spread-eagle with a bullet through his chest, and something lodged in her throat that grew until she couldn't speak.

Fishman touched her arm. "Try not to worry. He's okay."

She nodded, still unable to form a sentence. Fishman shrugged and went toward his SUV, where the other men waited. Gracie backed away from the door and went back to check on Michael. His feet were propped up. His brows were drawn together, and his lips were in a tight line.

Gracie's stomach did a cartwheel. "Is something wrong? I mean, other than the fact that you're hurting?"

"You tell me." He leaned over and slammed a piece of paper down on top of the coffee table.

His anger tasted like alum. Gracie stepped nearer and stared down at the paper. At the top was a photo of herself. The text below it instructed that she and her child were to be found immediately. She swallowed the bile that collected at the back of her throat.

"Wh-what is this?" Seeing the thunderous expression on his face, she wasn't sure she wanted to know.

He leaned back against the cushion and folded his arms across his chest. "It appears someone is searching for you. Someone who fired shots at me."

Gracie put her hand to her mouth. "Oh no," she whispered. "Was anyone else hurt?" Had Cid used his connections to the cartel to find her? An even more sinister thought was that the men who had murdered the federal agents were looking for her.

"Just the guy with this paper in his pocket. What's this all about, Gracie?"

"I . . . I'm not sure."

"You know more than you're saying. What made you run away from your wedding?"

"Who did you show this to?" She could barely get the words out. With his eyes boring a hole through her, she couldn't think.

"Just the Border Patrol. They found it."

"Border Patrol," she muttered. Though she trusted Michael, the more people who knew her whereabouts, the more likely her hiding place would be discovered.

With a monumental effort, Gracie forced back her desire to run. "It might be my fiancé. I suspect he has some ties to a Mexican cartel, and he might be using his connections to find me."

"What makes you think he's tied to a cartel? Is he dirty?"

She nodded. "Federal agents came to question me just before the wedding. They mentioned a cartel called La Loma. Gunmen showed up and killed the agents, then came looking for me."

"La Loma?" Michael asked.

"They're behind most of the drug trafficking in the Southwest."

"What did you tell the agents?"

"Nothing. The next thing I knew, a vanload of men was shooting and the agents were dead. I grabbed Hope and ran."

"What about Cid?"

She eyed his grim expression. "I thought he was dead—until he called me later."

"You didn't tell him where you were?"

She shook her head. "He has no idea."

His stern expression relaxed. "So this poster likely has nothing to do with the shots fired at me. Cid is trying to track you down. Is he dangerous?"

"I don't know," she whispered. Her eyes burned. She'd hoped never to see such disillusionment on Michael's face. "He's always seemed kind and gentle."

"Then why didn't you tell him where you were?"

She rubbed her temples where pain pulsed. "I . . . I didn't trust him. I overheard him taking a bribe. I told him to cut off ties with the cartel or it was over. He said he did, but when the agents showed up, I knew it was all a lie. And I was only marrying him to give Hope a home. But he seems to be . . . obsessed with finding me. He's called several times."

"I need any information you have about this gang you suspect he's involved with," Michael said. "If they're operating here, I'll stop them."

"I don't know anything important," she said, holding his gaze. "I didn't recognize the men who bribed him, and the men who killed the agents were too far away to identify."

"You could take a look at mug shots."

She shook her head. "They mutilate and kill anyone who talks about them. I just want this all to go away. I have Hope to consider."

A muscle jumped in his jaw. "So do I. Protecting you both is my responsibility."

When was the last time she'd had anyone want to protect her? Not since she left home. She understood his anger. "I doubt they're operating around here. Isn't this Vargas's territory?"

He nodded. "Yeah, you're right. I'm overreacting. You should have told me all this though, Gracie."

"I know," she said.

"Why didn't you? There was plenty of opportunity."

She pressed her lips together to keep them from trembling. "I was afraid."

The sternness on his face softened. "I don't want you to be afraid of me, Gracie. You can tell me anything. We're a team."

The intensity of his expression held her rapt. Their bond had been growing stronger, and she allowed herself a tiny glimmer of hope that they might make it to some kind of deeper relationship.

"I never would have come here if I thought it would put you or the kids in any danger," she said. "I thought Cid was dead at first, and I was sure the cartel wouldn't go to the trouble of finding me once I was out of state. It's not like I know anything."

He picked up the paper and waved it in her face. "This shows he's looking very hard."

"I need some air," she said, rushing for the door. He called after her, but she didn't want him to see her fear.

She let the screen door slam behind her, then she sank onto the porch swing. The sun was going down, and the rays of gold and red spread across the sky just above the desert hills. She took out her phone. The Feds might help. She could answer their questions and then ask them to keep Cid away from her. All the evidence pointed to his continued involvement with the cartel. The agents had been sure of their evidence, and the fact the gunmen had let him live suggested he was with them.

She opened her phone, then closed it again. What reason could she give for her panic over Cid's obsession to find her? He hadn't threatened her. She'd be opening a can of worms with their questions about the murders too. It was something she wanted to forget, not rehash endlessly to the Feds. Though her letter had explained all she knew, there was no guarantee they'd believe her.

Michael thought she should face unpleasant things. Maybe she could take a step in that direction. She opened her phone again and found the number of the agent who had called her. She couldn't bring herself to push the send button.

The screen door banged. Michael limped onto the porch. She quickly closed her phone. "You shouldn't be up!"

"I'm fine." He dropped onto a chair. "Who were you getting ready to call?"

"I . . . I thought about calling the FBI."

The dim wash of light from the porch lamp illuminated his face. "What have they said about the murders?"

"I haven't talked to them."

His lips tightened. "Surely they've called."

She clenched her hands together in her lap. "Yes, but I missed the call."

"And didn't call them back." His tone held cynicism.

She held his gaze with as much bravery as she could muster. "No."

He leaned forward. "Gracie, you have to quit avoiding anything unpleasant," his voice rose. "Life holds both good and bad, and you're just making it harder on yourself when you run. The FBI isn't going to be happy you've been out of touch."

"I don't know anything that can help them, but I was about to call."

"Were you really?"

She dropped her gaze. "I'd just chickened out when you showed up."

He sat back and sighed. "I thought so. Give me the number. I'll call them."

"They'll want to talk to me."

"I'll be with you if they do. I'm not going to abandon you to face this alone, honey."

The endearment made her inhale. "I've never met a man like you," she whispered.

He shrugged. "You're my wife. A man shields his wife."

Discipline and commitment. Was that all he felt for her? "I'd better get the kids ready for bed," she said.

Her own feelings were developing into something much stronger.

13

"CAREFUL OF DADDY'S LEG." GRACIE SCOOPED UP EVAN AS HE ATTEMPTED to clamber onto his father's lap. She deposited him on the sofa next to Michael. She'd brought him supper, bathed the kids, and put ice on his knee. She was so tired she could hardly keep her eyes open. She needed some downtime to digest what had happened today.

Michael lifted his arm so the boy could snuggle against him. "He won't hurt me. But it's time for bed, kiddo. It's nearly nine thirty."

"I haven't had a story," Even protested. "I want you to read to me, Daddy."

Evan needed some reassurance. He'd just lost his mother and feared losing his father. Jordan had handled news of Michael's injury a little better.

"I think we can bend the rules just a bit tonight," she said. "This scared him a little." She mouthed the last sentence at Michael.

He frowned. "They have school tomorrow. Kids need a schedule."

"It won't hurt them to stay up awhile. Fifteen minutes. You can read them a story."

Evan's lip came out. "I don't want to go to bed."

"Look at him. He's got dark circles under his eyes, and he's barely awake. Take him to bed, please." His voice was inflexible.

She scooped the boy off the sofa. "Let's go to bed, sweetie."

"No!" Evan wailed, squirming and reaching toward his father. "I want my daddy!"

"Daddy needs to rest too," she said, carrying him out of the living room and up the steps. The girls were playing with their dolls in Hope's room. They looked up as she went past with a still-howling Evan. She reached his bedroom and set him on the bed. "Want me to read you another story?" she asked. She ran her hand over his head in a soothing gesture, hoping it would calm him, and pressed him back against the pillow. After pulling the covers up, she kissed his cheek.

He hiccupped. "I want my daddy." But his eyes were already starting to close.

Gracie kept her cheek against his. "I know, sweetie, but you're so tired. If you get some rest, you can help me make pancakes for breakfast. I promise."

"Okay." He rolled to his side and began to breathe deeply.

That was easier than she'd expected. She stepped to Hope's room. "Time for bed, girls."

"Okay." Hope clutched Molly, her favorite new doll, to her chest.

"Can I sleep with Hope tonight?" Jordan asked.

Gracie smiled. It might be a comfort to both of them. "Okay." She pulled back the covers, and both girls climbed into the bed. After tucking them in, she kissed both fresh-smelling cheeks, even though Jordan flinched.

"Daddy always prays with me," Jordan said, her tone accusing.

Gracie's smile froze on her face. Her cheeks burned. She didn't deserve to go to God about anything, but she couldn't explain that to the children. She knelt beside the bed. "How about you pray?" she asked.

Jordan nodded and closed her eyes. "Jesus, take care of my dad and help his leg get better. Could you make Gracie go away? I don't want a new mommy. Amen."

Gracie winced and pressed her forehead against the mattress. She was so tired. She'd been making headway with the children until tonight. Their fear of losing their father had stirred their insecurities. She wasn't sure she was up to the challenge.

"That was mean," Hope said. "My mommy is really nice to you."

Jordan hunched under the covers. "I want my own mommy."

Gracie touched the little girl's dark hair and tried not to let it hurt when Jordan swatted her hand away. "I don't want to take the place of your mommy," she said. "I know you love her very much. Can you think of me as a new friend?"

"Like me," Hope said. "I'm your friend." She took Jordan's hand.

"Maybe," Jordan mumbled. "I don't want to talk anymore. I'm sleepy." She closed her eyes, but the snore that issued from her pursed lips was obviously fake.

Gracie rose from the floor. "Good night, sweetheart. Love you."

Hope rolled onto her stomach and closed her eyes. "Love you, too, Mommy."

There were no sweeter words in the English language. Gracie

flipped off the light and went toward the stairs. "Now to have it out with Michael," she muttered.

MICHAEL SHIFTED HIS LEG, BUT THE ACHE DIDN'T EASE. HE GLANCED AT

his watch. Time to pop another pill. It might be smart to take it before Gracie came back so he could calmly discuss how out of line she'd been. Evan was *his* son. Her footsteps sounded on the stairs, then she stepped into view in the doorway.

"How's your pain level?" she asked.

"Bad. I could use a pain pill."

"I'll get one and more ice," she said. She stepped back out of view.

He heard her popping ice from the ice trays. Couldn't she bring him the pill first? Waves of pain encased his kneecap and moved up his thigh and down his calf.

She came back into the living room carrying an ice bag, a glass of water, and a pill bottle. After handing him the water, she dug out a pill. He popped it in his mouth and chased it down with a gulp of water. "I should have gotten it myself," he grumbled. "I needed the pill more than the ice." Caesar licked his hand.

"My, my, aren't we in a lovely mood?" She positioned the ice pack on his knee. "The ice will help the pain faster than the pill. The meds will take at least half an hour to work."

He shifted his leg on the footrest. "Sorry, I'm a bear, and I know it." He gestured to the chair opposite him. "Sit down. I want to talk to you."

She tipped her chin up in a challenge. "I want to talk to you too."

He glared back. In his mood, he could stare down a grizzly. "We need to settle who's in charge of the kids."

She eased into the chair and folded her arms across her stomach. "I distinctly remember being hired for that position. And I was just promoted to be their mother."

He muted the TV. "I'm still their dad. If I want them to go to bed, they go to bed."

She leaned forward. "Michael, I'm a mother who has spent every minute with my daughter. Believe me when I tell you that your kids need structure *and* security."

He moved the ice to a different position on his knee. "I get that. But it was past his bedtime."

"They've just gone through the trauma of losing their mother. Evan realized you could have died today."

"I'm fine," he grumbled.

"Thank God for that. But in their minds you could be gone at any time. You haven't been around much."

He winced. "Nothing like hitting a man where it hurts," he said. "You think I wanted to miss out on their first steps, their first tooth?"

Her gaze locked with his. "Then why did you?"

He gritted his teeth. "I had to work, Gracie. I was supporting a family."

"I think you volunteered for overseas duty because you craved the adventure," she said, her voice quiet.

His jaw dropped. "Do you really think that?"

"That's not a bad thing," she said. She reached toward him, then her hand dropped back to her knee. "You're a crusader and you care about others. That adrenaline can get addictive. Or so I hear." Her smile came and went.

As her words penetrated, he swallowed hard, realizing she might have a point. "I don't want to be an absentee dad."

"You're making up for it now, Michael. I admire that."

She moved her hands to her knees and leaned forward. He tried not to look at the smooth column of throat where her blouse formed a V. Her curtain of blond hair fell across her cheek, and his hand itched to tuck it behind her ear. Why did she have to be so doggone cute? Her makeup was long gone, and the dusting of freckles across her cheeks gave her a wholesome, all-American-girl appearance. The quintessential girl next door.

"A divorce is never easy on anyone," she said. "Right now your kids are rudderless. If you give them any hint that we aren't united, they'll be uncontrollable. And still rudderless."

He opened his mouth, then closed it again. Who was he to argue? The absentee father who didn't know squat about raising kids? "So how do we present a united front?"

"A set bedtime, especially on school nights."

"You just broke that," he pointed out.

"Not rigid," she said. "We have to pay attention to the kids and their needs."

"I can do that. What else?"

"Enforcing regular mealtimes. Time spent outdoors. Homework time. The things that give structure to their days."

He nodded. "We can't let them play us against each other either."

Her smile came. "And they need to know that they are to mind me just as they do you. We have to be a team pulling in the harness together."

Even through the pain in his knee, he recognized the truth in her words. He'd always heard kids needed loving structure. Structure without love or love without structure didn't work. In his travels, he'd often been in a Target or other store and seen how kids ruled their parents. He'd always vowed never to raise kids like that, yet here he was, challenging the very woman who wanted to help shape them.

He gave a grudging nod. "Where does discipline fit in with that? I'm not going to raise uncontrollable hoodlums."

"We'll both be spending time with them. Cuddle time, bath time, reading time. Kids can tell when they're loved and important. But that doesn't mean giving in to every demand. We don't want to raise tyrants who expect to control things."

He leaned back against the sofa. "So what's my role? Shut up and do what you say?" He couldn't help the scowl that took over his facial muscles.

She chuckled. "Of course not. We need to both be on board. We discuss bedtimes and decide what's best together. We can talk about how their playtime is to be spent and who is interacting with them."

"Man, that sounds like a lot of work."

"No one said raising responsible kids is easy," she said primly.

"What if we disagree?" he asked.

"We don't argue about it."

"You run from conflict anyway, so that shouldn't be hard." He grinned when her cheeks flushed and she looked away.

"I'll try to do better about that," she said.

He leaned forward. "If we're going to be a family, Gracie, we have to be able to talk, to hash out conflicts."

Her chin came up. "I talked to you about this, didn't I?"

"Touché. It's a baby step, but I'm impressed."

"You were right though," she said. "About Evan."

He lifted a brow. "Oh?"

"He was asleep before I got out of the room," she said. "The ideal thing would have been for you to be able to put him to bed."

"I'll be well soon."

"We just have to be consistent—with the kids and with one another."

He shuffled the ice on his knee. "I'm sorry I'm such a bear. Thanks for the ice. It's helping."

The smile lit up her face. "You're welcome. Is there anything else I can get for you?"

"Could you get me the laptop? The tech said the wireless was up and going." It might get his mind off his pain. And off the delectable scent of her hair.

14

GRACIE FOUND MICHAEL'S LAPTOP IN HIS ROOM AND CARRIED IT TO HIM. Their talk soothed a hurt she hadn't realized she carried. It had been years since someone listened so carefully to her. She deserved a tongue-lashing for keeping secrets from him, and instead he'd offered protection even though a lecture accompanied it. The lecture was his right, though, considering her behavior.

"We have to talk about what happened this afternoon," Michael said when she settled the computer on his lap.

"Which part?" Gracie worried. With a pain pill in him, he might ask more questions than she could handle.

He opened the laptop. "The poster. I need more information about what's going on if I'm going to protect you and Hope." At the stress in his voice, Caesar stared up at him and whined.

Gracie wanted to believe Michael could protect her. He'd been in wars and faced gunfire. She knew he had no idea how fear could paralyze. If La Loma came through the door right now, she'd sit there unable to move. Knowing the cartel might be so close had sucked the will to fight them right out of her.

"I'm scared," she said.

His gaze left the computer screen and zeroed in on her face. "I won't let them hurt you, Gracie."

His blue eyes inspired trust, but she'd trusted and been hurt before. Maybe she had a deficit of good judgment. "I trust you, Michael, but those men are evil." A chill came over her and she hugged herself.

"It's going to be okay, Gracie." He looked at the laptop. "I'll see what I can find out about your fiancé," he said. "I'm sure Cid doesn't know you're here."

"But the flyer . . ."

He shrugged. "It's a common crossing. Just because the guys came across there doesn't mean they know you're here at our house."

"You're sure?"

"As far as they know, you're eighty miles away up in Alpine, so that crossing they took makes sense. From Alpine you could have gone anywhere. Now, talk to me."

"I've never known a man like you," she whispered. "Such a protector." Realizing her voice revealed more than she'd intended, she glanced away. "Maybe I should start at the beginning."

Michael set down his laptop on the cushion beside him. The dog lay down at his feet. "I'm all ears. First off, where did you come from? You mentioned LA."

She ran her finger around the rim of her glass. "I was living in San Diego."

"You're from there?"

"Not originally. I grew up, um, a few hours north of here."

"Where?"

She bit her lip. It was hard to open up so completely. "Pecos."

"Good place to grow up in. So you're a Texan too."

She nodded. "My childhood seems like an idyllic life to me now, though at the time I hated the restrictions they put on me." She swallowed hard. Could she admit the rest of it?

"Restrictions?"

"You know how teenagers are. I wanted to be with my friends. My parents insisted on a curfew."

He grinned. "We're going to find ourselves in that equation sooner than we realize."

She smiled back. Maybe she could tell him. She wet her lips. "I . . . I got pregnant."

Michael's lips sank back to a straight line. "With Hope?"

She nodded. "I took a home pregnancy test and couldn't believe it."

"What did your mother say?"

"I didn't tell her."

His brows lifted. "Not ever? What about your dad?"

She shook her head. "I couldn't."

His expression turned speculative. "When did you find out?"

She forced out the truth. "The night I got on Diablo." His eyes narrowed, and she wondered what he was thinking. "Say something."

"You said you don't know why you got on the horse, Gracie." His voice was gentle. "Did it have to do with your pregnancy?"

Heat flamed over her skin. *Don't go there.* "What do you mean?"

"You knew Diablo was dangerous."

Unable to look at him, she closed her eyes. "I knew."

"What did you expect would happen?"

Her lids flew open. Staring in his face, the truth crashed into her consciousness. She buried her face in her hands. "God help me, I think I wanted to kill my baby." She was hot, so hot. The flush burned its way from her cheeks to her chest.

He struggled to his feet, then pulled her into an embrace. "Don't cry, Gracie. I can't stand it."

She buried her nose in his chest. His shirt smelled of fresh air and man. The safety of his arms comforted her, even if she didn't deserve it. She choked back the sobs. "You should be sitting down."

When his embrace fell away, her skin chilled and she wished she'd said nothing. Why had she never faced the truth?

He dropped back to the sofa, then patted the cushion beside him. "Sit here beside me."

She settled next to him. "You know the rest of that story. How I killed my mother." She raised her eyes to meet Michael's. "It was punishment, I guess."

"God doesn't work that way," he said. "You left home then?"

She nodded. "I took the money I inherited from my grandmother and moved to San Diego. I'd always dreamed of living by the ocean."

"Why did you keep Hope instead of giving her up for adoption? Or actually aborting her?"

She bit her lip. "I was going to give the baby up for adoption, but I couldn't. I kept seeing my father's face when he was so angry with me. I . . . I thought of someday bringing Hope to see him. I thought maybe it would change things."

"Maybe it would. What about her father?"

"He lived in Phoenix at the time. He moved to San Diego with me, but I soon found out he only wanted my money. Then he spent most of it on other women. I kicked him out a month later."

She squeezed her eyes shut a moment. Remembering was something she avoided whenever she could. "Five months later I had Hope. And I was flat broke." Her voice cracked, and she swallowed hard. "I'd gone through every dime of my inheritance."

"You don't have to go into all this," Michael said. "You can jump to your involvement with Cid if you'd rather."

"It all ties together," she said. At least it did in her mind. She wanted him to understand how she'd come to be in such a bind, down on her luck and a charity case. The realization made her face burn again.

She laced her fingers together. "I had to get a job to support the baby, so I got hired at a day care. That way I got to keep Hope with me."

"You worked there a couple of years?"

She nodded. "Until I got the break to do interior design, which I told you about. I rented a small cottage and was getting by."

"Where did Cid come in?"

"I met him at a party a client invited me to attend. It was about six months ago. Cid was there with his sister. He was charismatic, charming."

Michael slipped his arm around her and drew her into an embrace. "You said you never loved him."

She could stay here forever. "Hope took to him right off. I liked him, but no, I never loved him."

His grip on her tightened. "Did he know how you felt?"

She nodded. "He said love would come in time, and that Hope was the important one. That she needed a father. I was so tired of trying to do everything on my own, and Hope, well, she adored him. So things were fine until . . ."

"Until?" he prompted. "Did you find out he had connections with the cartel?"

Gracie nodded. "I overheard a conversation and realized he'd taken a bribe from them. I told him to get out of it, or it was over between us. I couldn't have Hope exposed to that."

Michael pressed his lips against her hair. "You did the right thing, honey. So he cut ties with the cartel?"

If she turned her head, her lips would meet his. She forced away the thought. "I thought so. He said he did. But when those men showed up on the day of the wedding, I knew he'd lied."

Michael rubbed the five o'clock shadow on his chin. "You're sure they were part of the cartel?"

She thought back to that day. "Not completely, no. I mean, they didn't announce who they were, but they came in with guns and killed the federal agents the minute they exited the van. What else could they have been?"

"They were Hispanic?" he asked.

She nodded. "All of them. And they spoke Spanish, not English."

"Did you hear anything else?"

She nodded. "One of them said, 'Find the woman and kid.'"

"So you were specifically targeted. Why would they want Hope?"

Gracie hugged herself and shuddered. "That's the scariest part. It makes no sense that they'd want her too. Why not kill me and let her live?"

Michael's eyes turned thoughtful. "Unless they were afraid she could identify them. Has she ever been with Cid when you weren't along?"

"Lots of times. He would often pick her up after school and take her to the park. She loved him."

"You think he genuinely loved her?"

She nodded. "He was going to adopt her. Like I said, the marriage was all for Hope. I thought we could have a safe and happy life."

"Could she have seen something she shouldn't have?"

"I suppose so, but she's never mentioned anything odd to me."

"I'd like to ask her a few questions."

"No!" Gracie lowered her voice again. "She's been through enough, Michael. I don't want her to live in fear too. Right now she thinks we're safe, and I'd like to keep it that way. There's no reason to question her. I'm sure she would have told me if she'd seen anything strange."

"Even if Cid asked her not to?"

Gracie hesitated. "I think she'd still tell me. We're very close."

"Kids can be funny though," he said. "If she thinks she'll get in trouble, she might keep quiet. Maybe Cid took her somewhere you'd told him not to and she was afraid to tell you."

Gracie forgot to breathe. "The park," she whispered. "I told her she couldn't go to the park anymore. There had been too many shootings, even in broad daylight. Cid used to take her there several times a week. He argued with me about it but finally gave in." Could they have lied to her—Cid and her own daughter?

And if Cid had taken Hope there, had she seen something that put her life in danger now? Gracie glanced at Michael. Her story hadn't disgusted him. That had to count for something.

Michael sat a mere three inches away on the sofa, with the laptop open. The glare from the screen revealed the concentration on his face. Maybe she could sit here and study him without his noticing. His lashes were longer than she'd realized. His bulk was enough to make her seem like a child beside him. If she scooted closer, would he wrap his arm around her again?

She wasn't about to play with fire and try it.

She scooted to the edge of the sofa and stood. "I need something to drink. How about you?"

He nodded. "That'd be great. We have any iced tea?"

"I'll get it." She escaped to the kitchen and put her palms on her hot cheeks. She was thankful he'd been oblivious to her wayward thoughts. She poured tea over ice and carried the glasses back to the living room. This time she'd sit in the chair.

"Here you go." She handed him the glass and moved toward the chair.

His hand shot out and gripped hers. His gaze warmed her. "I'm sorry I was a grouch earlier."

"Well then, you're forgiven."

"Thanks. I think." He patted the cushion beside him. "Sit here with me. I'm going to find out what's going on, Gracie. I might need to ask you questions."

Just don't ask why my face is red. She perched on the edge of the sofa cushion and wished for a fan. The warm breeze through the screen did nothing to cool her hot cheeks. She felt like she was fifteen, having her first crush. Obsession, that's what she was experiencing. And probably only because he'd rescued her. What woman wouldn't develop a bit of a crush on the man who'd saved her and her daughter? Her knight in shining armor. That's all this feeling was. And it would pass.

"What is Hope's father's name?"

She leaned closer and glanced at the screen. "Jason Wheeler."

Michael typed in the name Jason Wheeler and Phoenix. He surfed through a few pages, clicking in and out again when it became obvious it was the wrong person. Gracie kept her eyes glued to the screen so she didn't watch Michael instead.

She had other senses that weren't easy to deceive. The warmth of his arm nearly touching hers permeated her skin. The spicy scent of his cologne filled her head. Even the deep timbre of his voice entranced her.

Michael made a noise, and she blinked to bring the screen into focus. "What is it?"

"An obituary. Is this the guy?" He turned the computer toward her.

She stared at the screen, saw the dark curls and even darker eyes. "That's Jason," she said.

He flipped the computer back around. "It says memorials are to go to the National Kidney Foundation. Maybe he had kidney disease. It doesn't mention a living daughter. Just his dad and a brother."

"Tyler?"

"Yes, that's the brother mentioned."

"I wonder if that's why Sam called me?"

"Didn't he say something about Jason's estate?"

She nodded. "He sounded upset. I never called him back." She leaned closer so she could read the screen. Big mistake, because her skin touched his arm. *Read the screen and get away*, she told herself.

"He died two months ago." She gasped. "It says Sam is the governor now. Wow. He's moved up in the world." She quickly moved back to her place.

"Governor? And you didn't know?"

She shook her head. "I haven't heard from the family in years. I wonder why Sam is just now calling."

"Maybe he wants to see Hope because she's all he has left of Jason."

"As far as I know, Sam didn't know Hope existed. I don't think Jason ever told his parents he had a child."

"He could have confessed it before he died."

She sucked in her lower lip. "I guess so. I should call Sam back." She glanced at the clock above the fireplace. "It's only nine thirty in Arizona."

"No rush, I guess. You can call him tomorrow." He closed the lid on the MacBook, then leaned forward and set it on the coffee table. When he leaned back, he stretched his arms above his head. "I'm sick and tired of sitting here. Wish we could go for a walk." When he put his arms down, his right one came down along the back of sofa, right above Gracie's head.

She smelled the musky scent of his skin. If she tipped her head back just a bit, it would rest on his arm. Would he slide it down into an embrace? Her pulse jumped in her throat when she turned her head and caught him staring at her. She glanced away before she was sure of his expression. If she didn't know better, she'd swear she saw longing in his eyes. Heat spread through her, and she knew if she didn't get up and leave, it would be too late. She'd turn and throw herself into his arms.

She eased her head back the tiniest fraction until her hair brushed his arm. The electricity from the contact enveloped her neck. Her cheeks were hot enough to melt marshmallows.

He leaned closer, and his breath stirred the air between them. "Gracie?" His voice was husky.

She was lost. Turning her head, she stared up into his face. The intensity in his eyes made her lean in to him. Her eyelids began to drift shut. His arm came down around her shoulders, and he pulled her closer. She lifted her face a fraction, and she felt herself nearly ooze into his arms, like a jellyfish. His head came down, and his lips brushed hers in a touch so soft it barely registered. His breath quickened, and so did hers. She reached up and touched the stubble on his cheeks in a caress. His lips came down again, firmer this time. Her hand slid to his chest and she entwined her fingers in his shirt.

She couldn't think, couldn't register anything more than the taste of his mouth and the scent of his breath.

"Daddy?"

They both jerked. Gracie tore her lips away from Michael's to see Jordan standing in the doorway, rubbing her eyes. Gracie leaped to her feet. "I'd better get her back to bed." She escaped up the stairs to the sound of Michael's low laughter.

15

EVEN THOUGH MICHAEL WAS TRAPPED ON THE SOFA FOR SEVERAL DAYS, Gracie managed to evade any reference to the charged kiss they'd shared. She didn't know how to deal with it herself, let alone talk about it with him. Several times he tried to bring it up, and she danced away from the subject.

She mulled over the realization of why she'd climbed on Diablo that night. The truth made her guilt all the more painful. Not only had she killed her mother, but she'd subconsciously wanted to get rid of her child. Hope, the light of her life. How could she ever face her father, even though that reunion was something she longed for?

By Saturday, Michael was hobbling around a bit, and by Sunday when he came into the kitchen while she was making breakfast, he had barely any limp. Dressed in jeans and a blue western shirt that deepened the color of his eyes, his presence filled the small room.

He raked his damp hair off his forehead. "I thought we might all go to church this morning as a family."

Her pulse stuttered. "You go ahead without me." She kept her back to him as she pulled fresh blueberry muffins from the oven. He stepped up behind her, so close she could smell the scent of his Dial soap. She nearly dropped the muffin tray on the floor but managed to save it, burning her hand in the process.

"Ouch." The tray clattered onto the top of the stove, and she thrust her burning fingers in her mouth.

He grabbed her wrist and pulled her to the sink, where he put her hand under running cold water. "Better?"

"Yes, thanks." Or she would be if he'd let go of her arm.

As if he'd read her mind, he removed his hand and stepped away. "You don't have to dress up for church here, if that's what's worrying you. No one will look at you funny if you show up in those cute jeans."

"I'm not worried about my clothes." She shut off the water and dried her hand with a paper towel, then went to the cupboard for milk glasses. "Since my mother died, it's hard to face God."

"You have to stop running from God sometime, Gracie." His words were low. "Besides, it's important for the kids to learn about God, to see the importance of church. United front, remember?"

She whirled and shook a finger at him. "Don't preach at me, Michael Wayne. I can manage my life by myself. I don't need you to tell me how to live."

"Yeah? You've got it all worked out, right? That's why you jumped on a train and ran. Because you know just what to do."

She winced at the sarcasm in his voice and decided not to answer it.

His big hands came down on her shoulders, nearly engulfing her. "Just put it all behind you for one day. I want to introduce you to the community."

"I need to think about dinner."

"After church we can stop for lunch at the café in town and give you a break from all the cooking. We can take the kids to Big Bend to see the exhibits. Have a family day."

A family day. She searched his expression for some hidden meaning. He might mean it, but in her own eyes, she was still just the hired help. The ring on her finger didn't mean she was a real wife.

Though she'd like to be.

She caught her breath and tore out of his grasp. "Fine, I'll go. Just don't preach at me." She glanced down at her jeans and blue fitted blouse. It wasn't church attire.

"Your clothes are fine," he said again.

Her mom and dad had brought her up differently. "I need to change. Can you feed the kids? I'll be down in a few minutes." She fled for her room without waiting for his response. When she passed the kids' rooms, she called for them to go down to breakfast.

After she shut the door behind her, she went to the closet. Allie and Shannon had both given her clothing, and a certain blue dress made her wonder what Michael would think if he saw her in it. She tore off her jeans and blouse, then slipped the silky dress over her head. It fit over her slim figure and flared at the knee. She gave an experimental twirl. The silk swished deliciously around her. It had been a long time since she'd worn anything so pretty. It had been Shannon's, and it cost the earth. The tags were still on it when Shannon brought it over, and Gracie wondered then if it had been purchased just for her.

She found the strappy sandals Shannon had brought to go with the dress, then grabbed a brush. Releasing her dark-blond hair from its ponytail, she brushed it until it lay in smooth waves on her shoulders. Cheek color wouldn't be necessary, not as prone as she was to blushing in Michael's presence. A touch of lipstick, and she was ready.

The shoes gave her the confidence she'd been lacking in the jeans and flip-flops, but they felt alien on her feet after not wearing heels for so long. Clinging to the banister, she made her way down the steps. Michael must have heard her approach, because he stepped through the kitchen doorway in the hall below her and stood watching her sashay down the steps. Or at least she hoped it was a decent sashay. As she got near to him, she could see his eyes were wide.

"Wow," he said. "Look at you."

She reached the bottom of the steps. "Shannon gave it to me."

He took her hand and lifted it so he could twirl her around. She obliged and the skirt swished around her legs. "You're making me dizzy."

He leaned close and whispered in her ear. "Not as dizzy as you make me."

She went hot again. That man was going to give her a heart attack yet.

ALL THROUGH CHURCH, MICHAEL WAS CONSCIOUS OF THE SCENT OF Gracie's hair, the delicate rustle of her silk dress when she shifted, and the soft, daintly curve of her cheek. She listened intently— or so it seemed—to Grady's message. The kids sat like small chicks to her right. He would have to tell them how proud he was of their behavior.

Friends gathered around after the service to welcome him home, and he introduced them to Gracie, who hung back with an uncertain smile. The shy mouse had returned. When Shannon and Jack approached to embrace her, she brightened, and he stared at her sudden animation. When would she come into her own as the woman God meant her to be? He'd love to see her throw off her mouse facade for good.

Shannon released her. "You're radiant in that dress. I knew the color would be amazing on you."

The flush came to Gracie's cheeks. "I love it."

So did Michael. *Eyes front and center, soldier.* He averted his gaze and tried not to listen to their conversation. It wasn't difficult, since Rick and Allie came up to talk too. Both couples invited them for dinner, but he begged off and promised to accept another day. With his knee finally stronger, he wanted to have the family day he'd promised Gracie.

And that promised honeymoon kept drifting through his thoughts.

When they finally escaped the building, he took her hand and tucked it into the crook of his elbow. "Let's walk. The café is just down the street, and it's a beautiful day. After lunch, we'll run by the house to change, then go to the park."

She clung to his arm, and as they went down the street, he realized she was struggling in the heels on the brick sidewalk. "Take them off," he said, gesturing to her shoes.

"What? No!" She tried to walk faster but tripped over a rise in the sidewalk.

"I can carry you," he offered.

"Absolutely not!"

"Carry her, Daddy," Hope said. Dancing around them, she began to chant, "Carry her, carry her."

Daddy. He loved to hear Hope call him that. He exchanged an amused glance with Gracie. "I've got my marching orders from my newest daughter."

A tide of red moved up her face. "You're still injured."

He swept her into his arms. "You're lighter than a kitten," he said.

"Put me down!" she ordered. She squirmed. "You'll hurt your knee again."

"I'm all well. Put your arms around my neck, or I'll hold you responsible if I get hurt." He acted as though he were losing his grip, and she shrieked, then threw her arms around his neck. With his nose pressed into her fruity-smelling hair, he could have carried her like this all day.

Then his children caught his attention. They both stomped along the sidewalk with identical scowls. Maybe this wasn't a good idea. He'd hoped this would be a bonding time for them to appreciate all Gracie was doing for them.

The café was just ahead, so he set Gracie's feet back on the concrete, then scooped up his kids, one in each arm. He swung them around to their delighted shrieks.

"I want on your shoulders," Jordan said.

"No, me!" Evan clawed up his arm.

"You can't both be there. Jordan asked first."

"It's my turn!" Evan said, his face crumbling.

Michael exchanged a helpless glance with Gracie. She smiled, and the adorable dimple in her left cheek flashed.

"You're a big, strong guy. Put one on each shoulder," she said. "But don't blame me if you have to ice your knee tonight."

"You're killing me." But he hefted the kids onto his shoulders. They both clung to his hair, and he expected to be bald the next time he looked in the mirror. His arms ached with the effort of keeping them from sliding down.

Gracie darted ahead and held open the door for him. With a

groan, he put the kids down. "Now that you've maimed me, we'll have lunch. Then we'll go to the park and see the ranger exhibits."

"Yay! I want to see the snakes," Jordan said. "The rattlers!"

"You would," Michael said, following the server to a table in the corner. The red and white–checked tablecloth made him remember the last time he was here. With Kate. Evan had barely started walking, and Jordan was hard to corral in her seat. Poor Kate. He was beginning to see she might have been lonely.

He studied the menu, then ordered a hamburger and fries. The kids wanted the same, but Gracie ordered grilled fish. "A health nut," he said. "You can go wild today and have something special."

"Maybe I'll have a turtle sundae for dessert," she said. "Be all wild and crazy."

"Hey kids, want to pick out some music on the jukebox?" He dug out some quarters for them.

Squealing, they ran off. "I'll have to read the list for you," Jordan said in a self-important voice.

Gracie steepled her fingers together and rested her chin on them. "You look different today," she said. "More carefree. It's been good for you to be off work a few days."

He sobered. "It's all waiting for me tomorrow."

"I wish you'd give it up, Michael. Do something else. What's your dream job?"

"Doing what I do now. I like being useful," he said. "Serving my country is all I know."

"What's the favorite part of the job you had in the army? You said you were a pararescueman before you got out. What is that exactly?"

"The plane would get us as close to an extraction as possible, and we'd go in and free prisoners."

"What does the *para* part of the word mean?"

"I was trained like a top-notch paramedic, since I would often have to treat the soldiers before the extraction. Sometimes they'd be in rough shape, and it would take all our expertise to save them."

She toyed with her napkin. "Important work. I can see why you loved it."

He leaned forward and stared into her eyes. "What I did really mattered then. Life-and-death stuff."

Her gaze never left his face. "What about doing paramedic work here? There's a real need in Big Bend for a medical chopper with paramedics."

"They probably have one already."

She shook her head. "I heard in church that a guy died on the way to the Alpine hospital, an hour and a half away. Guys like him would have a chance with a chopper."

He wasn't about to admit her idea made his pulse kick. "Where am I going to get the money to start an operation like that?"

"Grant money? There has to be a way if it's something you want to do."

He reached across the table and took her hand. "What about you? What's your dream?" Her fingers tightened on his, then she started to pull away, but he hung on. "Come on, turnabout's fair play. Give."

Her face shuttered, and she yanked her hand away. "Here come our drinks."

He eyed her haunted expression. What dream could cause her to look so bleak?

16

THEY'D SPENT THE DAY SPLASHING WITH THE KIDS IN THE HOT SPRINGS, and Gracie was gloriously relaxed. She kicked off her flip-flops and wiggled her toes against the carpet in the truck's cab. She'd loved spending the day as a family, once she got Michael to stop questioning her.

The sun slid down the sky in a brilliant display that set the desert on fire. The eroded rocks looked on like sentries guarding the ribbon of road that was empty except for Michael's big truck. The kids slept in the backseat. Caesar curled on the floor. They were just like any other family on an outing.

Except they weren't.

She stole a glance at Michael's firm jawline. Her gaze traced his strong nose and lips, the solid column of his neck, and the muscles in this arms as he maneuvered the truck along the narrow highway. "Thanks for the fun day," she said. "The kids enjoyed it too."

He smiled, glancing in the rearview mirror. "They're sacked out." He didn't sound displeased at the thought. "What do you want out of life, Gracie? You never said."

She looked away. "I haven't thought about it." What would he think if she told him her dream was always to be a wife and mother? To have that perfect home with a picket fence and a man who rushed home to her at night? Such an old-fashioned dream to admit to.

Her cell phone rang, and she exchanged a glance with him. "I wonder if that's Sam." She dug it out of her purse. "It is." She flipped it open. "Hello, Sam, this is Gracie."

"Gracie, finally," his voice boomed. "I wasn't sure you got the message I left."

His voice looked like a red sun surrounded by orange light. For some reason, it made her sit straighter. "Sam?"

"If he doesn't already know, don't tell him about Hope," Michael whispered.

She nodded and concentrated on her answer to Sam. "I got your message, but I haven't had a chance to call you back. I'm so sorry about Jason. I hadn't heard he died."

"Thank you. It's been hard. Now Tyler is sick." His voice choked. "Looks like I might outlive my boys."

She struggled to remember Tyler. It had been nearly six years since she'd seen any of the Wheelers. When she was dating Jason, his younger brother had been fifteen or so. Tyler would be twenty-one now. "What's wrong with Tyler?"

"Same thing as Jason. Polycystic kidney disease. They won't even let him have a transplant because they say the disease will just destroy the new kidney. He's on dialysis now."

"I'm so sorry, Sam." She wanted to ask why he was calling after all this time, but she didn't want to be rude. What was his wife's name? She couldn't remember the quiet woman who mostly stayed in the kitchen.

"Jason said something before he died. At first I thought he was out of his head and rambling. Then I got to wondering if it might be true. He said you had a baby. His baby. Is that true?"

She could lie. Or maybe hang up and not answer when he called back. Without stopping to consider the consequences, she closed the phone. After a few seconds, she opened it again and turned it off.

"What?" Michael asked.

She wrapped her arms around herself. "He knows. Jason told him. I hung up rather than answer him when he asked if I'd had a baby."

"Maybe you should tell him. He deserves to know he has a granddaughter."

"Why? Neither he nor Jason ever so much as called to see if I needed anything. I owe them nothing."

"You can't run from unpleasant things all the time, Gracie. It's always better to face trouble head-on."

She swiveled her head to stare at him. "Oh? Is that why you told me not to tell him about Hope when he first called?"

"I meant if he didn't know, don't tell him. He knows, so it's time to face the music."

"Well, this is one dance I'm going to sit out. He doesn't know where I am, and that's the way I want to keep it. Hope has enough to get adjusted to without throwing a new grandfather into the pot."

"Maybe she'd like a grandfather. Kids need grandparents. I wish mine had them."

The bleakness in his voice made her take a deep breath to try to come down off the ledge of her outrage. "I know you're trying to help, Michael, but let me handle my own life."

Caesar whined and pressed his cold nose against her cheek. She pushed him away. Not even the dog was going to keep her anger from spilling over.

"I thought it was *our* life now," he said.

"On paper. You know as well as I do that our marriage is in name only. It's for the kids, and that's *all*."

"Is it?" He slowed the truck to a crawl, then turned into their driveway and killed the engine in front of the house. "What were those kisses the other night? For the kids? Let's not deceive ourselves. I can't keep my eyes off you, and you're just as attracted to me."

She could tell him he was a conceited jerk. Or she could say she was just lonely, and he was better than no man at all. But she couldn't force from her tongue the lies that would make him back off. She laced her fingers together in her lap and stared at them.

"Gracie, look at me," he said, his voice softening.

"No."

"Please."

The coaxing smile in his voice was her undoing. She raised her eyes from her lap and peeked in his direction. Wrong move. The glow of the lights in the dash was enough to let her see the humor in his firm mouth, and the gentleness in his eyes. "Okay, so I like looking at you," she said. "And you're a very good kisser. That's not enough to build a real marriage on."

"Isn't it?" he whispered. "I think it's a good start. Every relationship has to start somewhere. I like you, Gracie. Your soft heart would be hard to resist, even if I wanted to. But I don't want to."

"You . . . you don't?" She tried to look away and couldn't. She was hypnotized . . . mesmerized . . .

He slid across the seat until he was close enough to slip his arm around her. His fingers touched her chin and tipped her lips up to meet his. "I don't think you want to resist either."

Run! Open the door and run. But as his lips claimed hers, all will to escape evaporated, and she let down her guard enough to pretend for a few minutes that this relationship might really last.

"MOMMY?" HOPE'S SLEEPY VOICE MADE GRACIE PULL AWAY FROM HIS embrace and reach for her door handle. Michael said nothing as she got the children out of the backseat.

He knew she would gather her reserve around her as soon as they were out of the truck, and she did.

As the kids raced for the house, she turned a shuttered gaze his way. "I'm going to check on King."

He watched her walk toward the barn. Even the grace in her movements intrigued him. The sunset lit her hair with a red halo, and he wished he had a camera. He followed her to the corral, where their sorry acquisition of a horse stood on spindly legs.

"He still looks like a candidate for the glue factory," he said when he stopped beside her.

She turned a fierce glance his way. "Don't say that! It's not his fault."

He held up his hands. "Sorry." He leaned on the top fence rail. "Have you touched him yet?"

"No, he's still afraid."

"You mean you are."

Her dimple flashed. "A gentleman wouldn't remind me."

"I'm a soldier, not a gentleman. You need to let him know you're in control. Get a lead on him and work him out."

"He needs to know he's loved first. When he's ready, he'll let me know."

"Animals respond to a firm hand."

She turned her head and their eyes locked. "Just like kids?"

Her tone reminded him of their previous conversation about raising the kids, and the way she'd worked with him to find middle ground. "I get your point."

"He's been abused," she said, her tone wistful. "It will take a while for him to trust enough to love."

Just like Gracie.

"Gracie," he said. He waited until she turned to look at him. "You can trust me."

Her eyes were full of tears. "Can I, Michael? I hope so, because it's impossible for me to resist you." She turned and ran for the house.

THE KIDS WERE IN BED. GRACIE HAD SLIPPED THEM INTO THEIR PAJAMAS after supper, then into bed without a murmur of protest. She pulled their doors shut, then stepped into the hall, where she found Michael waiting.

"I'll meet you downstairs," he said. He tucked a stray lock of hair behind her ear, then leaned forward and brushed his lips along her jawline.

Her face flamed as the ocean waves that were his voice enveloped her with warmth. It was all she could do to nod and step back. "I think I'll change." She fled to her room, shut the door behind her, then leaned back against it, completely winded.

Caesar had followed her, and he leaned against her leg. "I'm not afraid, Caesar," she said. His dark eyes were skeptical. She laughed. "Okay, maybe I'm scared out of my mind."

If a kiss made her react this way, what would she be like if they ever . . . ? She cut off the mental image. Gathering her pajamas and robe, she rushed to the bathroom, where she took a hasty shower and washed her hair. After the day in the sun, she needed to smell fresh and clean.

The hairdryer cut out several times before she finally got her locks semidry. Her kitten pajamas could hardly be called seductive. Which was a good thing. She wasn't planning on vamping him tonight. The robe swathed her figure even more. She stared at herself in the mirror.

She glanced at the dog watching her. "What do you think, Caesar?" His eyes stared back. "Pretty bad, huh?"

No one could possibly be attracted to this frumpy image. Besides, it was too hot for the stupid thing. She took off the robe. The pajamas were enough of a turnoff. He'd keep his distance. She stared at herself again. Her eyes held more anticipation than she wanted to reveal. Michael disrupted any peace she'd hoped to find here. Her obsession with him couldn't be healthy.

"It's obsession. *Not* love," she told her mirrored self. The eyes looking back at her communicated doubt, and she stuck her tongue out at the traitorous expression. "A lot *you* know," she muttered.

Butterflies had taken up residence in her stomach. She pressed her hand to her waistband. "He's just a man. Like any other man. There's no reason for your every thought to be consumed by him."

Straightening her shoulders, she marched to the door and opened it. Caesar followed her into the empty hallway. Banging from the kitchen echoed up the stairs. She went down the steps and peeked in. Michael stood at the counter, cutting squares of cheese and putting them on a plate with crackers. Two glasses of iced tea stood on a tray.

When she cleared her throat, he turned to face her with the cheese cutter in his hand. He glanced from her pajamas to her bare feet. "Cute," he said. "'Course, you'd look good in a gunnysack." He grinned. "Or a bedraggled wedding dress."

"I'm surprised seeing me like that didn't make you run," she said.

"I couldn't take my eyes off you. Besides, what soldier runs from a damsel in distress?"

The man was entirely too free with his compliments. She tore her gaze from his. "How's your knee? You probably ought to get those cowboy boots off. The heels have to be bothering you with all the walking we did."

"I'm indestructible," he said, grinning. "I'll take them off in a minute."

"Where are your slippers?"

"In my room. I'll get them when I'm done here." His scrutiny still pinned her in place.

"I'll run and get them." Anything to escape his skillful stripping of her self-control. She should take him his slippers, then go off to bed and try to put his face out of her mind. She ran up the stairs and down the hall to his room. He could eat the crackers by himself. It was safer that way.

As she approached his room, she noticed the door was tightly shut. He never closed his door except when he went to bed. Never. She put her hand on the doorknob, but before she turned it, she saw a tiny wire protruding from the jamb near the latch. Snatching her hand away, she took two steps back. With the bounty on his head, there was no telling how Vargas's cartel might try to attack him.

She turned and raced to the top of the stairs. "Michael, come here! Hurry!" She heard something clatter, then he appeared at the bottom of the steps.

Taking the steps two at a time, he reached her, with Caesar on his heels. The dog's ruff stood at attention. "What's wrong?" Michael asked.

She clasped her trembling hands together. "Did you shut your door this morning?"

"No. I never shut my door." He glanced down the hall, then frowned when he saw his closed door. He started toward it.

"Don't open it. I saw a wire by the latch. Be careful."

He'd reached the door and stood peering around the frame. "Get the kids out of here!" He barreled back toward her. Reaching Hope's door first, he threw it open and stepped inside.

Gracie ran to Jordan's room and scooped up the little girl. Jordan murmured a protest but didn't open her eyes. Gracie exited the room with the little girl's dead weight. Michael was entering Evan's room with Hope in one arm. Caesar was a hairsbreadth behind him.

"I'll take Jordan on down," she called. "Should I take her to the truck?"

"No, it might be rigged too," came his muffled reply. "Just get her away from the house. And call Rick. I'll call Pickens when I get downstairs. We need a bomb squad."

Huffing under Jordan's weight, Gracie hurried down the steps. A bomb. There was really a bomb in the house. She swallowed hard. If she'd opened the door, she'd be dead now. Probably the kids too. Maybe all of them.

17

SEEING HIS FRIGHTENED FAMILY HUDDLING OUTSIDE DID SOMETHING TO Michael's spirit. He wanted to pound his fist against the hood of his truck and kick a rock. Vargas's anger with Philip shouldn't have included Michael's family. It was all he could do to stand back with Gracie and the kids instead of searching his home like he wanted.

The sheriff exited the house and came to where he stood with his family. The sheriff tipped his hat back from his face. "I'd suggest you hightail it out of here for a few days until we get the place thoroughly checked. Got any relatives you can visit for the week?"

"I want to know what's happening. This is my house, my family the guy tried to blow up," Michael shot back. Beside him, Gracie stiffened and put her hand on his arm. He tensed. "Don't try to persuade me, Gracie. I'm going to find out who did this. If they have a beef with me, fine. But don't drag my family into it."

"You have kids to raise," she said, her voice soft and determined. "What about your duty to them?"

Caesar pressed against his leg, and Michael petted the dog's ears. "The best way I can protect them is to stop the cartel."

"Then what? Where does it all end, Michael? If you stop this guy, you'll only put yourself in the sights of the next one."

"So what would you have me do? Run? My kids will respect that, won't they? And where would I run? There's no safe place to hide."

Her fingers tightened on his arm. "Vargas has access to you here. Get out of Texas, and you have a better chance. Let's go far away."

"My life is here. I don't want to live in some frozen northland. Besides, I've never cut and run in my life, and I'm not about to start now. Not everyone runs from a problem." Her hand dropped away, and she stepped back, but not before he saw her lids come down to shutter her eyes.

He turned back to the sheriff. "What did you find?"

"A homemade bomb rigged to go off when the door opened. There was enough explosive to blow up the whole house."

Michael shut his eyes against the mental image. He struggled for his usual control. "Anything else?"

The sheriff shrugged. "My men haven't finished combing the place. I wouldn't go back in there yet, not until they're done. Might be another day before we can say for sure it's clean. We need to check the barn too."

"It was Vargas," Michael said. "You know that, right?"

"There's no evidence of his involvement yet. The explosive was made in the U.S. So was the detonator. I know Vargas has a price on your head, but he's got money on half a dozen people in West Texas. There hasn't been a single one of them hit."

"There's no one else who could be behind this." Michael rubbed his forehead. Was he wrong to jump to that conclusion? His glanced at the kids, who were rubbing sleepy eyes. If anything had happened to the kids . . .

He swallowed hard. "Did you check out my truck? Is it safe to drive?"

"It's clean. You can get your family to bed somewhere."

He nodded. "Thanks, Sheriff. You've got my cell number. Call when it's safe to return."

The sheriff put his hands on his hips. "If I were you, I'd hire some-one to watch the house 24-7."

Michael inclined his head but said nothing. Where was he going to get the money for that kind of help? The sheriff wasn't offering any of his men for the chore. The department was too short-staffed to devote men to something that might or might not happen. Michael took Gracie's elbow and steered her toward Rick and Allie, who were climb-ing out of Rick's truck. News traveled fast in this small community.

"You all come home with us," Allie said. "The kids are exhausted." She glanced to where the children sat on the ground with Caesar.

"Are you sure?" Michael asked. "Don't you have a full house right now? I thought a new group of teenagers just arrived."

"They're in the bunkhouse. All boys this time. We've got two spare rooms, and they're all yours."

Beside him, Gracie tensed at the unspoken implication that they'd be sharing a room. "The kids need reassurance," she said. "Maybe it would be best if I kept Hope with me and you stayed with your two."

"I want to sleep with Jordan," Hope said, trying to stifle a yawn.

"It's up to you," Rick said, "but the way the rooms are set up might make that a little difficult. The rooms have double beds. I'm not sure you can get one adult and two children in a double bed."

Allie nodded. "You might be able to squeeze three kids in one bed though. The rooms are right next to one another, so you'll be close if they call."

"We'll take a look at the setup and see how it works," Michael said. He glanced at Gracie, but she kept her face turned away. If he knew Rick better, Michael would tell him the truth about their marriage. As it was, they had to ride out the story. "I'd like to stay and help clear the property."

"You need to stay out of the sheriff's hair," Rick said. "He gets testy when his authority is challenged."

"I should probably call Pickens." Michael glanced at his watch.

The border patrol supervisor would be in bed, and really, there was nothing he could do. The sheriff had jurisdiction here. The border patrol could assist, but it would be up to the sheriff to turn over any information that might be beneficial.

"It's after midnight. Let's get to the Baileys' house," Gracie said. "These kids are about to drop."

"You look ready to collapse too," Allie said. "We'll meet you there."

Then what? Michael glanced at Gracie again, and this time she returned the question in his eyes. How would they get out of this one?

FEELING OUT OF PLACE IN HER PAJAMAS, GRACIE CARRIED HOPE UP THE steps of Rick and Allie's house. Stupid, stupid man. Sometimes discretion was the better part of valor. There was nothing wrong with Michael walking away from something that could hurt his family. He didn't have to make it look as though using his head was cowardice.

"Here's the first room," Allie said, opening the door on the right. She flipped on the wall switch, and soft light flooded the room.

Gracie glanced around the comfortable space. A braided rug was in front of the double bed. The only other furnishings were a chest of drawers and a lamp. The blue and yellow quilt on the bed invited her to fall onto the mattress.

Allie stepped forward and pulled back the covers. "Just lay her right here. The other room is identical to this one."

Gracie laid her daughter in the bed, then pulled the covers up around her. Hope was out cold. Gracie doubted she'd awaken before morning.

Michael loomed in the doorway, with his two children in his arms. "Where should I put them?"

Gracie stared at the bed. "Allie's right. There's no way you can get two kids in bed with you. Put them here with Hope."

She darted around to the other side of the bed and pulled back the covers, then stood aside for him to settle the children. They were small enough that they each had their space. Neither of them stirred when he laid them down. Gracie and Michael watched the sleeping children for a long moment.

"I think they'll sleep all night," Allie said, echoing Gracie's thoughts. "Your room is just past this one." A faint call came from across the hallway, and Allie tipped her head to one side. "That's my son. I'd better check on him. Your room is on this same side, the next door." She hurried out.

Gracie drew in a deep breath. "I could drag a chair in here and sleep in it. That way I'd be here if they needed me."

"I think Allie is right. They're dead to the world." Michael's voice was gentle. "You don't have to be afraid, Gracie. I won't touch you. You stay on your side of the bed, and I'll stay on mine."

That dratted heat washed up her face, and she couldn't look at him. "I'm not afraid."

"Liar," he said with a smile in his voice. "I'm exhausted. Honestly, I plan to drop into bed, roll over, and snore."

"Me too," she admitted, only now sensing the crushing fatigue weighing her down.

She went past him to the door, then turned for one last glance at the zonked kids. Evan was snoring. Caesar lay on the floor. She stepped into the hallway, then to the next door. The quilt on this bed was in shades of brown, and the walls were painted warm terracotta.

The bed dominated the room. She gulped and turned to see Michael watching her. "Which side do you want?"

He shrugged. "I don't care. I'm not picky."

"I'll take the side closest to the door, in case the kids call out." Still not looking at him, she sat on the edge of the bed to kick off her flip-flops. The bed springs creaked. "Sounds like I need to go on a diet," she muttered.

"You're perfect just the way you are," Michael said. He went around to the other side. The springs groaned under his weight as well. "Sounds like I'm the one who needs a diet."

"Muscle weighs more than fat," she said, then nearly groaned. What a stupid thing to say. She scampered under the covers. The sheets smelled of fresh air with a hint of lemon.

"I'll get the light," Michael said, getting back up and heading for the wall switch.

The room plunged into darkness. The curtains blocked any beams from the barn light or the moon. Gracie heard him fumble back across the room, then bang against the dresser before the covers rustled on the other side of the bed. She heard him unzip his jeans, then they hit the floor. He was getting undressed? Heat flooded her whole body. She rolled onto her side and lay as close to the edge as she could without falling onto the floor. She should have expected that. He didn't bring any pajamas, and jeans were hardly comfortable to sleep in.

"You still awake?" he asked.

She debated whether to answer, but she knew he had to sense her lying there barely breathing. "I'm awake."

"I'm glad you weren't hurt tonight, Gracie. Your perception saved us all. Was it your synesthesia?"

"No, I never pay much attention to that. It's just something I have."

"It's a sixth sense. It might tell you more than you realize."

Would it? "It hasn't kept me from making stupid decisions in the past."

"Maybe you just weren't listening."

She was listening now—to the deep tones of his voice. Michael's words made her feel as safe as when she was in her mother's lap, listening to a story. Did it mean anything at all?

He cleared his throat. "You kept your head, too, and helped me get the kids out. Some women would have gone into hysterics. Kate would have. I'd have had to carry her out as well as the kids."

"I've been on my own a long time," she said. If her pulse would quit pounding in her ears, she could hear better. The warmth from his body began to seep across the bed. He shifted, and the bed springs groaned again. "I want to hold up my end of the bargain." His breath touched the back of her neck.

"You're doing even more than that," he said. "You don't have to be afraid to tell me anything, Gracie. I'm not going to walk away."

"Because Hope and I are your responsibility now?"

"*Responsibility* isn't a dirty word."

It wasn't, but she was beginning to realize she wanted more than his obligation. "And it's not a bad thing to put family first," she whispered. "There's a balance."

"I'm trying to find it."

If she reached out, she'd be able to touch him. "So am I."

The covers rustled, then his warm hand encased her shoulder. "There's something between us, Gracie. We both know it. The question is, what are we going to do about it?"

With him so near, she couldn't think. She wet her lips. "What do you want to do about it?"

"I'd like to think about making this a real marriage someday. I think I could love you, Gracie. In fact, I think I'm already halfway there." There was an audible clicking when he swallowed.

He had just bared his soul. Gracie couldn't leave him with his backside hanging out the barn door. She rolled onto her other side to face him, close enough for his breath to touch her face. "I'd like that, Michael. I . . . I care about you. I don't want to, but I do."

"Why don't you want to? I won't hurt you."

She wasn't worthy of his love, but oh, how she wanted it. "I want a husband who loves me more than he loves his job. Who puts me first. Think that will ever happen, Michael?"

She heard him exhale. "Can you stop running, Gracie? I'll try if you will."

She inched a bit closer, and so did he, until they lay nose to nose in the middle of the bed. His lips brushed her forehead. She lifted her face to meet his kiss. His lips were so warm and tender. She could stay wrapped in his embrace the rest of her life. Her palm flattened against his chest.

Then, with a deafening creak, the mattress crashed to the floor and they were entangled in sheets. In the next room, Caesar began to bark ferociously. Gracie giggled, then couldn't stop until tears ran down her cheeks. So much for romance.

18

MICHAEL'S NECK ACHED FROM SLEEPING ON THE SOFA. AFTER LAST NIGHT'S fiasco with the broken bed, he and Gracie had each taken a couch, and he'd been too tired to follow up on their intriguing conversation. But this morning he sat up, rubbed his eyes, and glanced over to where she had spent the night on the love seat.

He saw only rumpled covers, but he heard the sound of laughter from the kitchen. Caesar was barking too. The kids were up. Allie and Rick too. Was he the last one out of bed? That never happened. He stumbled to his feet, nearly tripping when they became entangled in the sheet. He hopped into his jeans, then tucked in his T-shirt before heading in the direction of the kitchen.

The laughter died when he stepped into the kitchen. Gracie's cheeks flushed the second she saw him, but at least she didn't glance away like usual. Her eyes drew him in.

Bacon sizzled in the skillet and mingled with the aroma of the coffee. "Smells good," he said. Caesar came to greet him, and Michael rubbed his dog's ears.

"Daddy!" Jordan ran to him, and he scooped her up. "We get to ride to school with Betsy today. Was there really a bomb at our house?" Her dark eyes expressed doubt at what she remembered from the night before.

"Yes, but it's gone," he assured her. "I'm not going to let anything hurt you."

"Are you going to find the bad guy?" Evan asked, biting into a piece of toast smeared with strawberry jam.

"You bet I am." Michael set Jordan in the chair by her half-eaten breakfast. "Better chow down. The bus will be here soon."

"Aw, Daddy, I want to stay home with you," Evan said. "What if the bad guy comes back?"

"He won't. You don't have to be afraid he'll hurt me. I'm tough." Michael flexed his arm. "Feel that?" He let Evan press on his biceps. "You think anyone can hurt your dad?"

"No!" Evan yelled. "Daddy is the strongest." He pushed away his empty plate, then clambered up Michael's leg and into his arms, where he planted a sticky kiss on his dad's cheek. "I love you, Daddy."

A boulder rolled into place in Michael's throat. "Love you, big guy." He gave his son a squeeze. A flash of yellow at the window caught his eye. "Uh-oh, here comes the bus. Got your lunches? Books?"

"They're by the door," Allie said. She herded the three kids toward the front door. Hope watched with a forlorn expression.

"Want some breakfast?" Gracie rose and went to the stove.

"Sure," Michael said, "if there's enough. I can get it. You don't need to wait on me."

"I want to, and there's plenty." She forked up bacon from the skillet and mounded scrambled eggs on the plate. "Toast?"

"No, just bacon and eggs." He liked watching her. Her movements were economical and efficient. The kitchen was her natural element. "Thanks," he said when she put the plate in front of him.

He should be focused on finding the cartel that had targeted him, but he couldn't marshal his thoughts past the faint fruity scent that clung to her. "I'm going to go to work today."

"But you're still on sick leave!"

"I'm just going to poke around, not report for duty. I'd like you to stay here."

Her slim shoulders lifted in a shrug. "There's nowhere else for me to go. The sheriff said we couldn't go back to the house until he gave the all-clear."

"Right. Remember what's happening today?"

She nibbled on a piece of toast. "You and I need to meet at the judge's chambers to finalize the adoptions at four. I thought I could help Allie with the chores. And, of course, do Hope's lessons."

"After the adoption papers are signed, we can admit her to school and let her take the admissions test under her new name," he said.

She lifted her blue eyes to his. "I can never repay you for that, Michael," she said.

"I love Hope," he said, realizing it was true.

Her dimple flashed. "She's easy to love."

So are you. His tongue wouldn't release the words. "Those chores might be in the barn," he warned her. "Around the horses."

She laid down the toast. "I'm not going to ride the horses. Just feed and water them. Allie won't let anything happen to me."

He smiled. "You don't sound too sure of that."

"I'm in no danger today. Unlike you. The bomb was on *your* door." Her gaze met his. "I wish you'd listen to reason. We could move far away. Vargas put a reward on your head for revenge. If you get deeper into the investigation, your actions may spike the intensity. Instead of bounty hunters after you, Vargas will have his men trying to take you out."

"I can't keep looking over my shoulder. We all need to see this threat resolved. I'm going to stop Vargas's men."

"What if you can't stop him, and there's no resolution to be found?" She rose and stepped to where he sat. Cupping his face in her hands, she stared into his eyes, stealing his breath, "What about last night?"

"I meant every word."

"That talk about seeing where this relationship would lead? It won't lead anywhere if you're dead."

He seized her hand. "I'm not going to be dead. All I'll do today is feed the livestock at our place, then go into the border patrol office and go through some records."

"What records?"

"I thought I'd start with the records of the incident that started all this. The shooting that turned deadly."

"Your brother?"

He nodded. "Pickens wants me to stay out of that, but I don't think I can."

"Will Pickens let you look at the files?"

"He's out of the office today. A meeting in El Paso. What he doesn't know won't hurt him."

Her eyes widened, and a smile lifted the corners of her mouth. "What? Going against orders? What about duty and all that?"

"I have no choice."

"But how can you just walk in there and go through stuff? Do they let the army have access to the computers?"

He shrugged. "I'll just give it a try and see if anyone stops me. My first responsibility is to my family, even if it gets me written up."

His own words rocked him, but he managed to hide it. He hadn't always put his duty to his family first. Being with her was changing him, stirring something inside that he wasn't sure how to name.

AFTER MICHAEL LEFT, GRACIE DRAINED THE LAST OF HER COFFEE AND SET her cup on the table. "What can I help you with today?" She wished she could sit around and daydream about what had almost happened last night. Touching her lips, she thought of Michael's kiss. And the promised honeymoon from their friends. Maybe they could actually talk about that.

"You okay, Gracie?" Allie asked.

Gracie jerked her hand down and forced herself to pay attention. "I'm fine. Did you decide how I might help?"

"I'm teaching some of the kids their first lessons about horses today. You can join me if you like." Allie wiped her toddler's face with a damp washcloth. Matthew screwed up his face and banged on the tray of the high chair with his fist.

Gracie shuddered. She didn't want to do horse stuff. The alternative plan she'd considered this morning began to coalesce.

"All done," Allie said, lifting down her son. He ran off toward the living room. "You're welcome to join in, but don't feel you have to. If you'd like to take my car and run up to Alpine or do some shopping, go right ahead."

She could go past the house. Gracie imagined herself driving up the lane, knocking on the door, seeing her father. The action might require more courage than she possessed. But it wouldn't hurt to drive by, would it?

She glanced at her watch. She had to meet Michael in eight hours. There was barely time. "If you're sure you wouldn't mind, I do have some errands I could run."

"Leave Hope with me. She'll like playing with the new kittens." Allie stepped to a hook on the wall and retrieved a keychain. "Here you go. There's a map in the car."

"Thanks." Gracie knew every inch of the road to Pecos. "I might be gone most of the day. You've got my cell number if you need me or the car."

Allie made a shooing motion. "If I need a vehicle, we've got others. Go, enjoy yourself. Don't worry about anything here."

Gracie's fingers closed around the keys. "Thanks."

Allie walked her to the door. "Should you call Michael and let him know you'll be out? He might worry."

"He won't worry if he doesn't know. I'll be fine. The guy was after Michael, not me. I'm the one who should be worried."

A frown furrowed Allie's forehead. "What if he calls here?"

"Tell him to call me on my cell. I'm not hiding anything from him, but he's such a worrywart I'm not going out of my way to tell him about it." She hugged Allie, then Hope. "You be good, honey. Miss Allie has some kittens for you to play with."

Hope's eyes widened. "Can I have one?"

"We'll have to ask Daddy."

She hurried to the car. Under a blue bowl of sky, the ribbon of highway snaked through the desert past the striated rocks standing sentry along the road. When she was a kid, she used to imagine they were Apaches with their bows drawn, ready to attack. Allie's car, a red Ford Escort, performed well on the narrow road. Recent rains had brought the wildflowers into full bloom, and Gracie ran her window down to inhale their aroma. Sage and creosote overshadowed the slight floral scent of the colorful blossoms.

She followed Highway 67 north to 17. Once on the familiar road, the crushing weight of what she was about to do pressed on her chest. What if someone recognized her? The years hadn't changed her much since she was a green eighteen-year-old. At the same time, maybe *they'd* changed and moved on. Pecos was hardly a Mecca for job seekers. There had always been people moving in and out when she was growing up. She could hope for a town very different from the one she left.

Her father used to tell her stories about his first trip to Pecos. He was a hippie in the sixties. The local police arrested him and cut his hair before they turned him loose. He swore he'd never set foot there again, but then he met her mother, and she convinced him to give the town another try.

Gracie's lips curved up at the memory, and she accelerated when she saw the sign that said the town was two miles away. Salt flats and exposed gypsum fled past her window. She pressed harder on the gas when she saw the water tower in the distance.

She slowed as she came to the road that led to the ranch. Should she turn in or not? The steering wheel cranked, almost by itself, and she was driving past the oak and cottonwood trees that lined the narrow humped road. Her old home was just ahead on the right. Her foot eased off the accelerator, and she stared as the ranch came into view.

The gray-green paint on the one-story glistened in the sun. It must have been redone lately, but it was the same shade it had always been. White shutters and a red door and trim gave it a smart, hip appearance. The barns beyond the house had new roofs and fresh red paint on their boards. She stopped the car in the middle of the road.

Taking the inheritance from her grandmother apparently hadn't harmed her father's financial footing. All she had to do was turn in to the blacktopped driveway and pull up to the porch. She could get out and press that doorbell. Her dad would open the door. He'd either embrace her or shut the door in her face.

She discovered she didn't have the courage to find out. When a movement flickered behind the curtain, her foot came down on the accelerator and she sped away, her pulse pounding against her throat.

No one paid any attention when Michael entered headquarters, flashed his badge, then walked back to the bank of gray metal filing cabinets. Caesar trotted at his feet. The building reeked with the smell of ink. Computer keyboards clacked, and printers whirred as they spit out papers. He glanced at the wanted board but saw no one he recognized. He nodded to a woman who brushed by with a stack of papers, then found the filing cabinet he needed. Most of this would be digitized, but the tactile sensation of paper and pictures in hand would help him marshal his thoughts.

Sliding open the filing drawer, he found the file marked with his brother's name. Once he saw the details of the case, it would become even more real, and he doubted he'd be able to turn his back until his brother's killer was brought to justice. He was disobeying a direct order by even looking through this file. He carried it down the hall to an unassigned cubicle and turned on the computer. As it hummed to life, he flipped open the file. Caesar curled at his feet. His brother's face assaulted him with memories.

He picked up the glossy eight-by-ten photo and stared into Philip's crinkled blue eyes. "I miss you, man," he whispered. *I love you* had never been part of their vocabulary, and he wished he had a second chance.

Laying aside the picture, he began to read the paperwork. Phil had told his boss that he suspected Vargas would move a massive stock of high-tech weapons into Mexico. At first, most of the Border Patrol thought Phil's suspicions were based on faulty information. Pickens in particular thought the tip most likely came from someone with a grudge against Vargas who was deliberately trying to mislead the patrol.

The doubt of his colleagues did nothing to deter Phil. He pressed on, and when no one would believe him, he went to the designated meeting place to find it swarming with Mexican paramilitary who were packing a van full of weapons. Phil called for reinforcements, then waited for their arrival. When most of the gang left and the van was about to pull out, Phil intercepted the two drivers. A shoot-out followed, with both the driver and his accomplice being killed in the confrontation.

While not the best outcome, Phil had prevented the arms from reaching the cartel, where they would have killed more innocent Mexicans. Instead of applauding Phil, though, a newspaper article focused on his partner, Hector Estevez, as the hero who arrived in time to prevent Phil's death. Weird. A week later, Phil was forced off the road and killed. Phil was a good driver and he knew these roads. How had they managed to blindside him?

Caesar sat up with a low growl rumbling in his chest.

"What are you doing?" Estevez stared at him from the cubicle entry. "I thought you were still on sick leave."

Michael flipped the file closed. "Just checking out a few things."

"That's Phil's file." Estevez folded his arms across his chest. "Pickens said he didn't want you involved. This is Border Patrol business, not army. How'd you get access to this anyway?"

Michael rose and stepped past Estevez to return the file to its home. Estevez followed. "Someone tried to bomb my house last night. With my wife and kids there."

"I heard about that. Not very popular, are you?"

Michael narrowed his eyes. "You don't sound upset about it."

Estevez shrugged. "What do you expect? You come in here playing the big man because of your service overseas. We've seen as much enemy fire as you. Most of us serve in this forsaken place with never a thank-you for risking our lives every day."

"I thought we were on the same team." Michael barely managed to shut the drawer without slamming it. "Don't you want Phil's killer brought in? You two were partners for five years."

Estevez grimaced. "Yeah, I want him caught. But I always knew Phil was going to end up dead. He took too many chances. His heart always ruled his head."

"I can't dispute that. It's what made him good at what he did, though." Michael nodded to the filing cabinet. "He was the only one who figured out that arms shipment was going through. The rest of you sat on your thumbs and did nothing to help him."

A dull red ran up Estevez's neck. "He nearly got himself killed, and we saved his bacon."

"That's bull. You and the rest of the posse came riding in after he'd done the work. For some reason, the newspaper mentions you as the big hero, not Phil. What's up with that?"

The other man's lips tightened. "I don't write for the paper, so I couldn't say what they had in mind."

"What are you and Pickens doing to find my brother's killer? Pickens said he had some leads, but I don't see anything in the file."

"You'd have to ask Pickens. That's not my case, just like it's not yours." Estevez's name blared on the speaker. "If I find you here after I take this call, I'm notifying Pickens." He stomped down the hall.

Michael might have five minutes. He went back to the cubicle. Maybe there was more information on the computer. The Border Patrol wouldn't just let this case go uninvestigated. Was it possible Pickens had shut out Estevez because he suspected Phil's partner of some duplicity? Michael found it hard to believe that anyone who knew Phil would want him dead, but no one was above the right kind of bribe or threat. Phil had never mentioned his partner's background to Michael. Maybe now was the time to find out.

He called up the case file, then clicked on the investigation tab. DNA hadn't turned up anything. No witnesses. An anonymous tip had told the patrol where to find Phil's vehicle, which seemed odd to Michael. Why not let the desert do its work and hide the evidence? It could have been weeks or months before the site was found, especially since his truck had gone into an area that was hard to see. The truck ended up in a grove of cottonwood trees. Finding him from the air would have been difficult. Only dogs might have found him. So the killer *wanted* Phil's death to be discovered. As a warning, or something else?

Michael skimmed the rest of the short file. No real leads. So why had Pickens lied about it? Because he knew the trail led back to one of his men? After closing the file, Michael launched a browser window. He typed in *Hector Estevez* and quickly found several links. The son of immigrants, he'd worked his way through college and had plenty of accolades from the university and the Border Patrol. There was a picture of Estevez with Phil, and Michael allowed himself to linger over it a minute. Maybe Estevez really had cared about Phil.

He sat staring at the search box. There was so much he didn't know about Gracie, and while he hated digging into things behind her back, he suspected there was much she hadn't told him. She'd been looking up something in the San Diego paper last week. He knew her fiancé's name. And, of course, hers. He found the site for the paper, then put both names in the Google search box. Several articles came up, and he navigated to the first one, which reported the discovery of the dead federal agents. Scanning it, he paused when he remembered the Feds were looking for her and he had forgotten to call them.

If he abided by his duty, he'd have to tell her to turn herself in. While logically he knew that was what *should* be done, he found himself reluctant to call the federal agent. In spite of what the article said about her not being under suspicion, he knew better. The FBI would assume her guilt because she fled the scene.

It had to be done. Grimacing, he dug the number out of his wallet and placed the call. When he asked for Special Agent Adams, he was transferred right away. He identified himself as Gracie's husband.

"We'd like to talk to her, Lieutenant Wayne," Adams said, his voice sharp with interest.

"I can tell you all she saw. The federal agents recommended she go into hiding. They said the cartel would seek revenge because she talked to them." Michael recounted everything Gracie had told him.

"I appreciate your call, but please ask your wife to come in. She might be able to give our artist a composite of the men she saw. And we need a better description of the van."

"We're in Texas. It's not just a stroll across town."

"Your wife is in serious trouble. She's the only witness to a brutal slaying. If she doesn't cooperate, I'll get a warrant for her arrest as a material witness." Adams's voice was inflexible.

Michael wished he hadn't called. "Can you send someone here? We've got three kids to care for."

"I'll be there on Friday," Adams said. "Give me your address."

Michael rattled it off. "Call when you get your itinerary." He hung up. Gracie would freak at this news.

He glanced at his watch. It was nearly time to meet Gracie at the courthouse. He grabbed his hat and headed for his truck.

19

GRACIE'S FLIP-FLOPS SLAPPED AGAINST THE TILE AS SHE PACED THE HALL, waiting for Michael. She heard the precise march of Michael's regulation shoes along the ceramic. Watching him walk with head up and shoulders squared, the agitation humming along her spine calmed.

"Ready?" he asked.

"Are you? Once we do this, it won't be easy to get rid of me."

He stopped and stared into her face. His blue eyes probed hers. "I don't want to be rid of you. I'm a man of my word, Gracie."

Such a good man. She didn't deserve him. "It's the only reason I'm here today."

He cupped her cheek in his palm. "The only reason?"

She felt the blush travel up her neck and lodge where his skin rested against hers. "Maybe not the only reason," she whispered. "You're a good man, Michael Wayne."

He colored a little, then dropped his hand. He offered his arm. "Let's go finalize our family."

She linked her arm with his. "'Our family' has a nice ring to it, doesn't it?"

"There's no phrase that's better."

She smiled as he led her to the judge's chambers, and the bailiff showed them in.

"Your Honor," he said when they reached the judge's desk.

Judge Thompson glanced over the top of the bifocals perched on the end of her nose. "Right on time, I see." She rustled through the papers. "This is pretty straightforward. You kids didn't waste any time in getting this done, and Wally assures me there are good reasons for this haste. You've asked for the custodial period to be waived as well. You want to share with me what those reasons are?"

Gracie exchanged a glance with Michael. "I . . . I'd rather not, Your Honor. Those reasons are . . . personal."

The judge frowned. "What about Hope's father?"

"He's dead, Your Honor."

The judge nodded. "You're both alone, then. Well, I see no reason to withhold your petition. You're adults and in your right mind. Your children are small and need the stability of two parents. I'm granting the adoptions. The clerk will have papers for you to sign and will issue new birth certificates in Hope's new name. Congratulations." She rose and shook their hands.

As Gracie grasped the judge's hand, the implications hit her. She was the mother of three children now. Three little ones, not just Hope, who needed her.

Michael escorted her from the room, and she paused in the hall. "I . . . I wasn't sure I was going to get through that," she whispered.

He gripped her hand. "Thank you, honey. You're going to make a great mother. You already are."

"You're welcome," she mumbled. Her gut clenched. "I need to find the ladies' room," she said.

She bolted for the marked door and barely made it before she lost her lunch in the toilet. Her stomach cramped again, then calmed. She rinsed her mouth with cold water, then patted her face with a damp towel. Her lip gloss was in the bottom of her purse, but she found it.

Her cell phone rang, and she froze, then relaxed. The caller ID read *Unknown*. She stared, then forced herself to answer it.

Cid's voice assaulted her ear. "Where are you, Gracie?"

"Cid," she said, her voice failing. She faced the light of a low window.

"That's right. Cid. The man you were going to marry. You've got to come back *now*, Gracie. It's best for Hope. She misses me, I know."

She put her hand to her throat. "Hope is fine. Just fine now that you're out of her life. You've lied to me at every step. I'm not coming back. Not now, not ever."

His voice took on an edge. "Something could happen to you, and then where would Hope be?"

Her fingers tightened on the phone. "Cid, did you put out a poster offering a reward to whoever found me?"

"What if I did? I *will* find you, Gracie. You had no right to leave me the day of our wedding."

A relieved sigh eased out her lips. "I . . . I thought the men who killed the federal agents were the ones looking for me." A long silence followed her words. Her stomach dipped. "Cid?"

"Your leaving ruined everything. You must tell me where you are. I will come get you, no questions asked. If you do not . . ." His voice was thick with menace.

Her head swam, and she sank onto the sill of the window. "Cid, did you do the poster?"

But she was talking to dead air. She closed her phone and sat shaking and crying. When the phone rang again almost immediately, she turned it off and dropped it back into her purse. If he was trying to scare her, he was doing a good job of it.

THE AROMA OF ENCHILADAS STRUCK GRACIE AS SHE ENTERED ALLIE'S kitchen. The clock over the sink showed nearly five. Her hands still shook from Cid's call, but she didn't want anyone to suspect her frayed nerves. Not now, when they should be rejoicing with the children about becoming a family. There would be time to talk to Michael later.

Fear tactics, that's all Cid's call was. She should be used to it from him. On top of that, Michael told her the federal agent in charge wanted to talk to her. The man had called back while she was in the restroom and made arrangements to be here at the end of the week.

"Got everything done in town?" Allie asked.

"I'm the mother of three now." Gracie meant the smile that stretched her lips. Whatever else happened, she was going to help Michael and the kids. "We stopped by the school and got Hope enrolled too."

"Perfect!"

Allie's smile was too gay, her tone too cheerful. Gracie was afraid to ask what drove Allie's good mood. "Anything I can do to help?"

"Just one thing." Allie's eyes danced, and she turned Gracie around toward the doorway. "Come with me."

"What on earth?" Gracie allowed herself to be propelled into the living room, where she found a mound of clothes and two suitcases. "What's all this?"

"This is the packing for your honeymoon. Jack and Michael are about the same size, so Shannon brought over some stuff for him. I dug out some things and Shannon brought more, and she stopped and bought underwear for you both. It's just up to you to decide what you want to take to Chisos Mountains Lodge."

"We can't go to the lodge now! Someone tried to bomb the house."

Allie waved away her protests. "That's exactly right. All the more reason to lay low until the sheriff finds out who is behind this and grabs him."

"But the kids . . ."

"The kids are perfectly safe here. This place is like a fortress, with plenty of people around to watch out for them. They can catch the bus from here."

Gracie backed away from the suitcases. "I appreciate the thought, Allie, but it's just a bad time. Michael will never go for it either."

"If you're all packed up and ready to go, he won't turn you down. You *need* this time alone with him, Gracie. You've been surrounded by kids and problems ever since your wedding."

"This is such short notice," Gracie muttered.

Allie's impish grin widened. "I've already made the reservations for tonight. When Michael gets home, you grab him and go."

"You've got enough on your plate without more kids."

"I love it! Shannon and I are going to share the fun with them. Betsy and her girls are all looking forward to a sleepover." Allie grabbed the nearest suitcase and flipped it open. "The reservation is for two nights. I've thrown in incidentals, but you need to go through the jeans and blouses and pick out what you like."

Gracie swallowed hard, then turned as the screen door slammed and Michael entered. He could deal with this situation. She didn't have the emotional resources.

"What's all this?" Michael stood in the doorway with his eyes crinkled in a smile. "Are you going somewhere, Allie?"

"No, you are." Allie's smile widened. "You two have a reservation tonight at the Chisos Mountains Lodge. You can be there in an hour." She peered at her watch. "In time for dinner alone."

Michael's smile faltered. "I have to work."

"You're still on sick leave," Allie said.

His face flushed, and he took a step back. "But our house was nearly bombed. I can't go running off when I need to find who did it."

Allie shook her finger in his face. "Listen to me, you big blockhead! You just married this woman. There has been problem after problem slamming into her—and you—ever since you signed that license."

"All the more reason to stay and face them," he muttered, glancing at Gracie.

Allie rolled her eyes. "You can't get into the house yet anyway. This is the sheriff's investigation, not yours, right now. All you'll be able to do is pace and worry. Why not do that in a beautiful setting with your new bride?"

He blinked, then shot a glance at Gracie. "Okay," he said. A grin spread across his face.

Gracie gasped. "We're going?" The promise in his gaze made her catch her breath.

"I'm game if you are." He nodded toward the sofa. "But what is all this?"

Allie's eyes were sparkling again. "Pick out some clothes and stuff them in a suitcase. You can't get into your house, so Jack sent some loaners."

He picked up a pair of jeans. "Nice duds. Bet he paid more for them than I do." He folded up two pairs of jeans, then grabbed several T-shirts. He stuffed a package of new briefs into the top.

Gracie moved to the sofa. This couldn't be happening. How could he cave so easily? And what on earth were they going to talk about for two days? The memory of last night seared her cheeks, and she bent her head so her hair would hide her blush. She didn't know if she was ready to move this relationship to a different level quite so fast.

Without looking, she grabbed some jeans and shirts and stuffed them in the suitcase. Her hand touched a filmy negligee Shannon had bought, and she gulped. This was all wrong. She couldn't go through with it. Once they were in the truck, she'd talk Michael into getting separate rooms or something. He would see the wisdom of moving slower.

"Where are the kids?" Michael asked.

"At Shannon and Jack's. They claimed the rascals for the first night."

Michael frowned. "Does he know what happened at our place?"

Allie held up her hand. "Don't worry, Michael. Jack has a dozen hands, and he'll watch your babies like a hawk. But we both know Vargas is after you, not them."

"He might use them to get to me, though." He rubbed his forehead. "I'm not so sure about this, Allie."

"I *am*," Allie said, shutting the suitcase and zipping it. "Now, get out of here. Both of you. Put all this out of your mind. Let go of the stress for a few days. Hike in the ponderosa pines. Go rock climbing. Or rafting on the river. Laugh, cry, let the wind run through your hair."

"Stop! You're making it sound too fun," Gracie said, half laughing. "I'm not sure about this either."

"You have no choice. It's all arranged. Call your commanding officer on your way."

Michael grinned. "I hear it's a terrific place."

Allie nodded. "You'll never want to leave the mountains. The restaurant at the lodge has the most amazing view of the sunset. If you hurry, you can get there in time to see it."

"Wait—the livestock," Gracie said.

Allie shoved a suitcase at each of them. "We'll care for your horses. I'm not taking no for an answer."

"I can see that," Michael said slowly, glancing at Gracie. He grabbed her suitcase. "I'll put these in the truck. You have everything you need for tonight?"

She could say no. She could sit on the sofa and refuse to budge. But in the end she just nodded and followed him out the door, with her heart about to jump from her throat.

20

SUNSET HIGHLIGHTED THE MOUNTAINS WITH RED AND GOLD. THE CHISOS Mountains Lodge Restaurant had a panorama of windows that looked out over the best view in Texas. Delicious Tex-Mex aromas hung in the air—peppers, chili, onion. Gracie sneaked another glimpse of the mountains, then went back to studying her menu. There was a large variety of food, so it was hard to choose from so many dishes she loved. Settling on chicken enchiladas, she closed her menu and studied Michael's bent head.

They'd barely talked on the way here. She hadn't known what to say and suspected he felt the same. "Did you find out anything today?" she asked after the server took their order.

He lifted a blank expression. "Find out anything?"

"At Border Patrol. About your brother's death."

"Oh. Nothing concrete. Pickens said he had some leads, but if he did, they're not in the file."

"That doesn't make sense. Wouldn't he have to put them in the file?"

He sipped his coffee. "That's standard protocol. Estevez was openly hostile to me looking over the file too. I'm wondering if someone in Border Patrol had a hand in Phil's murder."

"How can you find out?"

"By talking to people. Digging. Pickens isn't going to like it."

The server interrupted with their salads. Gracie waited until she left. The sound of Michael's voice was a blue wave cresting on the beach. She liked listening to it, seeing it. Someday she wanted to close her eyes and let it carry her away. She didn't realize she was staring until he laughed uncomfortably.

"Do I have something on my nose?" he asked.

She glanced down at her salad. "Sorry. I was lost in thought."

"Care to share it? Tell me more about yourself, Gracie. I still don't know whether you have siblings, or anything about your life before you showed up here. Other than your mother's death."

With his blue eyes boring into her, she couldn't think. "There's nothing much to tell. I'm an only child." She toyed with her napkin. "Did you know I left Allie's ranch today?"

"Where'd you go?"

She tucked a lock of hair behind her ear. "I can't believe I'm telling you this."

He reached across the table and took her hand. "I'm listening."

But she had ceased to think, with his thumb rubbing across the skin on top of her hand. "I went to Pecos," she said. "To the place where I grew up."

His thumb stopped its movement, then resumed. "Pecos? You got there and back and still made it to the courthouse?"

She smiled. "I didn't let the grass grow under my tires. The house looks the same."

"Did you stop?"

She opened her mouth, then closed it again. "No, I chickened out. Maybe next time."

"I could go with you."

Her pulse stuttered, then resumed its rhythm. When she tried to withdraw her hand, he maintained possession. "I shouldn't have mentioned it," she said. "I don't want to talk about it."

"I think you do. You brought it up."

All she had to do was open her mouth. Bare her soul. How hard could it be? But the weight of years of silence pressed hard.

"I bet your dad wants to see you as much as you want to see him."

A hummingbird darted from blossom to blossom outside the window. The bird's wings moved so fast they could hardly be seen. Her life had been like that. She moved from place to place quickly so she could come and go without being noticed. If she was noticed, she might have to give a part of herself to someone. Michael was pushing her to do what she'd avoided for six years.

Something squeezed her chest. Maybe a cry that wanted to escape. She managed to hold it at bay behind the lump in her throat. She shook her head.

"He hates me," she choked out. "When he found her in the stall, I saw his stricken expression, the hatred in his eyes. I didn't have to tell him—he knew what I'd done."

Michael smiled. "No one could hate you, Gracie."

"I killed my mother and broke his heart. Then I took the money my grandmother left me and sneaked off in the night so I wouldn't have to see the condemnation in his face over breakfast every morning. That money is gone, all of it. I used it trying to forget, but it didn't work. Nothing works." She was crying now, barely aware of the curious stares around her.

"Hang on a minute, love." He rose and went to speak to the server. When he returned, he took her hand. "Let's finish this in our room. Our server says our food is up, and she's going to put it in boxes. We can eat in our cabin."

"I'm sorry I ruined our dinner," she said, the tears still running down her cheeks.

Where had this fountain sprung from? She couldn't turn off the tap of tears. Sobs welled in her chest as well, and only a monumental effort kept them back.

"It's not ruined at all. We'll just have some privacy."

With his fingers on her elbow, she followed his lead through the restaurant toward the door. Their server met them with boxes of food. She flicked a curious glance in Gracie's direction, then wished them a good night. Michael quickly paid for their meal, left a generous tip, then took her to the truck, which was parked on the steep hillside. He drove up the even steeper incline to their cabin, a low-slung log structure hidden by ponderosa pines. It had a great view of the Casa Grande Peak.

Gracie sniffled her way up the walk to the front door. Her tears flowed until she stepped inside. Seeing the big king-size bed in the cabin dried them right up.

THE ROOM WAS A LITTLE SHABBY, BUT CLEAN. THE BED HAD A PILLOW-TOP mattress. *Don't look at the bed.* Michael deliberately turned his back and pulled out a chair at the small dining table. "Here. Sit. Let's eat before it gets cold."

She smiled at him. "Are you always so perceptive?'

"Me, perceptive? Like a tank. No one has ever accused me of that before."

She scooted up to the table and opened the Styrofoam boxes. The aroma of roasted peppers vied with the desert scents wafting in through the open window. A gecko ran from the window ledge onto the table, then back again.

Gracie watched it until it disappeared. "When I was a little girl, I could watch them by the hour. Their red squeaky noises."

"Red?"

"I . . . I told you I see color and shape in sounds. The synesthesia? It's lots of sounds I see, not just music."

"You're kidding." But he could see from her expression that she was serious. "In every sound?"

"Not always. Music, yes. Voices too. But not every sound I hear."

"Do you see color in my voice?"

She nodded. "It's like a deep blue wave." Color ran up her face and settled in her cheeks. "It surrounds me and lifts me up like I'm body-surfing."

"What about your own voice?"

She shook her head. "Nothing there." She picked up her plastic fork. "I shouldn't have said anything. People look at me differently when they know."

"Sure, they do! You're even more amazing." He watched her eat, then wolfed down his food. "What about your dad, Gracie? Have you talked to him since you left?"

She put down her fork and carefully closed her box over the half-eaten enchiladas. The dying light shone in her face, and she shielded her eyes. She shook her head, and her hair fell forward to obscure her cheeks. "I've picked up the phone several times, but I never dial."

"He may long to see you as much as you want to see him."

"I don't think so. I was a huge disappointment to him."

"Because of getting pregnant? Or because of your mother?"

She tore her paper napkin into strips. "I didn't tell him I was pregnant. But he shouted at me when he found her. He kept saying, 'You knew Diablo was a killer.' And I did." She ended on a whisper.

"He probably doesn't blame you."

She shook her head. "He does. He must."

"What if you went back and confessed it all to him? Confront it head-on?" He nodded toward her purse. "That Bible of his fell open to the story of the prodigal. Maybe he's waiting to welcome you home."

Her head came up. "That's always your answer. I'm not good at confrontation. If he wanted to see me, he has the money to track me down."

"I thought you said you'd moved around a lot."

"A good PI could find me. I've always kept the same cell phone number, even when I moved."

"So he could call you," Michael said. He wanted to sweep her into his arms and protect her. All these years she'd hoped to hear from the man, and her father couldn't pick up the phone and call her.

She nodded. "But he never has. So I know he hates me still."

"Like I said, I'd go with you." He took her hand.

She squeezed his fingers. "You always know how to say the right thing."

"Let's go for a walk along the trail and watch the last of the sunset."

She nodded after a surreptitious glance toward the bed. He held out his hand, and she took it. Her head barely came to his chest. He liked her smallness, compact but perfectly proportioned. Being around her made him feel he could climb mountains and conquer the world. Her hand nestled in his, and he led her along the stony path up to the top of the hill. It was deserted up here. A flat rock jutted out over the canyon and was the perfect spot for viewing the last glimpses of the sun.

"Let's sit here," he said, leading her to the rock. He glanced over the edge. "There's another ledge just under this one, so it's safe to dangle your feet if you want."

She knelt and scooted forward. He settled beside her with his arm around her waist. "Cold?" The wind had a bite to it.

"Not with you here." She leaned against him and rested her head against his shoulder, then lifted her head and stared into his face.

When their gazes locked, something expanded in his chest, right around the region of his heart. The warmth spread as he sank into the depth of her eyes. He read the loneliness there, the tentative hope that this relationship might be something more.

It already was to him.

The realization made him dizzy, and he clutched her a little tighter. "I don't want to scare you," he muttered, pressing his lips to her hair. "If I'm moving too fast, tell me."

Lifting his head, he smoothed her hair, silken and sweet scented. He lifted his right hand up to cup her cheek and tilt her lips to meet his. Their breath mingled as he bent his head. Kissing her was like bungee jumping off the cliff. He was in freefall and wasn't sure when he would reach the end of the cord. Her lips were soft and pliant, with the faint taste of her mint lip gloss.

She pulled away with a question in her eyes. He realized she wasn't going to let him that close unless he spilled the truth. "I love you, Gracie." His thumb traced her jawline. "I love your heart and the way you love other people. I love the way you blush so easily and pay such close attention to the kids." The strand of hair that tangled in his fingers was fine and silky, and he couldn't resist raising it to his lips. "I love your hair and the way you smile."

Tears were welling in her eyes, and he wasn't sure what that meant, so he rushed on before he lost his courage. "This wasn't supposed to happen, and if it's too soon for you, that's okay. I'm a patient man."

Her tremulous smile finally came. "I love you, too, Michael. How could I not fall in love with a man who is so quick to accept me and overlook circumstances that would make most people walk right on by?"

"Anyone would have helped you."

She shook her head. "You're a knight on a white horse to me." Her hand came up and caressed his face. "I'm so afraid of disappointing you, that you'll find out I'm not who you think I am."

"We'll discover each other's layers together," he said. "I look forward to years of finding out more about you every day."

"You're too good to be true." She kissed him, a lingering caress full of promise. "Let's go back to our room."

His pulse galloped at the passion in her eyes as he rose and took her hand.

21

GRACIE FLOATED IN A WARM, SAFE PLACE WITH THE FRESHNESS OF A NEW morning enveloping her. From a distance, she heard someone calling her name, but she didn't want to leave this haven. She drifted in and out of sleep for a few moments before her eyes flew open and she remembered where she was.

"Good morning, sleepyhead," Michael said. He leaned on one elbow and looked down at her where she rested in the crook of his other arm.

She smiled up at him. If her heart swelled any more, it would burst from her chest. Her fingers traced the cleft in his chin. "Good morning. What time is it?"

He kissed her fingertips. "Late. Nearly nine. But we have the whole day to do whatever we want." He wound a lock of her hair around one finger. "We don't have to get up."

She snuggled against him. "My stomach is growling loud enough to be mistaken for a mountain lion."

"I'm ignoring it." He nuzzled her neck until her stomach complained again. "Fine. I'm getting up." He threw back the covers and sat up.

"I need coffee too," she announced, watching him rise and grab his jeans. "I thought I smelled it."

He opened the curtains and light streamed into the room. "You did. I got up and made it a few minutes ago when you refused to open your eyes. It's all ready." He stepped to the table and poured her a cup.

"A man after my heart. My creamer is in my purse." She crawled from the covers and sat on the edge of the bed.

"Only a woman would bring her own creamer." He grabbed her handbag from under the table and handed it to her.

She dug out her plastic sack of hazelnut creamer and handed two packettes to him. She watched him dump them into the cup, then stir the coffee. "I rather like having a maid in the morning."

Grinning, he handed her the cup. "If that's what it takes to keep a smile like that on your face, it's a small price to pay."

She carried it to the window and looked out. Sunlight dappled the desert plants and rocks, inviting her to come out and play. "I'd like to go rafting on the Rio Grande."

His arms came around her and he rested his chin on her head. "As long as you promise not to fall overboard."

"You can't get rid of me that easily." She turned to face him and wrapped her arms around his waist. "I'm so happy, Michael, but what about the future? You're in danger every day. How am I supposed to live with kissing you good-bye in the mornings and never being sure if you'll come home?"

He stiffened in her arms. "Gracie, it's my job."

"And I'm your wife. You have three kids to raise. What's more important? The job or your family?"

"Not fair, Gracie, and you know it."

When he pulled away, she knew she'd gone too far too fast. Men always compartmentalized their lives. Jobs in this box, friends in this one, family in this one. To a woman it was all interconnected. She didn't know about the men being from Mars thing, but they were sure from some other planet.

"I'm going to take a shower." He grabbed his clean clothes and walked off to the bathroom.

She sank onto the chair. Now she'd spoiled their perfect day. Michael knew his responsibilities. It wasn't her job to change his mind about what he thought was important. Would she never learn to keep her mouth shut? She leaned her head into her hands.

Her cell phone rang, and she froze. Maybe something was wrong with one of the children. She sprang toward her purse and grabbed her phone, not bothering to glance at the caller ID. "Hello?"

"You never called me back," said Sam Wheeler.

Gracie sank back onto the chair with the phone clamped to her ear. *Hang up.* "Hello? Is anyone there?" Her heart slammed against her ribs. "I don't know if you can hear me, but I'm in the mountains with poor reception."

She closed her phone without waiting for a response and drew a ragged breath. Flipping it open again, she pressed the button to power it down.

Michael exited the bathroom toweling his hair. "Who was that?"

She couldn't lie to him. Not now. "Sam Wheeler."

"What did he want?" he asked, coming closer.

"I don't know. I pretended I couldn't hear him and hung up."

"Gracie, you can't avoid this forever. If he knows about Hope and hires an attorney, what then? If you know what to expect, you can plan for it."

"I'm scared," she whispered, hugging herself. "What if he wants to see her? I couldn't bear for Hope to be hurt or for him to try to fight for custody of her. I don't want anything to disrupt our lives."

His eyes softened, and he took her hand and drew her to her feet. "Honey, it's not going to go away. Those kinds of things never do. If he thinks you're avoiding him, what might have been a cordial discussion will turn into a free-for-all."

"You're right. I know you're right. But Hope is all I have. I can't risk her."

"What am I? Chopped liver? This isn't anything we can't handle together. Do you want me to call him?"

He reached for the phone, and she grabbed for his hand. "No!" She forced a smile. "I'm hungry. Besides, I don't want to spoil the only honeymoon we're likely to have."

Though he smiled and shrugged, she knew he wouldn't let it rest for long. But the danger was averted for now. He smacked her bottom and told her to get dressed, and he'd buy her the biggest breakfast in Texas.

ON THEIR LAST DAY IN THE CHISOS MOUNTAINS, THE LOT AT RIO GRANDE Village held only a battered pickup. Dawn had barely arrived. Michael parked his truck under a cottonwood tree. "Sure you're up for a hike?"

Gracie leaned over to brush a kiss across his lips. A few hours could change so much. This time two days ago, she wouldn't have dared. "I'd climb Mount Everest as long as you were there to haul me up."

He grinned. "We could just sit here and neck."

What confidence love brought. Who knew? She patted his cheek. "We both need the exercise. Besides, you promised me beavers. That's the only thing that got me out of bed at this hour."

"Slave driver." He released her with obvious reluctance and shoved open his door, then came around to open hers.

His chivalry brought an even broader smile. "Bet this doesn't last long," she teased.

He took her hand. "You keep waiting for me to open it, and I'll keep coming around."

They found the nature trail and moved toward the scent of water. A boardwalk crossed over the wetlands, and they followed it to a side trail toward the river. The Rio Grande flowed placidly along the grassy bank, reflecting the blue of the sky.

Michael's grip tightened, and he pointed with his other hand. "There. See the beaver's head in the water?"

She squinted, then saw the water's movement. And a black nose above the river. "I'd hoped to see more than a nose," she said.

"Glutton. Come with me." He led her along the bank of the river, where the marshy ground sucked at their shoes. "Beavers here build their homes in the riverbank. There's always been one under this big cane growth." A few feet from the river, he pointed to a boulder. "Have a seat, and maybe we'll see some action."

Once he scoured the underbrush for snakes and other undesirables, she settled on the rock. Water lapped at the bank in a soothing sound, and she squinted to see in the dim light. Within a couple of minutes, two beavers came waddling toward the water, with twigs in their mouths. They splashed into the water and disappeared under the canopy of cane. "Are they repairing their den?" she asked.

Michael joined her on the rock. "Or storing up food. There's a reason for the phrase 'busy beaver.' These rodents never seem to stop working."

"Kind of like someone else I know," she said.

He smiled. "They have an extended family, and sometimes the mother beaver raises kits that aren't her own. Beavers are territorial, too, and will fight for their families. And they mate for a lifetime."

"What is it you're trying to tell me?" she asked, trying to decipher the deliberate meaning in his voice.

His gaze held hers. "We can build a new family unit, the five of us. I'll work hard and make sure you have a good life."

She ran her fingertips over the stubble on his cheeks. "Don't make the mistake of thinking you need to provide us *things* when we need you, Michael."

"I know, I know," he said. "But I want to get us a nice house, some land. You need a car."

"I can see where this is headed, and I don't want to go there. The kids and I need shelter, food, and clothing."

"A man takes pleasure in providing for his family."

"We don't have to have a house like Shannon's or a field full of horses. I like the simple life we've found here. I'm content staying in our old rental and fixing it like we want it."

He grimaced. "The place is a dump."

She held his gaze. "It's got good bones, and I love it. Forget what you *should* do and focus on what we really need. Your love and attention."

"I thought that's what I was doing."

"The night we came here, you mentioned the prodigal son. I've been thinking about what my dad said about the story." She wet her lips. "He always said too much emphasis was placed on the prodigal's return and too little on the attitude of the son who stayed behind."

"He was a selfish dude. He should have been happier to see his brother."

"That's not what Dad meant, though." She hadn't thought about this in years, and she struggled to remember what her father had said. "Dad said the son who remained did what was expected out of duty instead of love."

"What do you have against duty? It's why people go to work every day."

She twisted a lock of her hair between her fingers. "Dad struggled with his tendency to put his duty to the church above his family. Some days he'd come home and take me and mom out for ice cream or kite flying. The next day he'd be deep in a new sermon series, and I'd have orders not to so much as put my toe in his office for weeks on end."

"You're remembering it as a kid remembers. He was a grown-up with responsibilities."

"I always knew he loved me." She released her hair and leaned back on the heels of her hands. "I just know he never overcame that defect. Now he doesn't have anything to worry about besides his congregation."

"Doing our duty is not a defect," Michael growled through gritted teeth.

His head turned away, and she couldn't tell if she was getting through or not. "I'm cold. Let's go back to the room."

He rose without protest and held her hand as they walked back to the truck. Could two people be less alike? He steered his life by logic and responsibility, and she navigated hers by emotion and conflict avoidance. She wasn't sure there was a happy medium between them.

They were silent on the return trip. After the long morning hiking, Gracie's muscles ached, but in a good way. She clung to Michael's hand as they walked the last few feet to their cabin. This afternoon they'd have to go home, and while she missed the kids, the time spent with Michael had cemented the love she'd been afraid to admit to herself. And to him.

He pulled her back when she would have gone into the cabin. "The door's cracked open."

"Maybe the maid is still here."

"Maybe." He moved her out of the way, then pushed open the door. He reached inside and flipped on the light.

Gracie peered over his shoulder. The bed was neatly made up, and the room appeared empty. "She's been here. Maybe she forgot to lock up."

"I hope none of our stuff is stolen." Michael put one boot inside the room, then the other. After striding the length of the room and peering into the bathroom, he motioned for Gracie to come in. "Looks clear."

She joined him. "Mr. Paranoid."

"Hey, it pays to be careful." He embraced her, and his lips grazed her forehead. "I want to stay around a long time."

She circled her arms around his waist. "You're not going anywhere, buster." She nuzzled his neck. "Um, you smell like sage and desert sun."

"Doesn't sound like a good combination to me."

She raised her head at his distracted tone. "What's wrong?"

He tipped his head to the side. "I thought I heard something."

Moving away from her, he approached their suitcases. He prodded one with his foot, and a frantic rattle sounded. His gaze met hers. "A rattler is in my suitcase. And it's zipped."

"Don't touch it!" She shuddered. "What if it bites you? We're a long way from help."

"It's inside the suitcase, and we have to get it out." Lifting the suitcase by the handle, he carried it outside and laid it down on the path. The rattle from inside the case intensified. "Stand back." Once he moved behind the suitcase, he unzipped it slowly. "I'm going to open it now. Go inside."

She retreated to the front door of the room. "I'm staying here. I'm far enough away."

He scowled but didn't say more. "Be ready to run inside."

She watched Michael and the case. The snake would exit the suitcase and run for cover, so she didn't think she was in danger. But what if she was wrong, and the snake struck at Michael?

Michael grasped the top of the suitcase and flipped it open, then leaped away. The rattling grew louder, then a triangular head appeared. The snake's tongue flickered as it tested the air. The rattling stopped, and the greenish-brown snake slithered out of the suitcase. The rattlesnake slipped sideways down the hill and across the road, where it disappeared into the brush on the other side.

"That was a Mojave green," Michael said. "You don't see them often. Their venom is sixteen times more deadly than a regular rattler's." He stooped and retrieved something from the suitcase.

Gracie shuddered. "I thought it was a diamondback. I saw the diamonds."

"The two are similar, but the greenish color gave it away. And did you see how the diamonds faded out near the end of its tail?"

"I didn't look that closely." Suddenly cold, Gracie hugged herself. "How did it get in your suitcase?"

"Someone had to have put it there. Whoever it was meant business. This far away from help, if one of us had been bitten on the face or chest, it would have been lights out."

Gracie clutched Michael's arm. "Someone was trying to kill you." She peered into the luggage. "Is it empty?"

He held up a paper. "Except for this."

She craned her head to try to read the scrawled handwriting. "What's it say?"

His mouth tightened. "'Gotcha.'"

She suppressed a shudder. "That's it?"

"Yep."

"How'd they know we were here?"

"That's what I'd like to know," he said. His eyes narrowed to slits. "I'm going to find out."

She hugged herself. "Maybe we should get on home and check on the kids."

"Let me call Allie." He grabbed his cell phone and punched in the number.

While he was on the phone, Gracie wandered over to a rock wall and sat down. The pungent scent of pine from the trees wafted down to her nose. The bright sun illuminated the striated rocks of red and brown. Her phone rang in her pocket, and she pulled it out, then nearly put it back when she recognized Cid's number.

Why couldn't he leave her alone? She'd been gone for weeks. Turning her back to Michael, she opened it. "Cid, what do you want from me? Can't you leave me alone?"

"Gracie, I miss you," Cid said. "I do not understand you. You promised to marry me. I think of Hope as my daughter. How can you rip us apart in this way?"

"You lied to me. You never intended to get out of the cartel. I can't trust you, Cid."

His voice grew eager. "I am out of it, Gracie, I swear."

She shouldn't have left the door open for him. The only thing to do now was to tell him the truth. "Cid, I've married someone else. I want you to leave me alone." The words had barely left her mouth when she wished she could snatch them back.

Cid's voice growled. "Married? What is this craziness?"

She dropped her head. "I'm married, Cid. It's over. Quit calling me, and get on with your life. I'm getting on with mine."

"Gracie, what have you done? It is not that easy to walk away from me. I hope this is not true, or you will have ruined everything."

The phone clicked off in her ear, then she stared at it in her hand. His tone left her queasy.

"The kids are fine." Michael dropped his cell phone back into his pocket. "You're pale. What's wrong? Who was on the phone?" He put his arm around her.

"It was Cid. I told him I was married. Maybe that was a mistake. He was so angry." His voice had held a dark threat, but Michael was right. She was safe here.

"The guy's a nutcase. He can't have you." He nuzzled his face in her hair. "Um, your hair smells like oranges."

The tension dropped from her shoulders in degrees until she leaned into his embrace. "Think it's safe to go back into our room?"

"I checked it out. No more snakes. The gecko is still waiting for you though."

"I can handle the gecko."

22

THE HOT SUN BEAT DOWN ON GRACIE'S UNCOVERED HEAD, AND SHE WISHED for a cowboy hat. On the way home, the sheriff had called and told them they could occupy their house again, so they'd picked up the kids and headed home. Michael had them in the barn, helping muck out the stables. She'd invited the Baileys for supper and only had an hour before she needed to start cooking.

She tried to push Cid's call from her mind as she leaned her bare arms on the rough wood of the corral. What had he meant? The only plans she'd ruined were the ones he'd made for their marriage. She had to keep reminding herself that she was hundreds of miles away from San Diego. Cid would be hard-pressed to find her in this remote location.

A new life stretched in front of her—one with promise and purpose. She didn't need her father's forgiveness now. Not when she was making a new life without him. The old life was gone anyway. It couldn't hurt her anymore. She ignored the internal ache that said otherwise.

She focused on the scene in front of her. Poor King had sores and a dull coat. The kids squealed in the barn, and she heard complaints of "Ooh, it stinks, Daddy!" She laughed, and King lifted his head and stared at her. His dark, liquid eyes seemed to ask what could be funny in life.

An impulse she couldn't explain to herself made her prop her foot on the lowest rung. All she had to do was climb the fence, and she could begin to interact with the horse. After the time with Michael, she wanted to be braver, stronger. King continued to stare at her, and the misery in his eyes drew her.

"Hey, boy," she said softly. The horse had been as frightened of her as she was of him. Maybe they could both find wholeness and fearlessness. She swung her leg over the top rail and landed on the other side of the fence.

King snorted and backed up. He neighed, and Gracie saw clouds tinged with orange. Fear? His tail swished the flies from his rump. The strong scent of horse closed her throat, but she forced herself to approach with her hand out.

"Hey, boy," she said softly.

King's eyes rolled to white, and she froze but kept her hand out. The horse snorted again, and his head came down. He pawed the ground. His nose lowered. She took another step and reached toward him. The horse nickered, then nuzzled the hand she extended. Her pulse stuttered, and she expected to feel his teeth on her skin, but the only sensation that registered was the softness of his muzzle.

"Good boy," she said. If only she'd brought a lead with her. She ran her hand down his neck. "You need to be curried," she said when her fingers detected the roughness of his coat. The horse stepped nearer and lifted his nose to her cheek. She forced herself to stand and wished Michael could see how brave she'd gotten. It was all his doing.

His voice came from over by the barn door. "Gracie, are you okay?"

She wasn't brave enough yet to turn her back on the horse, so she didn't turn. "I'm fine. More than fine. He likes me, Michael."

Boots thumped over the fence, then he was beside her with his hand on her shoulder. "You did it! He was as afraid of you as you were of him. Now you both have one another's measure. If you can do this, you can do anything. Like go see your dad."

She stroked the velvet softness of King's nose. "You're pushing again." But she smiled. She glanced at him from the corner of her eye, and the pride in his face choked her up. "I need a brush."

He handed her the one he held. "Here."

She took it and began to curry King. He stood still and let her run the brush through his rough hair. The dead, dry remains drifted to the ground like the leftovers of her fear. She was conscious of Michael's stare, but she silently continued with her task. There would be time for words later.

THE SCENT OF ALLSPICE AND SPARERIBS FILLED THE WARM KITCHEN. Gracie wiped her forehead with the back of her arm and opened the oven door to check on the Swedish ribs. The brown beans were done, and so were the dill potatoes. The Baileys would be here any minute.

Had there ever been such a perfect day? It didn't seem possible that everything she'd ever hoped for in her life would all land in her lap so swiftly. Her dream was complete, even down to the sweet dog sleeping on the rug by the door.

Michael dropped a kiss on her neck. "Anything I can do to help?"

She leaned back against him a moment. "Set the table?"

"I'm on it."

She watched Michael's face as he grabbed a stack of plates. He was such a thoughtful man who always wanted to do the right thing. Even if she was normally a bad judge of character, she knew she wasn't wrong about him. She wished she could believe that God cared so much about her that he was responsible for bringing her into her new husband's loving embrace.

"I can see the wheels turning. What are you thinking?"

"That you're a wonderful man, and I'm a lucky, lucky woman."

He grinned and kissed her on his way to grab the dinnerware. "Just make sure you remember that the next time I make you mad."

Allie stepped through the screen door, followed by her husband, who carried their son, Matthew. "Smells wonderful!"

"I hope you like it. We have apple pie for dessert."

"My mouth is already watering," Rick said, setting Matthew down. The toddler quickly rushed to grab Gracie's leg. She gave him a gingersnap cookie. "Where's Betsy?"

"Outside with Hope and Jordan," Rick said. "They're checking out King's progress. He's looking much better."

She glanced at Michael. "You want to call the girls and have them wash up?"

"Be right back."

As he started for the door, an earsplitting scream rattled the windows. Gracie recognized her daughter's cry and sprang for the door Michael was already rushing through. The dog crowded through with her. Caesar whined, then began to bark. He overtook Michael, then turned and barked as if to tell them to follow. Rick and Allie came running behind them. Allie had scooped up the little boy on the way.

Hope stood by the barn door. Betsy was beside her. Screams pealed from Hope's mouth. Michael reached her first and lifted her in his arms. "Hope, what's wrong?"

"The man!" she screamed, pointing to the back of the barn. "He took Jordan!"

Michael passed Hope to Gracie and ran with Rick to the back of the barn. Rick yelled for Allie to get the rest of the kids inside. "Go inside with Miss Allie," she told Hope.

Please, God, let us get Jordan back. Gracie thought she heard a child cry out as she followed the others. Her breath gasped in and out of her mouth as she ran. Her lungs burned with the exertion. Rick and Michael were just ahead. The men rounded the corner of the barn, and she heard Michael shout.

A cry from Jordan followed, and Gracie put on an extra burst of speed. Her chest laboring, she reached the back of the barn and veered behind it in time to see a horse galloping away.

A man sat atop it with her daughter pinned in front of him. Caesar was on the horse's heels.

A cry escaped Gracie's lips. "Jordan!"

Jordan glanced back, her eyes dark pools of terror. "Mommy!"

Even though her brain knew it was hopeless, Gracie ran after the horse and rider, which quickly pulled away from her. Sobbing, she fell to her knees with the last of her strength spent. The thunderous pounding of hooves came from behind her. Michael bent over the bare back of Fabio as he chased the kidnapper. She struggled to her feet and made another attempt to follow. Their daughter needed her. She had to catch them.

Michael's hand came down on the horse's rump. "Giddup!" he yelled. The horse began to gain on the kidnapper bearing Jordan away. Caesar's snapping at the horse's heels was slowing down the swarthy man, who kept glancing back at them.

Gracie stumbled on a rock and fell headlong to the ground. She struggled to her feet. Rick was beside her before she could stand, and he pulled her upright.

"Stay here," he said. He puckered his lips and a shrill whistle pierced the air. Another horse whinnied and trotted toward him. Gracie had never seen it, but the animal was a beautiful black stallion. He grabbed the horse's mane and swung onto its back, then set out after Michael and the kidnapper.

Gracie squinted after Michael as he neared the man with their daughter. Michael's horse was almost level with the other one. His arm went out in a karate chop movement that caught the other man in the throat. The kidnapper fell from the horse, and Michael reached over and scooped Jordan from the saddle. The riderless horse snorted and stopped by a large rocky outcropping.

Michael's horse turned and started back toward them. All Gracie wanted was to have Jordan in her arms again. Her pain forgotten, she stumbled to meet them. Her chest was on fire, but she had to run.

Rick had nearly reached Michael and Jordan. He glanced back at Gracie. "Look out!" he shouted.

She stopped and realized the kidnapper had regained his feet in the path ahead of her. He pulled a revolver from a holster. She stopped and turned to run. A lasso sailed from Rick's hand and snaked over the man's hand. Rick yanked and the gun went flying. The man swore, then turned and ran. Rick pulled the rope back toward him, but before he had it looped and ready to go again, the man had reached his horse and vaulted into the saddle.

Gracie didn't care about him. Michael was in front of her with Jordan in his arms. The little girl was crying and clinging to her daddy. When she saw Gracie, she lunged for her. "Mommy!" she cried.

The word was the sweetest in the world. Gracie took Jordan in her arms. "You're safe, sweetheart," she crooned, rocking the child in her arms. Jordan clung to her, and Gracie hugged her tight. She mustn't show the child how frightened she was.

"It's okay," she whispered, running a soothing hand over her daughter's hair. Her gaze met Michael's over Jordan's head.

Vargas would stop at nothing to punish the Wayne family.

MICHAEL LOCKED EVERY DOOR OF THEIR HOME AFTER THE SHERIFF LEFT with his notes. They'd managed to force down the dried-out remains of supper. Rick and Allie had wanted the family to come home with them again, but Michael assured them they'd be fine.

Finding the man who had tried to snatch Jordan wouldn't be easy. It was a big country out there. The guy would vanish back into his hole like the rattlesnake he was. Michael marveled at the resiliency of kids. Jordan was giggling with Hope as they played with dolls in the living room. His wife was a different matter, though. Gracie was still white and shaken.

He thrust a cup of coffee into her hands. "Drink."

She curled her fingers around it as though she were cold, but he didn't see how she could be. The air-conditioning wasn't working well, and it had to be nearly eighty in the house. When she sipped the coffee, he saw goose bumps on her arms. Shock maybe. He stepped to the living room and grabbed a red throw. Back in the kitchen, he draped it around her shoulders.

"Thanks," she whispered. Her blue eyes focused on his face. "That man is despicable, Michael."

"That's what I've been saying." He ran his hand through his hair. "But why grab Jordan? What could he possibly gain by taking her?"

"I don't know. It makes no sense. The only thing I know is we've got to get out of here."

He took her shoulders in his hands and stared into her face. Her blue eyes were wide and fearful. "Honey, there's no place to run. We have to stand and face this together as a family."

Her eyes blinking rapidly, she wrenched away from him. "We can't stay here with the kids in danger, Michael. How can you even think of it?"

He crossed his arms over his chest. "If we run, we'll just be lulled into a false sense of security. The cartel is everywhere, Gracie. *Everywhere*. Where could we possibly be safe?"

She waved her hands in the air. "North! Maybe Michigan. Or North Dakota. Anyplace where there are people nearby to call for help."

"Why do we need people when we have God?"

Her eyes widened, then shuttered. When her nod finally came, it was reluctant. "God lets bad things happen sometimes."

Her mother again. Everything always went back to that. "I know, honey. He does, and we don't always understand it. But we can choose how we respond to the challenges that come—with fear or with faith. I choose faith."

Her lips trembled when she pressed them together. "I want to choose faith, but I don't deserve it."

He shook her gently. "Gracie, Gracie, you've got to face your father and go on. As long as you have that cloud over your head, you're never going to let go of fear. You've been running for years. From yourself, from God. Isn't it time you faced your problems and solved them?"

"What would you know about problems?" She tucked a lock of hair behind her ear.

"You think I don't have problems?"

"Look at you—the officer everyone looks up to. The rescuer who fights off the attacker wherever he might appear. You don't know anything about guilt."

"Calm down. You'll scare the kids," he said quietly.

"I bet the metallic taste of fear has never rested on your tongue for a minute." Her voice rose with every sentence.

Don't get mad. She's just scared. "Life hasn't been perfect for me, Gracie. I wasn't there for a wife and she divorced me. I haven't been around to raise Jordan and Evan. You don't think I feel guilty about that?"

"No, I don't think you do," she said. "You're a man who executes his responsibilities to the letter. Do you ever get upset about anything? Really *mad* with your passions engaged? I don't think so."

His heart rate increased, and he slowed it with a few deep breaths. She was trying to push his buttons, and he couldn't let her. "I'm trying to help you," he said, his tone even. "This is about you, not me. Fighting with me helps you get on top of your fear, and I understand that. But it's not going to protect the kids."

Her face crumpled. "I'm so scared." She hugged herself, and the blanket around her shoulders slipped to the floor. "I keep thinking about Cid's call." She rubbed her head. "He said my marriage to you ruined things. I keep expecting to see him."

"Is that why you want to run?"

She put her hands over her face. "A few hours ago everything was perfect. Now it's slipping out of my hands—again."

He dropped his hands, picked up the throw and put it around her again, leaving his hands on her shoulders. With her this close, he could see the dusting of freckles across her nose. He struggled to keep his tone even when he wanted to yell at her for not giving him the details of the call sooner.

"I want to help you," he said, accenting each word. "Exactly what did he say?"

She clutched the throw and stepped away. "He said I needed to come back. That I'd ruined everything. It made no sense, and I . . . I hung up."

"Did he threaten you?"

She shook her head. "Not overtly, but there was something in his voice that scared me."

"Did you ask him what he meant?"

She sighed and shook her head. "I didn't want to hear it. I should have made him tell me what he meant."

"I should call him," he said.

"I can handle him."

He would have pointed out she wasn't doing such a hot job of that, but he didn't want to see the clouds return to her eyes. He could get lost in those blue pools of trust. He nodded toward the fading light outside. "Let's go. I want to teach you to shoot."

"I don't think I can."

"I'll show you." He led her to the hall and stopped by the doorway into the living room, where the kids played. "Mommy is going to learn to shoot a gun," he called to them.

They squealed and came running. "I want to watch," Hope said. She took her mother's hand.

Michael smiled when Jordan took the other one.

They reached the yard and Gracie pointed. "There's that horse Rick rode. The black one I've never seen."

"The stallion roams the area. He belongs to Shannon." Michael went to his truck and got a pistol. "Now, we're going to teach you to stand and face danger when it comes."

23

THE SUN WAS ON ITS RETURN TRIP, RADIATING SHARDS OF GOLD AND RED low on the horizon. If Gracie wasn't so scared, she'd drink in the surroundings. The air held the crisp edge of coming twilight.

How could such a perfect two days have ended this way—with fear coating her tongue, and every muscle on full alert? She wanted to go back to last night, when she lay in Michael's arms and listened to the birds sing outside their window. Was there to be no happiness for her anywhere? Would God expect her to pay for her past mistakes the rest of her life?

"Gracie?"

She came out of her trance to see Michael holding out the butt of the gun to her. She wanted to tell Michael it was too dark to see the target, but he'd know it was a lie. It was gloomy, but not dark.

Michael pointed to an aluminum pan attached to a fence post. "There's your target. You need to learn to protect yourself and the kids when I'm not around."

"I don't like guns." She stared at the gleaming silver and black revolver in his hand. It looked big and dangerous.

"Neither will a kidnapper. You sight down the barrel at him with this thing, and he'll run."

"Who are you fooling? No one has ever taken me seriously." Even Cid treated her like a child.

He winked at her. "It's because you're so cute."

"Cute," she grumbled. "What woman wants to be called cute? We want to be called beautiful, mesmerizing, addictive. If I were three inches taller, you wouldn't call me cute."

Michael chuckled, then curled her fingers around the grip. "Here, take the gun."

She nearly dropped the heavy thing in the sand. "It will take two hands to hold it."

He studied her. "You're right. Wait here a minute."

She watched him jog across the yard to the house and disappear inside. When he came back, he held a snub-nosed revolver with a wood handle. She eyed it and said nothing.

"This is a Smith & Wesson 327 revolver."

"Cute," she said.

"It's easy to use, and you can conceal it in an ankle holster." He guided her arms into position. "Support your arm with your left one."

"You can do it, Mommy," Hope called from behind her.

All three kids were perched on a fence post far enough away from the action to stay safe. Knowing her daughter would see her ineptitude made Gracie want to drop the gun and run to the house. "I can't do this," she whispered. "Don't make me."

His fingers tightened on her hand. "You can and you will. Think about our kids."

He knew where to hit her. She'd do anything for the children. "Okay."

"Spread your legs apart a little to take a firm stance." He waited until she complied. "Now sight down the barrel. See that little raised nub there? Aim it at the pie pan."

Her arms shook as she tried to obey. She got the little nub aimed at the center of the aluminum plate. Her index finger curled around the trigger. "Now what?"

He was behind her with his arms around each side of her as he guided her movements. "Squeeze gently. Don't just jerk back on the trigger. It will throw off your aim."

His breath moved gently across her cheek. The strength in his arms and hands radiated to her. She forced herself to concentrate on the job at hand. Her finger tightened on the trigger. More, just a little more. When the report came from the gun, she flinched, and the shot went high. It zinged against the rocky outcropping on the other side of the fence.

Adrenaline pumped through her muscles, and she was instantly in flight mode. For a moment she was back in San Diego as the men poured from the van with their guns popping. She labored to inhale through tight lungs.

"What's wrong?" Michael asked.

"Nothing, just stunned." She struggled to regain her composure.

"If you hadn't flinched, you would have been right on the money. Try it again, and this time hold the gun steady."

His arms tightened around her again, and she wanted to yell for him to get away so she could concentrate. She gritted her teeth and raised the gun into place again. This time when she squeezed the trigger, Michael helped her hold it steady, and the bullet hit the plate. "I did it!"

Michael smiled and nodded but stepped away. "Try it by yourself."

Okay, maybe she hadn't done it. Biting her lip, she took her stance and raised the gun. Her hands shook, and she tightened her grip. With the nub on the plate, she squeezed off another shot. It nicked the outer edge of the plate, and she nearly dropped the gun, not quite believing she'd hit it.

The kids clapped their approval. "Yay, Mommy," Hope called.

"Good shot. Again."

"Slave driver." But she smiled and lifted the revolver again. Shooting wasn't as hard as she'd thought. In five shots, she hit the plate three times.

"Not bad for a first try. We'll practice every night. For now, I want you to go to Rick's every day. Let the kids get on the school bus from there and stay until they come home."

"I'll be fine here with the kids in school. I don't need to go to Allie's."

His lips formed a firm line. "You're the one who wanted to move to a city so you could be near people."

She wanted to protest again but knew it was no use. Once the kids were on the bus tomorrow, she'd come home and clean, then go back over. He wouldn't be the wiser. She could lock the house and take the gun with her. While she liked Allie, Gracie wasn't a child who had to be looked after.

"I see the wheels turning," he said. "It's for your own good, Gracie."

"I know," she said, handing the gun back to him.

"Wait." He strapped a holster to her ankle, shoved the gun into it, then pulled her jeans back over the revolver. "No one will suspect you're packing heat."

"I don't have a permit," she protested.

"We'll get you one as soon as we can." He unbuckled it. "I wanted to show you how it fit."

She chuckled. "I never thought the day would come." She motioned to the kids, who jumped from the fence and ran to join them.

Hope took her hand. Gracie glanced at Michael as he walked toward the house, shoulders back, head erect. A man's man. And one a woman could trust if she had any faith in her own judgment. She was ready to believe she might have made a good decision for once in her life.

GRACIE LAY AWAKE IN THE PREDAWN. THE ROOSTER CROWED. SHE HEARD the distant rumble of a truck's tires on the macadam road in front of the house. Michael's breathing was slow and deep. He hadn't yet begun to swim toward consciousness. She wasn't sure she'd slept at all, even though Michael had herded the kids into one room and put Caesar on guard in the hall last night.

She sat up and eased out of bed. Her feet felt the floor for her slippers, and once she had them on, she moved to the door and into the hallway. Caesar raised his head when Gracie peeked into the room where the children slept. The security light shone in the window and touched Hope's sweet cheeks as she lay with one hand under her cheek. All arms and legs, Evan was sprawled at the end of the bed, and Jordan was curled with her back to Hope. All was well here.

She went downstairs and stepped outside onto the back stoop that faced the barn. Predawn had a certain smell. Freshness mixed with new hope. She needed to find a bright lining wherever she could.

King nickered to her from the corral, and she stepped into the weedy yard and approached the fence. "I don't have any sugar, boy." He stretched his head across the fence, and she instinctually stepped back.

Hesitantly, she held out her hand and let him press his velvety nose against her fingers. "You wouldn't hurt me, would you?" Yesterday's bond would continue to grow.

"Gracie? You okay?"

She turned to see Michael standing on the stoop in his pajama bottoms without a shirt. Just the way she'd left him. "I couldn't sleep."

"You should have woken me. I don't like you out here by yourself."

After rubbing King's nose a final time, she retraced her steps to the house. Michael opened his arms, and she went into them. His musky scent buried her fears, and she pressed her lips against the warm skin of his chest.

"It'll be okay," he said. "I won't let anything happen."

She said nothing. He'd try his best, but she knew the dragon waited out there to devour any happiness she might find. She should never have dragged this good man and his children into the pit of God's rejection with her.

"I have to go to work early this morning," Michael said. "Could you come back after the kids are on the bus, just long enough to feed and water my horse and King? Fabio's in the pen inside the barn. He can't hurt you."

"Fabio wouldn't mean to hurt anyone." Though she knew and agreed with her words, her pulse sped up at the thought of entering the barn. The smells would be enough to bring back the fear.

"Thanks, honey. I'd better get in the shower." He kissed her, his lips warm and reassuring. "Want to join me?"

She laughed. "Don't tempt me."

"It's what I hope to do best." He kissed her again, this time with more hunger.

She broke away and laughed. "You have to go to work early, remember?"

"Yeah, yeah." He patted her bottom, then stepped back into the house.

Gracie got the kids up and ready for school. Michael dropped them all at Bluebird. It was all she could do to watch the children get on the bus. Last night Michael's arguments about maintaining as much normalcy as possible had been persuasive. In the bright daylight, she wasn't so sure it was the right decision. What if a gunman held up the bus and took the children off of it? Several different scenarios played out in her imagination.

She asked to borrow Allie's car to run back and feed the horses. The silence at the house made Gracie's nerves jitterbug as she found a dented metal bucket. She filled it with water from the garden hose on the side of the house, then carried it toward the barn. She watered King first to delay stepping inside.

The closed barn door beckoned her. She heard Fabio whinny and snort from inside his stall. She could do this. Fabio wasn't dangerous. Michael knew she needed to stop running and face some of her fears. This was one small step in that direction. Setting down the bucket, she slid open the barn door. The scent of hay and dust rushed at her, evoking a tornado of emotion. It took every bit of strength she had to stand still as the winds of memory buffeted her.

Her mother wasn't lying in a pool of blood inside. There was nothing but a hungry and thirsty animal in the stall in front of her. Gradually, her heart resumed its rhythm. Her eyes adjusted to the gloom. Though her legs trembled, they supported her as she carried the bucket to Fabio.

"Here you go," she said, falling into a soothing tone. She climbed onto the railing, then poured the water into his trough.

Fabio plunged his nose into the water and drank. Gracie turned around and spied the bag of feed by the door. By the time she dumped his food into the feed bag and attached it to the gelding, it was as if she'd never left this part of her life behind. Why, she could even curry him if she wanted to. She started toward the comb and brush, when a shadow moved in the doorway. Squinting through the gloom, she saw a Hispanic woman peering into the dim interior of the barn.

Gracie took in the crisp appearance of the woman's jeans and shirt, the expensive athletic shoes. Alarms rang in Gracie's head even though the woman didn't appear dangerous. "Can I help you?" she asked. A pitchfork hung on a peg nearby. If she had to, she could lunge for it.

Glancing outside, the woman stepped into the barn, then sidled out of the light. "No, *señora,* but I can help you. You must leave this place. Go far away before he arrives to take you and the *niña.*"

Gracie gasped and put her hand to her throat. She smelled oranges in the woman's voice. Only Cid's voice had ever caused her to have that reaction. She took a closer glance and realized the woman was familiar, though Gracie couldn't place her.

"Before who arrives?" She took a step back.

The woman shook her head. "Ask no questions. If he discovers I have come here to warn you, the journalists will report my head lying in a schoolyard. He thinks I have come to deliver his message. Leave, *señora.* Leave right now, before it's too late."

"His message?"

The woman clutched her hands together. "He says if you will meet him when he calls, he will spare your husband and his children. But I know him and I do not believe it."

"Spare my husband and children." She shook her head. "Why would Vargas want to talk to me?"

"It is not Vargas I speak of."

"Then who?" She studied the woman's strangely familiar face. "Cid has a half sister. Are you her?"

The woman held up her hand. "Please, no questions!"

She'd guessed right. "What does Cid want with me? I'm married now. It's over between us."

"For you, perhaps. For Cid, it is not over. His obsession only grows."

"I don't understand any of this."

"I have no time to explain it. Listen to my warning. I do not want your blood on my hands."

Blood. Gracie felt her own drain from her head. "He means to kill me?"

"When you and your daughter are of no more use to them."

"What does my daughter have to do with this?"

"Everything. He panicked when they failed to take the child yesterday."

Spots danced in Gracie's vision. "Hope was the target?"

The woman inclined her head. "A mistake was made that will not be repeated. They are out of time."

"They? You mean the men who killed the federal agents?"

The woman backed toward the door. "If you stay here, the children will be in danger also, and your husband will be a dead man."

"They've done nothing!"

"It is no matter. You must leave this place. Today. Do not take his call. Run, and do not look back." She held out her hand. "Tell no one you have seen me. If he hears . . ." She shuddered. "My life is in your hands. I could not stand by and see innocents harmed."

"Stay with me, then," Gracie urged. "Don't go back."

The woman wiped her eyes. "There is no help for me. Too many times have I turned from the right path and chosen the wrong. This thing I could not do. Maybe I will find grace in God's eyes for the one good deed I could do."

Gracie stepped closer to her, but the woman backed away. "Please. Do not look on my face. It is not that I do not trust you, but he might make you describe me. Forget what you see. Please, say nothing to your husband. To anyone. If you do, my blood is on your hands." Glancing outside first, the woman stepped through the doorway, and the sound of her feet running on the dirt faded.

Gracie reached for her cell phone to call Michael, then stopped. He would rush right home. And what if the woman was right—what if Cid would make sure Michael and the children were killed? She couldn't live with herself if she brought danger to the ones she loved more than life.

Her choices had brought her to this place. Now she had to run again. At least until she could get Hope to safety. The face of Gracie's father flashed into her mind. He would take in Hope. Would Cid know to look in Pecos? She'd never told him where she was from, but how hard could that be to figure out?

She rubbed her forehead where pain began to pulse. Was there no way out?

With the horses cared for, she walked back to the house and strapped the tiny gun onto her ankle. Permit or not, she was taking it.

The tick of the clock on the wall in the living room was the only sound, so she flipped on the TV. A morning talk show came on, and she sat down to try to think.

What right did she have to drag Michael, Jordan, and Evan into this morass? Her choices loomed in front of her. She could stay and hope Michael could be vigilant enough to protect them all, or take Hope to safety and confront Cid. Make him see that it was over. She wanted to run and hide somewhere, but Michael was right. There was nowhere to go. She had to have faith he could protect their family.

The talk-show hostess was replaced by a reporter standing on the sidewalk in front of a modest home. Gracie listened as the newscaster reported seven people shot and killed in El Paso.

"The man and woman were beheaded," the reporter said. "The police suspect a Mexican cartel involvement. The family had been under a death threat and were being watched by police, but the policeman was shot first, then the family."

Nausea roiled in Gracie's stomach. "Michael can't be everywhere at once," she whispered. "I have to fix this myself if I want to save my family."

She flipped off the TV and went to the car. King whinnied when he saw her, and she paused before crossing the weedy yard to the corral. "Hey, King," she whispered, rubbing his nose. He huffed into her palm.

"I don't want to leave here, but I have to." She wiped her nose with a paper hanky, but tears clogged it again. "You'll be fine without me. Michael will take good care of you. So will the kids. And you'll forget about me."

His dark eyes denied the statement, and he nuzzled her neck. His warm breath and horsey smell made her want to throw her arms around him and sob for the happiness that had been all too fleeting. She'd named her daughter for the hope she'd dreamed of having for the future, but it had been nothing but a mockery. She should have expected this.

She kissed King's nose, then ran back to the car. When the vehicle reached the end of the driveway, she stopped and glanced back at the house. For a brief time she'd had a home.

CAESAR LOPED AT MICHAEL'S SIDE AS HE EXITED THE TRUCK AND JOGGED toward the Rio Grande, where Estevez waited. A vehicle had left ruts in the dirt, and Michael saw where the tracks crossed the shallow riverbed to the other side.

When he reached Estevez, he knelt and examined the ruts. "Looks like it was loaded down."

"Probably a coyote bringing a truckload of illegals through," Estevez said.

"Or a load of guns and ammo," Michael said.

Estevez's lips tightened. "You sound like your brother."

"He was right, though, wasn't he?"

"That's been the only time arms came through here."

"That you know of." Michael glared at his brother's former partner. "What is it with you, Estevez? You don't like me. I get it. But I've done nothing to warrant your antagonism. We're on the same side. And since you brought up my brother's name, listen: I've been thinking about what I found in the file on his death."

"What?"

"Nothing. And that bugs me. There doesn't look to have been a real investigation into his death. It's like the incident was logged in and forgotten. He deserved better than that."

Estevez's mouth turned grimmer. "He was my friend. I've been investigating it."

"Then why is nothing in the file?"

"You just missed it. I personally input the evidence I've found."

"What evidence? I went through every shred of the physical file and every bit of the electronic one."

"Fingerprints, shell casings, a shoe. Eyewitness evidence. An informant's testimony."

"There's none of that in the files. Check for yourself. It's all gone. Now, why would that be?"

Estevez studied Michael's face as if to gauge whether he was lying. "For real?"

"Yeah. So that tells me someone in the department scrubbed it. Which means only one of two things."

"Blackmail or payoff," Estevez said. He let loose with a string of profanity.

Michael felt the weight of the knowledge like a physical blow. Anyone in the department could be to blame. In fact, how could he know Estevez wasn't covering up his involvement by pointing his finger at someone else? He ran through the list of possible suspects: Estevez, Parker, Fishman. Even Pickens himself could be behind this.

"Sometimes I hate this business," he muttered.

Estevez glanced at him. "Then why stay?"

"It's my job. It's part of who I am."

"Not a very good reason."

"Maybe not." Was it reason enough anymore? He'd wearied of the constant threat of violence, the looking over his shoulder, the red tape and politics.

A movement caught Michael's attention. A woman darted from

shrub to shrub, making her way toward a crossing farther down the river. "Look there," he said, starting in that direction.

Caesar bounded ahead of him. He reached the woman before the men did and backed her up against a boulder. Every time she tried to move, he bared his teeth and hedged her away from the crossing. Michael squinted against the glare of the sun and studied her. About thirty. Hispanic. Dressed in expensive jeans and a blouse. New athletic shoes. Not your typical illegal alien.

"Where you headed?" he asked, forcing a smile into his voice.

She clutched trembling hands in front of her. "Please. Call off your dog."

"Caesar, sit," Michael commanded. The dog padded back to his side and lay down. "Do you have any identification?"

She shook her head and stared at the dirt.

Estevez joined them. "Why are you out here?"

"I walk. There." She pointed across the river.

"You live over there?" Michael saw the way she continued to tremble.

Her shoulders slumped. "*Sí.*"

He and Estevez exchanged glances. Their job was to stop incoming illegal aliens, not prevent them from returning to Mexico. He should have escorted her to the water and made sure she exited the country, but there was something about the way she glanced at him that aroused his curiosity. He almost thought she knew him. "What's your name?"

"It is of no matter," she said, finally raising her head enough to show her dark eyes. Those eyes held a flare of rebellion.

"Humor me," he said, hardening his tone.

"I will not. You cannot keep me. I am leaving."

He caught her arm. "I could take you in as an alien with no papers. What are you doing here?"

She glared at his hand on her arm, then up into his face. "You should attend to your own business, Mr. Wayne."

"How do you know my name?"

"It is enough that I know. Watch your wife. And her child." She jerked, and her arm tore from his grasp.

"Wait!" He sprang after her, but Caesar collided with him and slowed him down. She crossed the rocks poking above the river's surface and reached the haven of Mexico.

"I need to go home," he told Estevez. Without waiting for an answer, he ran for his truck.

24

GRACIE'S FLIP-FLOPS SMACKED THE TILES IN THE SCHOOL HALL AS SHE
ran to the office. Bursting through the door, she told the receptionist
she wanted to take her daughter out. The woman eyed her with suspicion, so without being asked, Gracie pulled out her ID. "Just get my
daughter," she snapped.

"Sorry, Mrs. Wayne. We have to be careful, of course."

"Of course," Gracie echoed. "Hurry, please." At least the receptionist didn't question why she wanted her daughter. The woman left the
office. Gracie glanced at the clock above the door. Nearly ten. She'd be
to her father's by one, even if she stopped to grab some food for Hope.

The door opened, and the receptionist came in with Hope, whose
eyes were wide and scared. She carried her new Winnie-the-Pooh
book bag.

"What's wrong, Mommy?"

"It's okay, honey," Gracie said, running her hand over her daughter's silken hair. "Don't be scared. Thank you," she said to the receptionist before taking Hope's hand and exiting the office.

"Where are we going?" Hope asked once they were in the hall.

"I have a surprise for you," Gracie said, forcing a smile. "I'm taking you to meet your grandfather."

Hope stopped and gripped her mom's hand tighter. "I have a grandpa?"

"Yes, honey. He and I—well, we've kind of been mad at each other. But it's time we got over that. I want him to see he has the most beautiful granddaughter in the world."

Hope's smile burst out. "I like it when you tell me I'm pretty. Am I pretty, Mommy?"

"The prettiest little girl ever born," Gracie said. They reached Allie's car, and she buckled Hope into the back. "It's going to be a long drive," she told her. "I brought you some coloring books and crayons and a few stories. Or you can take a nap if you like."

"Are we going to stop and have lunch? I might get hungry. My tummy is already making noises. Our class was just getting ready to go to lunch."

"We sure are. In about an hour, we'll stop and have something to eat." Gracie buckled her seat belt, then pulled onto the street.

The note she'd left Michael said only that she was taking Hope and leaving, but he'd check at her dad's. Which was fine, because once she saw how her father responded to her sudden reappearance, she'd call Michael and explain better. Keeping her burning eyes on the road, she tried to convince herself this was best all the way around.

His earnest blue eyes came to mind, and she nearly turned

around. How could she leave him and the children? How could she not? Staying would put them all in terrible danger. She'd seen those federal agents gunned down right in front of her. They would all be safer without her, and she had the power to protect them.

She wasn't meant to be happy. It was clear God would thwart her at every turn. And how could she blame him? Look at what she'd done with her life. Her mother was in the grave because of Gracie's selfishness. Her money was gone, with nothing to show for it. Now the man she loved would die because of her poor choices. Unless she stopped it somehow. She was done. At the bottom of life's barrel.

The road blurred, and she blinked twice to clear her vision. Self-pity wouldn't save them. In the rearview mirror, she could see Hope's beautiful eyes drooping in sleep. No sacrifice was too great for her daughter. Once she was sure her daughter was safe, she needed to find Cid and get to the bottom of his obsession. If she could convince him to make a new life without her, she'd go back to Michael and the kids.

Her pulse kicked. The woman had said Cid wanted Hope. Why? It made no sense. If she threw herself on the mercy of an evil man, who would protect Hope? Her father was sixty years old. How could he protect a child? Her thoughts scattered like cottonwood seeds on the wind. There seemed no way out for her.

I'm here.

The words, though inaudible, hit her heart. She gasped and jerked the car to the side of the road. The pounding in her chest was only her heart, not God trying to get her attention. Or was it? "Is that you, God?" she whispered. "Are you here?"

Air, she had to have air. She ran the window down and tried to draw enough oxygen into her lungs. It was as if a horse stood on her chest, squeezing the air from her. Her eyes burned, then tears slid down her cheeks. She was tired, so tired, of dealing with her shame. Could God really forgive her? The reality sank in with a gentle breeze through the window.

He'd never left her. She was the one who left him. He was waiting in the same place where she'd turned and walked away. The tears came faster now, obscuring her vision, clogging her throat. The steering wheel was her only support, and she collapsed against it.

"I want to move back to you. Show me how," she choked out. Though she lay still against the wheel, her head spun, faster and faster, as though she sailed through time and space. Gradually, her panting stilled, her pulse slowed, her vision cleared. Warmth enveloped her as though someone held her in his arms, safer than she'd ever been.

God was here, right here. Closing her eyes, she unburdened herself on the Lord. All the vile, selfish things she'd done over the past years flooded into her memory, and she confessed them all. With each one behind her, it was as though she floated higher and higher above the seat grounding her in place. When she opened her eyes, she was clean. And she couldn't stop smiling.

Returning to God had been so easy. Why had she turned it into a mountain when it was only a groundhog hill? Clean. She was clean. The shame, the knowledge of how she'd disappointed God, was washed away. God had never let go of her, though she'd ignored his gentle promptings. There was only one more person whose pardon she had to seek.

She pulled onto the road again. Her father's house was only five miles away. The closer the car rolled to her destination, the slower she went. Facing God with her failures had been easier than what lay ahead of her. Her father could order her off the property. He might shut the door in her face.

The road loomed just ahead. She forced herself to slow, then turn down the road. The macadam strummed a message against her tires. *Turn back, turn back*, it said. As she came to the driveway, she nearly obeyed the insistent command. But no. She'd come this far. Hope deserved a better life. She deserved a grandfather, and the dad Gracie remembered would dote on her daughter.

Even if he threw Gracie to the vultures.

Her cell phone rang. She slowed the car and grabbed it. "Hello, Cid," she said, keeping her voice low. "I thought you'd call."

"It is now time to come home, Gracie. I know where you are. If you do not come, the next bomb we leave for your husband will not be discovered. And we will make sure to put one in the little ones' rooms too."

She couldn't breathe, couldn't speak. In her mind's eye, she saw the explosion, the blood on dear Michael's face, the screams of the children. "Cid, I'm married. What's the point of this?"

"I will tell you when you come," he said, his voice inflexible. "And do not think of refusing. I have your horse, and he will go to the pet food factory if you do not show up."

She gasped. "King? You took my horse?"

"If you can call that piece of flesh a horse."

No plea would move him. The obsession in his voice had grown more strident. She smelled oranges. "You're cruel, Cid," she whispered. "Take him home. I'll come."

"I thought so."

"Where should I meet you?" she finally managed to whisper.

"Davis Mountains Indian Lodge. At five."

"Davis Mountains Indian Lodge," she repeated. "Where?"

"There's a picnic area."

He gave her directions, and she committed them to memory. "I'll be there," she said.

"Yes, you will. Or your new husband and his brats are dead."

The phone clicked in her ear, then fell out of her nerveless fingers. "Oranges, just like his sister," she muttered.

Her hands trembled, and she clutched them in her lap. She swallowed hard and put the phone away. Her father's house peeked over the hill. She accelerated the last few feet, then slowed. The tires quit their litany when they hit the smooth blacktop driveway.

The car rolled to a stop. She shut off the engine, then sat looking at the house. Glancing in the rearview mirror, she saw Hope was still asleep. Good. This was a conversation best made between her and her father first. She ran down the windows, then eased open her door. A gentle click latched it without waking Hope. The sun glared in her eyes, and she squinted. The door to the house stood open, barred only with the screen door. Dad must be outside, in the barn or the garden.

After making sure Hope still slept, she walked to the side of the house. The sweet smell of freshly turned earth told her where to find her father. She stood watching him as he stooped among the last of the tomatoes. He was a little grayer, a little heavier, but still the man she remembered. The man who used to play horsey with her. The father who took her for ice cream on Saturdays. The daddy who read her a story at night before he tucked her into bed.

Then he turned and their eyes met.

"GRACIE?" MICHAEL CALLED. HE LET THE FRONT DOOR BANG BEHIND HIM. The house held a still quality that put his senses on high alert. "Anyone here?"

Caesar's ears stood up, and he padded to the kitchen, where Michael heard him lap from his water bowl. The dog detected no intruders. Michael followed him. "Find Gracie, boy." The dog licked his chops and whined but made no move to leave.

She wasn't here.

She was at Bluebird Ranch. His terror had driven today's plans from his mind. Even as his relief blew from his lips, a paper on the table caught his attention. He recognized Gracie's handwriting. His name was at the top.

Michael, I'm so sorry, but I have to leave. It's better for you and the kids if you don't try to find me. I love you too much to stay. Gracie.

It took a moment for the words to penetrate. Leave? As in go for good? No, he wouldn't accept that. Gracie loved him. She wouldn't go off and leave a cold note behind. Pain crushed his chest. His hand spasmed around the paper, and it crumpled under the pressure.

"Don't do this to me, Gracie," he muttered.

He released his grip on the note and smoothed it to reread it. That's what she meant—that she was leaving him for good. The strength ran out of his legs, and he sat heavily in the chair. A family didn't disintegrate when times got tough. Not if they loved one another. Could someone have made her write this? The warning from the woman at the river came to mind. He had to find Gracie, protect her. She had very little money, so she couldn't have gone far.

She had no vehicle. She either left here with help, or under duress. He grabbed his cell phone and dialed Allie.

"Hey, Michael," she said when she answered.

"Has Gracie been back since she went to feed the livestock?"

The smile left her voice, and she shook her head. "Is everything okay?"

He sagged against the wall. "She left a note at the house saying it would be better for us if she was gone. Did she say anything at all?"

"She just said she'd be back after feeding the horses. Um, Michael, speaking of the horses, did you give King away?"

"Of course not. Gracie loves that horse."

"I could have sworn that was him in a trailer that went by about half an hour ago."

Michael went to the window and stared toward the barn. He didn't see the horse, but Allie must have been mistaken. "Where could she have gone?" he muttered.

"Is it because Jordan was nearly kidnapped yesterday?"

Caesar whined and Michael stooped to rub his ears. "I think her old boyfriend has found her. She's trying to escape again. But he'll just find her like he did this time. It's not that hard these days."

"Does she have any family who would help?"

"Her father," he said, suddenly remembering. "I bet she's gone to Pecos."

"That's not running very far."

"No. No, it's not. Which means if she's there, it's just her first stop. I've got to figure out his name and where he lives. Thanks, Allie."

"You want Rick to come with you? I can get him from the barn. He could fly you there."

"That's a great idea! I'll be down as soon as I have an address. Is it okay if I call the school and have the kids get off the bus at your house?"

"Of course. And we'll take care of the horses if you're not back in time."

He closed his phone, then went to the living room, where he got his laptop and ran a search for the last name of Lister. Bingo. Only one in Pecos. That narrowed it down. He printed out the address, then yelled for Caesar and ran to the truck.

When he reached it, he glanced toward the barn. The corral gate was open. He jogged across the scruffy yard. King wasn't anywhere to be seen. Michael walked around the barn. Still no sign of the horse. The barn held only Fabio, who nickered when he saw Michael.

Could someone have stolen King? But why would someone steal a poor, broken-down horse? Frowning, he jogged back to the truck, then drove toward town. He dialed the school on the way.

Fifteen minutes later, he sat back in the front passenger seat of Rick's Cessna as the small plane soared over the desert landscape. From this vantage point, the Rio Grande was a blue ribbon in a brown, gold, and red tapestry. The roar of the engines filled his head, but it couldn't drown out the voices inside. Since he found the note, he hadn't stopped begging God to lead him to his wife.

Rick glanced at him. "You doing okay, buddy?"

"Not really. I can't believe she'd do anything like this. Look. There are things you don't know." Michael filled him in on how their marriage had begun and why.

Rick listened intently as he guided the plane. "So this Hispanic woman said to take care of your wife and her daughter. And she knew your name. That doesn't sound good."

"I rushed home to find Gracie gone. I'm wondering if she got another call, or if the incident yesterday spooked her." He wanted to pound something. "She doesn't have any way to protect herself or Hope. I had no trouble finding her dad. They won't either."

"Unless she isn't planning on staying there. Maybe she hopes to ask for money or some other kind of help."

"They haven't spoken in years. If he turns her away, what then? She'll be at the mercy of whoever is looking for her."

"Any idea who that is?"

"She thinks it's an old boyfriend with ties to a cartel. I'm not so sure. And why try to take Jordan yesterday? Is that part of this, or was it Vargas?" Michael took off his cowboy hat and rubbed his forehead.

He saw the runway ahead. He'd soon have answers. He hoped.

25

Gracie's muscles froze when her eyes met her father's. It had been so very long since she'd last looked into those blue orbs. Her own eyes were carbon copies, right down to the long, straight lashes. The veins in her neck pulsed and expanded as she waited for his reaction.

His hand came up to shade his eyes, and she realized the glare of the sun might be obscuring a clear vision of who she was. She could have called out, but she waited, willing him to recognize her. A bird called from the fence post and the breeze lifted the hair from her hot neck. Maybe she'd have no choice but to tell him. When recognition claimed his expression, she would know whether to turn and run away or walk forward.

He squinted, and his jaw dropped. The shovel fell from his hand.

He started forward in a gait that changed to a run. His arms opened. "Gracie, oh, baby girl!"

The sound of his voice filled her vision with soft green clouds, and she smelled fresh-mown hay. Only her dad's voice was like that. A sob erupted from her throat, and she leaped toward him. Her feet barely skimmed the ground, and she watched his face. His face contorted as tears ran down his cheeks. His shambling lope stopped three feet from her. His gaze roamed her face as though he feared she would vanish.

He opened his arms. "Gracie? It *is* you. You've come home."

Gracie stepped into the shelter of his embrace. Her face pressed against his shirt. It smelled of damp dirt and Juicy Fruit gum. His arms were tight bands around her, and she knew he wouldn't let her go anytime soon. She had no plans to leave his embrace either.

"Daddy," she choked out. "Daddy, I've missed you."

His rough hands, still smelling of earth, smoothed her hair. "I wasn't even sure you were alive. I've prayed for you every day, honey. And listened for the sound of your footsteps."

Tears squeezed from under her shut lids. "I didn't mean to hurt you," she choked out. "I'm so sorry, Daddy. For everything."

She burrowed her face tighter against his chest. A million memories flooded her mind: Laughing with her parents over Scrabble in the evenings. She and her dad mucking out the barn every Saturday. Hanging clothes on the line out back with her mom. She'd ruined it all by her cowardice and selfishness.

"Hush, baby girl," he crooned. "You're home now. That's all I want."

She raised her head. "Mom died because of me."

"It was an accident, Gracie," he said gently. "It's not your fault."

Hoarse sobs burst from her throat. "It was, Daddy. You don't know. I didn't tell you."

He held up his hand. "Gracie, I found the pregnancy test in the trash in your room. I know." His voice was heavy with sorrow.

She gulped and went on. "It's not just that. I knew that horse was dangerous. I got on the horse because I thought it would throw me. I . . . I hoped a fall would make me miscarry." She searched his face to see if her words had killed his love.

He nodded heavily. "I'm not stupid, honey. When I found the positive test, I thought that's what you'd done. We all knew how dangerous Diablo was."

"Can you ever forgive me?"

"Can you forgive me? I said terrible things to you that night."

"I deserved them all," she whispered.

The light in his eyes dimmed but didn't go out. "Did you make that horse rear? No, Gracie. You didn't. It was an accident."

She buried her face in his shirt again. "I wanted to get rid of Hope. I'm so ashamed."

He pulled her away and studied her face. "You . . . you have a child, honey?" His voice wobbled.

She nodded. "Her name is Hope. She's five."

"You named her after your mother," he said, his voice awed.

"Yes. She looks like Mom too." Every time she looked in Hope's face, she remembered what she'd done. The penance had been terrible.

His eyes grew wet. "It's a beautiful name."

"I thought it would bring me luck and give us hope for a future, but I couldn't outrun what I'd done."

He glanced over her shoulder. "Where is she?"

"In the car. I'll get her." But she didn't want to move from his embrace. "Daddy, you didn't answer. Do you forgive me?"

His eyes widened. "Forgive you? Of course, Gracie, of course." He hugged her again. "There's nothing you could do that would make me stop loving you."

"You never called. I always had the same cell phone number, so I thought you hated me."

He rubbed his chin. "I tried to do it so many times. Every time I picked up the phone, I heard God whisper, 'No.'"

Her throat constricted. "Maybe I had to be ready too," she whispered.

He nodded. "God has his ways, honey."

His face blurred in her vision again. "I'll get Hope." She stepped back, and his hands fell to his side.

He walked beside her toward the car. "I have a granddaughter. I've always wanted another little Gracie."

"She looks more like Mom than like me. Dark hair and eyes. The dimple in her cheek is on the same side as Mom's." She opened the back door. Hope still slept in the booster seat. Gracie touched her daughter's arm. "Hope. Wake up, honey."

Hope's eyes flew open. "Are we there, Mommy? At my grandpa's house?" She rubbed her eyes, and the crayons fell from her lap.

"We sure are." Gracie unbuckled the seat belt and lifted Hope's sturdy little body out of the car. She turned with her daughter in her arms. "Hope, this is your poppy."

She slipped into the nickname she'd called her own grandfather. Judging by the way her father's face lit, she knew it was the right choice.

"Hello, Hope," her dad said, his voice choked. "I'm very glad to meet you. Do you know I've always wanted a granddaughter? There's something very special about baby girls." His gaze flickered to Gracie, then back again.

"I'm not a baby," Hope said, her voice rising on the last word.

"Of course not," he said gravely. "I'd say you're big enough to help me muck out the stables, aren't you? And you're certainly big enough to pull weeds in the garden." He held out his arms. "Would you like to come with me?"

Hope glanced at her mother, then she held out her arms and went straight into her grandpa's embrace. "You don't have to carry me, Poppy. I can walk." But she made no move to squirm down.

"I rather like carrying you," he said with a quaver in his voice. "Let me show you the barn."

Gracie watched them walk away. She pressed a hand against her chest to calm herself. A fresh sense of cleanness washed over her. This was the right thing. Opening her car door, she found a small notebook in her purse and jotted a note to her dad. When she put it in the screen door, she went to her car and got in.

A WELL-KEPT WINDMILL ROTATED IN THE BRISK BREEZE THAT BLEW IN OFF the desert. Michael turned the rental car into the driveway. "Allie's car isn't here. I was so sure Gracie would be here." He pounded the steering wheel.

"Maybe she called her dad. We should at least talk to him," Rick said.

"Yeah." Michael ran down the windows and shoved open his door. "Stay, Caesar," he ordered before heading to the front porch.

"Nice place," Rick observed. "Looks like her family has money."

Michael rarely noticed such things, but he took note of the large house, well-kept outbuildings, and yard. The iron fence all the way around the property cost plenty too. "Guess so. Gracie never mentioned it."

Gracie hadn't mentioned a lot of things. He bounded up the steps to the front door and pressed the doorbell.

"Gracie?" The door flew open, and an older man appeared. He held Hope by the hand. The light in his eyes died when he saw Michael and Rick.

"Daddy!" Hope said. "Did you bring Mommy back?"

The man glanced down at the little girl, then back to Michael. "You're Michael?"

Michael nodded. "Gracie isn't here?"

The man held open the door. "Come on in. I think there's a lot to sort out."

Michael and Rick stepped inside onto travertine floors and followed Lister through the entry to the living room. Nice paintings and pottery. Like Rick had said, the guy had money.

When he sat down, Hope clambered into his lap. "Where's my mommy?" she asked, her dark eyes anxious.

"We'll find her," Michael said, smoothing her hair. He adjusted her so her head rested against his chest. She clutched his shirt as if for comfort.

"Can I offer you a soda or coffee?" Lister asked. "I'm Paul Lister, by the way, but you probably knew that much."

Michael studied the man's face. He guessed Gracie's father to be around sixty. Lister's hair was mostly gray, but it still held a few streaks of blond the same color as Gracie's. And she had inherited the man's vivid blue eyes. "How long ago did she leave?"

"About an hour ago. I was in the garden when they came. I can't tell you what a joy it was to . . ." His voice choked and died. "I've watched for her for five years." He looked at Hope. "And to find out I had a granddaughter—it was the best day of my life. Until I came around to the front of the house and found she'd left me a note." He fished a paper from his pocket.

Michael leaned forward to take it from his hand. He caught his breath as he skimmed it.

Daddy, I'm so sorry I have to leave. A very bad man is after me, and I had to make sure Hope would be all right before I tried to fix this problem. I'll never forget the look on your face when you saw me. It will keep me strong for what I have to do. Keep Hope happy. If I can come back, I will. Michael will probably find you. He won't understand, but tell him I love him and the kids. This is the only way I know to keep everyone safe. Love, Gracie

He wanted to crumple the note and fling it to the floor. "It's insanity! She can't go up against the cartel by herself." He handed it to Rick to read. "Did she say *anything* that might tell you where she planned to go?"

Lister shook his head. "I had no inkling she wasn't planning on staying. She didn't seem upset or frightened. Just glad to be home. Then she was gone."

"I know where she went," Hope said in a small voice.

Michael glanced down at the little girl. "You do? Where did Mommy go?"

"She went to see Daddy Cid. He called when we were in the car. Mommy said she'd meet him."

"Did you hear her say where to meet?" Michael kept his voice low and soothing.

Hope scrunched up her face. "I can't 'member."

"Think, honey. If I can find Mommy, I can bring her home."

Hope chewed on her lip. "She said an engine lodge."

"Good, honey. You're such a good helper!" He turned to Rick. "Engine lodge?"

"Or Indian?" Rick suggested. "Davis Mountains State Park has the Indian Lodge. We could start there."

"What's the fastest way to get there?"

Rick considered the question. "Probably flying into Alpine and driving out there from town."

"Did Mommy say anything else?" Michael asked Hope. If they had no other clues, all they could do was drive the roads through the park and hope to spot the car.

"She said something about oranges," Hope said.

"Oranges?"

Hope scrunched her face. She rubbed her head. "I was sort of sleeping. Don't be mad."

Michael hugged her. "Oh honey, I'm not mad." *At least not at her.* "You've helped me a lot."

"Will you find Mommy?"

"I'm sure I will." He prayed he would find her in time. Though the thought of her lying dead in Allie's car was enough to make his heart seize.

"Can I stay here with Poppy?"

Michael exchanged a long glance with Lister. "I'd suggest you, um, go to town where there are other people," he said, picking his words with care and shooting a meaningful stare Lister's way.

"There's a nice hotel with a pool in town," Lister said. "Sounds like a party waiting to happen."

"A pool?" Hope sat up. "Can I go swimming?"

"You sure can," her grandfather said. "I'll buy you a new swimsuit."

Michael stood and handed Hope over to Lister. "Take good care of her," he said.

"Find my daughter," Lister said in a low voice. "I'll be praying."

"We'll need all the prayers we can get," Michael said grimly, heading for the door.

26

HIGHWAY 118 WOUND THROUGH BREATHTAKING MOUNTAIN SCENERY, BUT
Gracie barely noticed the mountains and canyons along the double-
yellow-lined road. The turnoff should be just ahead. She couldn't let
herself think too much, or she'd turn tail and run. A sign announced
the entrance to Skyline Drive.

The road to perdition.

She slowed the car and turned onto the drive. Cid was probably
already at the appointed place. The question was whether he was
alone. For all she knew, he was waiting with a gun to shoot her and
would throw her body over the side of the overlook. She found she
was okay with whatever happened. While she didn't want to leave her
family, her soul was clean. Anything that happened now, God was
allowing. She could accept that.

The road proceeded up Limpia Canyon, past the McDonald Observatory. Her cell phone lost its signal. The picnic area in Madera Canyon wasn't far now. She saw the sign and turned into the parking lot. There was one other car in the lot. A gray Mercedes. Though she didn't recognize it, the fact that it was a Mercedes told her Cid was close by. She parked and got out. There was no one in the other car, so she started toward the trees. The scent of pine washed away her fear, and she straightened her shoulders.

If Cid thought he would be meeting the meek woman he'd nearly forced to marry him, he was going to find her much changed.

"Gracie." Cid's voice spoke to her right.

She turned toward the gloom of deeper forest. "Cid? Where are you?"

He stepped out from a grove of pines. "I am here." He wore pressed jeans. The first three buttons of his red silk shirt were undone to reveal two gold chains around his neck. His leather loafers looked new. A diamond earring glinted in one ear. Beside him, Gracie was a common sparrow. It always amazed her that he had ever looked at her twice.

He held out his hand. "I will take your cell phone."

Reluctantly, she handed it to him. His smile broadened as he looked her over. "Gracie, I have missed you so much."

His voice was like the stream murmuring so seductively in the background, inviting her to step closer. The problem was she'd nearly drowned in the bottomless pool of his deceit last time. And his exterior was like a coral snake—beautiful but deadly. The orange scent she smelled was a warning.

"Hello, Cid," she said. He held out his arms, but she stepped back. "I'm married."

His eyes darkened. "Where is my amenable little Gracie?"

"She's had enough of letting you pull the wool over her eyes."

"Yet you came when I called."

"Cid, you *threatened* my family. Of course I came."

He snorted. "Your family. It did not take you long to run from my arms to another man. I do not like that, Gracie."

She could have told him she had to hide from him and his cronies. She could have said she loved Michael. But in the end she said nothing and stared at him until he glanced away. A tiny triumph, but an important one. He needed to realize she wasn't going to let him browbeat her. Not anymore.

"I brought food. Some sub sandwiches." He took her elbow and guided her toward the picnic table. A red and white cooler was on a white plastic tablecloth.

"I'm not hungry."

His fingers tightened on her elbow until she winced. "You are not going to waste the food I bought, Gracie. Enough with your defiance." He forced her onto the picnic bench and slammed a sandwich in front of her. "It is your favorite. Turkey with a kick. I had them put on lots of banana peppers."

Her hands folded in her lap, she stared at the sub. She'd choke if she had to swallow his food. Let him shoot her now and be done with it. His hand touched her hair in a caress. He bent toward her, and his lips touched her neck. She barely suppressed a shudder, but he must have sensed it because his lips tightened, and he moved across the table from her.

He unwrapped her sandwich. "Eat."

Her pulse stuttered at the dark threat in his voice. She picked up the sandwich, but her insides roiled. She took a tiny bite and got only bread. With no moisture in her mouth, the bread was like sandpaper.

She chewed it as best she could, then washed it down with a sip of the bottled water in front of her.

"Hope is asleep in the car? I have a sandwich for her too."

"No. I didn't bring her with me."

He put down his sandwich. His dark eyes narrowed to slits, and his mouth twisted. "What do you mean, you did not bring her? You agreed you would come back to me. Is this some kind of trick?"

She shook her head. "No trick, Cid. You are forcing me to come back, but I'm not letting you raise my daughter. I'm willing to sacrifice my own happiness, but not hers."

He rose and came toward her. She scrambled to her feet and backed away, but he sprang and gripped her forearms in a bruising hold. "I suppose you left her with that perfect husband of yours. No matter. One of my men can pick her up. We will make sure that family doesn't disturb our happiness again."

She struggled but couldn't escape his punishing fingers. "She's where you'll never find her."

He shook her hard enough that her head flopped back and forth. "Idiot woman! It is not *you* I want!"

He shoved her. Gracie reeled back, then hit the ground. Gravel dug into her back. Ignoring the bite of the rocks in her palms, she scooted away from him.

Cid glowered over her. "Hope is the key to everything. I never wanted you." His hand swept dismissively. "Look at you. Shy and timid."

"I never pretended to be anything else."

"You never tried. Always jeans and T-shirts. A real man wants a woman with some plumage."

"What do you want with me, then?" she whispered.

Not listening to her, he paced the clearing. "I was willing to put up with you in my bed for my father's sake." He leaned down and hoisted her to her feet. "Where is she?"

She stared up at him defiantly. "I won't tell you."

"You will tell me where to find Hope, or the crows will pick the flesh from your bones. And I will find her anyway, only she will not have her mother."

Looking into his dark eyes, she didn't doubt he spoke the truth. "No," she said.

His hand went to his pocket, and she knew he concealed a weapon there. She bolted for the trees. He shouted after her, but she plunged into the cool sanctuary of the pines.

A PINE BRANCH SLAPPED GRACIE IN THE FACE. SHE STUMBLED AND WENT down on one knee, then regained her feet and rushed across the blanket of pine needles. *Stupid, so stupid.* He'd set a trap, and she'd walked right into it. She had to get away, warn Michael, so he could help her save Hope. She should have done that in the first place, but she'd thought she could fix this problem herself.

If she could lose Cid, she might be able to circle back around to her car. He bellowed her name, but he wasn't close. The trees were so thick through here, he would have trouble spotting her. She needed a place to hide.

She kicked off her flip-flops, pausing long enough to angle them in a different direction. It might throw him off. A ridge of rocks poked up just across the creek. When she plunged into the stream, the cold shock of water made her gasp. She struggled against the suction of the muddy bottom but managed to reach the shelter of the rocks and hunker down behind them. She lay on her stomach and peered through a wedge in the rocks.

Cid emerged from the trees, then stood, staring around. He stooped and picked up one of her flip-flops, then stared in the direction they pointed. She willed him to follow the false trail she'd laid. When he kept the slipper and headed away from the creek, she let out the breath she'd been holding. Once he was out of sight, she rose and rushed away.

For the next two hours she hid, then watched before finally circling back to the parking lot. The dying sun threw rays of red and gold across the tops of the piñon pine trees and cast shadows deeper into the forest. Cid surely assumed that she'd found help somewhere by now. He would have run away before the law showed up here. Glancing around the area one last time, she exited the forest and ran for her car. Cid's Mercedes was gone, just as she'd suspected.

She dug her key out of her pocket, then opened her car door. The lights didn't come on inside. Surely she hadn't left the lights on or done something else stupid to drain the battery. Jamming the key into the ignition, she turned the key. The engine clicked, but nothing happened. "No!" she muttered.

"You stupid *chica*," Cid said from behind her. A steel barrel pressed against her neck. "Get out of the car."

Her hands dropped from the steering wheel. She glanced around for a weapon, but the front seat held only her purse. Her ankle gun was out of reach.

"Move before I blow a hole in your head right here," Cid snarled.

She got out and went to stand near the front of the car, where she'd be closest to the woods. If she got a chance, she'd bolt again. Cid had a length of rope in one hand and a revolver in the other.

"Turn around," he barked. When she complied, he roughly wound the rope around her wrists. He jabbed her between her shoulder blades. "Move. Over there." He pointed.

She saw his car parked down the road in a turnout. Stupid, stupid. If only she'd paid better attention. She stumbled along on sore feet. When she neared his car, the passenger door opened. A black-haired man she didn't recognize got out, but she had no eyes for him. Her attention was riveted by what the lighted interior of the car revealed: her daughter's frightened face in the backseat.

She started forward. "Hope!"

Cid grabbed her bound hands and yanked her back cruelly. "Not so fast." He shoved her face-first onto the hood of the car. "Stay right there."

The heat of the engine radiated through the hood against her cheek. She turned her head to watch the two men. And a woman, who stepped from the passenger seat. The woman who had warned her.

"Watch her, Zita."

"I am sorry," Zita whispered when she stopped behind Gracie.

Cid stepped nearer to the other man. "You get ahold of Wheeler?"

"Yeah. I sent him a picture of the kid crying in the backseat. That should make him see reason."

Gracie shoved herself upright. "What's Sam Wheeler got to do with this?"

Cid quirked an eyebrow. "You will be quiet or I will shoot you right here in front of Hope. You don't deserve to live after the way you treated me. I am letting you live to keep her calm." He gestured to the car hood. "Lie down on there again. Not another word."

"Do as he says," Zita said.

She did. With the heat baking her cheek again and the stink of the engine in her nose, she tried to think. Had Sam learned from Cid that she had a child? Hope was being used as a pawn, but Gracie couldn't quite ferret out how. She hoped Zita might turn out to be an ally.

Cid grabbed her bound wrists again and thrust her toward the backseat of the car. "Get in."

She half fell onto the seat, then crawled the rest of the way. "Hope," she croaked. "Are you okay?"

"Mommy!" Hope crawled into her lap. "The bad man hit Poppy. He had blood on his head." She started crying and pressed her wet face into Gracie's neck.

Gracie wished she could embrace her daughter. "It's going to be okay, honey," she whispered. She kissed her daughter, tasting the salt on Hope's wet cheeks.

The car shifted as both men climbed in. Cid glanced in the back. "Better get comfortable. We have a long night ahead of us."

Zita opened the door and got in back with them. She didn't look at Gracie.

"Where are you taking us?" Gracie asked Cid.

"To visit the kid's grandpa. One look at her face and he will do whatever we tell him."

"What do you want him to do?"

"Nothing that concerns you. A few hours and it will be all over." He leaned over the seat. "Turn around and I will untie you. Do not try anything." His gaze flickered to Hope.

Gracie caught his unspoken threat. She turned around and he loosened the ropes. If only there was some way to leave a message for Michael. She had no doubt he'd come looking for her.

27

"WE'VE BEEN DRIVING FOR HOURS." MICHAEL HIT THE STEERING WHEEL with his hand. "We've scoured the lodge and driven every mile of roads. The last call I made to the sheriff was useless too. They haven't seen a thing."

Rick leaned forward with an intent expression. "I thought maybe she'd be at the observatory." He glanced at his watch. "We need to get out of these mountains so I can check voice mail. Just in case Allie needs something for the kids or . . . or if Gracie called."

Fat chance of that, Michael thought. He turned the car around and headed out of the valley. He passed a turnoff to a picnic area that had been closed the last time they came through.

Rick turned his head to stare down the drive to the parking lot.

"That had a chain and a closed sign on it two hours ago. Turn around. That's one place we haven't checked."

"Okay." Michael turned the car around on the deserted Skyline Drive and approached the turnoff. One of the car's tires bounced over a hole, then out again. "It sure wasn't closed to fix the road," he grumbled. His car's headlamps pierced the darkness. "There's a car parked here," he said, squinting.

"It's Allie's!" Rick threw open his door before their vehicle rolled to a stop.

Michael slammed the gearshift into park, then hurtled from the car. Not bothering to shut the door behind him, he approached the driver's door, where Rick stood peering inside. "Anything?"

"Nope. Empty."

Michael cupped his hands to his mouth. "Gracie!" His voice rang into the trees. "I'll get a flashlight. I have a little one on my key ring." He jogged back to his car and retrieved it. Starting toward the picnic area, he flipped it on. The tiny beam of light touched something on the ground, and he paused. A flip-flop. He picked it up and shone the light on it. "This is Gracie's," he said. "Look. Here's Caesar's teeth marks."

The dog woofed beside him, and he realized Caesar had gotten out of the car. He held it to the dog's nose. "Find Gracie, boy." Caesar whined, then trotted toward the woods. "Come on," Michael said.

He'd only taken two steps when his cell phone dinged its voice mail notification. "We must have cell coverage here." He hoped Gracie had left a message. He scrolled through the calls and saw one from Lister.

"Gracie's dad called while the cell phone was out of range," he told Rick. He returned the call. It seemed to ring forever before Lister picked up. "Mr. Lister? It's Michael Wayne. I saw you called. I didn't bother to listen to the message. Is everything okay?"

"No, son. No, it's not." The older man's voice was weak and thready. "They took Hope."

Michael closed his eyes, then opened them again. "Who took her?"

"I don't know. Two guys. Hispanic, both of them. I was packing a few things to take to town, and they busted in here about two hours after you left. It's all my fault. I should have moved faster, but I had livestock to care for."

"It's not your fault. What happened?"

"One of them scooped Hope up and started for the door. I grabbed a vase and was going to cream him with it, but the other smashed the butt of a gun against my head. I fell and was out a few seconds. Even when I came to, I was so disoriented, I couldn't move. I think they thought I was still unconscious, because they wouldn't have talked like that if they'd known I was awake."

"Like what?" Michael prayed for a clue, any clue to the men's—and his daughter's—whereabouts.

"They told her to quit crying. Said they were taking her to see her grandfather. *I'm* her grandfather and I was lying right there, so I'm guessing it must be her dad's father."

"Sam Wheeler," Michael muttered. "Anything else?"

"That's all I heard." His voice trailed away.

"Are you okay? Where are you?"

"In the hospital. They tried to take my phone away, but I wouldn't let them. Not until I talked to you. The police have been and gone. They're looking too."

"If the doctor is keeping you, it must be serious! What's wrong?"

"I have a slight concussion but I'll be fine. Find my Gracie. And my granddaughter. I have a lot of lost time to make up for."

"I'll do my best. When I find them, I'll call you." He hung up his phone and repeated the conversation to Rick.

"Her other grandfather?" Rick said. "Any idea who that is?"

Michael nodded. "Sam Wheeler. He's been trying to get hold of Gracie for days. The first time she talked to him, he asked her if she'd had his son's child. She didn't know how he found out. It appears he's all wrapped up in this."

"Any idea where he lives?"

"No, but I can find out." Michael dialed Pickens's number and got his voice mail. He left a message asking for Wheeler's address. When he hung up, he dialed Estevez. This time the call was answered. He told Estevez what was going on.

"Hold on," Estevez said. "I'm right by the computer."

Michael heard the clicking of a keyboard. He didn't dare move from his spot in case he lost the signal. "Hurry up. My wife's and daughter's lives are in the balance," he said.

"I can only go as fast as the computer will let me," Estevez grumbled. "Got it." He rattled off an address. "He's the governor of Arizona," he said. "Did you know that?"

"Yeah, I did." He rubbed his chin. "Hmm, Vargas is locked up in Arizona."

"Yeah. So what?"

"I don't know, but it's interesting."

Estevez gave an impatient huff. "That all you need? I have to go."

"One more thing." What he was thinking was crazy. "Look up Vargas's bio. What's his background? Does he have any kids?"

"Got it," Estevez said. "He's got a son. Cid Ortega. Must be illegitimate since the last name isn't the same."

Nausea rolled in Michael's gut. He didn't see the full puzzle yet, but the pieces showing were enough to terrify him. "Thanks for your help," he told Estevez.

"You need backup?" Estevez asked.

"I don't have time to get to you," he said. "We'll need to head to Wheeler's right now."

"I can call agents in Arizona, and I'll get on the road myself. Let me call Fishman and get his authorization."

"All right. Thanks." He closed his phone. "Rick, we need to get to your plane. This beast has tentacles I didn't see until now."

AFTER A FAST CAR TRIP FOLLOWED BY A PLANE RIDE, THEN ANOTHER CAR ride, Gracie could barely keep her eyes open. Her feet throbbed from the cuts and bruises she received on her run through the forest. Her throat was parched, and her tummy rumbled. Hope had eaten the sandwich Cid handed to her, but Gracie hadn't been able to choke down a morsel. She had to find some way to save Hope.

She shifted and crossed her ankles. When she did, the holster rubbed against her leg. Somehow she managed to maintain her expression. If she could get out her gun, they'd have a chance. But she didn't dare try it with Zita watching. Cid's sister had given her no indication that she'd help. Gracie hoped once Sam Wheeler did what was asked of him, Cid would let them go. A futile thought. He'd be more apt to kill them and bury them in the desert. She could only pray she had the opportunity to try to use the gun.

She'd been so stupid. Another wrong choice. Would she never learn?

"What about King? Did you take him home?"

Cid laughed. "He has a new home. At the rendering plant."

Her fingers curled into her palms and she struggled not to cry. They may all be in the horse's shoes before the night was over.

They reached the gated drive back to the ranch house, and she suddenly recognized the place. It was the Wheelers' ranch getaway, where she'd gone four-wheeling with Jason a lifetime ago. She'd been to the Wheelers' big house in Scottsdale more often than this remote spot near Douglas. Was Sam even here?

Douglas. She remembered Jason telling her about the underground passages to Mexico tunneling this area. It was a dangerous place.

A shadow moved inside the small guardhouse and a man stepped out. He wore a revolver at his hip. Gracie put her hand to her mouth when Cid's cohort pulled out a gun and rolled down the window. She clutched Hope to her so the child wouldn't see and closed her eyes when a shot rang out. It was more than she could bear to watch. Cid's partner got out of the car and took the electronic opener from the guard's belt. Moments later the gate slid open and the car pulled through. Cid paused for the other man to get in, then drove to the ranch house.

"Not a word from you," Cid said, opening her door. He dragged her from the seat. She turned to help Hope out, and he shoved Gracie away. "Zita will get her."

Curling her hands into fists, she stood back while Zita pulled her daughter from the car and pushed Hope toward her. Gracie lifted her tired daughter in her arms.

"Go back to sleep, Hope," she murmured.

The little girl relaxed in her arms, and Gracie shuffled the weight a little as she followed Cid to the house. The door opened, and a man stood silhouetted in the light from inside the house. Sam had aged. His dark head of hair was shot through with gray now. Lines etched the skin around his mouth. He'd suffered.

His eye shifted to Hope in Gracie's arms. "Is that her?" he asked, his voice trembling.

"Hi, Sam. Let's let her sleep for now. She's had a rough day." Gracie stepped past him with her daughter in her arms. "Is there anywhere I can lay her down?"

Sam didn't take his eyes off Hope. "The first bedroom on the left in the hall was Jason's," he said.

Gracie started for the hall, but Cid stopped her. "We're all staying together."

"She's tired, Cid. You've dragged her halfway across the country today. She'll sleep and we can talk," Gracie said, keeping her voice reasonable.

He hesitated. "I'll go with you."

"Fine." But her gut clenched.

She'd hoped to awaken Hope and tell her to sneak out the back door. Conscious of Cid's narrowed gaze, she entered the bedroom and laid her daughter on the twin bed covered with an Arizona Cardinals spread. Jason had made so little impact on her that it seemed to be a stranger's bedroom. She brushed a kiss across Hope's forehead before backing out of the room.

Cid pushed her toward the living room. Had he always been so aggressive? What possible joy could he get from shoving her around? Her jaw hurt from clenching her teeth so tightly. When she entered the living room, both Sam and Cid's partner were sitting in chairs pulled close to the sofa. Zita stood behind them. Cid directed her to join everyone. He sat beside her and kept the gun in his hand.

Sam leaned forward. "Look, just let them go, okay? You and I can do what needs to be done."

"Yesterday we might have agreed, Governor," Cid said. "But today is a day too late. You will do exactly as I say or they will both die."

Wheeler nodded. "Whatever you want. Just don't hurt Hope."

Another person who didn't know Cid might have believed him when he assured Sam they would all live if he did as directed, but Gracie saw the flicker in Cid's eyes. He had a plan, and it didn't include letting them walk away to report him to the authorities. She had to figure out a way to get Hope free.

"Here is how we will do this," Cid said. "You will place a call to the warden at the prison and tell him new evidence has come to light and you are overturning the sentence of Lazaro Vargas. You will instruct the warden to turn him over to Teo, who will be waiting to pick him up. In the meantime, a truck loaded with guns is on its way here. When Vargas arrives, he and the truck will cross into Mexico unhindered. Then our business is over and we will be on our way. We will leave and never see you again."

Vargas. The man who had ordered Michael's death. "You'll kill us," Gracie said flatly. "There's no need, Cid. We know if we tell anyone, the cartel will kill us. I won't say anything. Neither will Sam. Right, Sam?"

"I wouldn't do anything to endanger my granddaughter's life," he said, twisting his hands in his lap. "You can count on me."

Cid's eyes were as dark as the night outside and just as soulless. "When we are all safe, you will be free to go."

Lies, all lies. Gracie tried to signal Sam with her eyes to tell him to do something, anything to get Hope away, but he wasn't looking at her.

"I'll make that call right now," Sam said. He reached for the cordless phone on the table beside his chair, then grabbed for his pocket, but Cid waved the gun at him. "I have to look up the number of the prison," Sam said.

Cid sat back again, and Sam pulled out his cell phone, then scrolled through it. He punched in the number on the cordless. "This is Governor Wheeler. I'd like to speak to the warden, please. I realize he's gone home for the day, but I need you to patch me through to his house. I'll wait."

Gracie bit her lip. The die was about to be thrown, and she had no way of seeing how it could turn up okay for her and Hope. If only Michael were here. She glanced at Zita, who was biting her lip as well.

Then she turned accusing eyes to Cid. "Vargas is your father? You don't share the same name."

His eyes gave a sullen flicker. "He never married my mother."

"Is he the reason you got involved in the cartel?"

Cid paced to the window, then came back. "What does it matter?"

"Why do you let him use you this way?" Zita burst out in Spanish. "I do not know you anymore."

"Shut up," Cid answered her in the same language.

Zita waved her arms. "Never do you hear from him until a year ago, and you become a crazy man. This father's love is not worth earning. He is using you, but you are too stupid to realize, my brother."

Cid's mouth worked. He turned his back on his sister and went to stand by the window. "We will wait in silence."

28

Two hours later, headlamps swept across the room from a truck rumbling by outside. Gracie tensed and scooted to the edge of the sofa cushion. Whatever was going to happen was about to start. Cid's cell phone rang, and he answered it. He spoke a few words in Spanish too softly for Gracie to hear, then closed it.

"Your *husband* will be joining you soon," he said. "This will be faster and less painful than divorce."

Gracie gasped and started to stand until he stepped to the sofa and shoved her back down. "This has nothing to do with Michael. Please, Cid, leave him out of it. He has two kids to raise."

"He has no one to blame but himself. He should have stayed out of my business." He glanced at his watch and spoke to Sam. "The warden said two hours. The time is past. I think you should call him again." He motioned with his gun at Sam, who nodded and picked up the phone.

Gracie heard a cry from the bedroom. "Hope is awake. I need to go get her."

Cid was watching the truck through the window. "Fine. Just hurry up."

This might be her only chance. She had to save Hope and get help for Michael. She quickened her step and rushed toward the bedroom. She paused a moment to glance down the hall. Only bedroom doors. Maybe one of them had a sliding glass door to the outside. Or a window big enough to climb through. Hope wailed again, and Gracie hurried into the room.

Rubbing her eyes, Hope sat crying on the edge of the bed. "It's okay, honey. I'm right here," Gracie said. She took Hope's hand and helped her from the bed, then leaned down and whispered in her ear. "We have to try to get away. Can you be very quiet, sweetheart?" Hope's tears dried, and she nodded.

Gracie lifted Hope in her arms and stepped to the doorway. "I'm taking Hope to potty. I'll be right there," she called.

"Five minutes," Cid barked.

Carrying her daughter, she stepped down the hallway and stopped at the bathroom door. She flipped on the light and the exhaust fan, then shut the door harder than necessary. Tiptoeing away, she went down the hall and peered through each doorway. The first two rooms only had windows that were too high for her to lift Hope through. The last one was the master bedroom, and it had a sliding glass door out onto a backyard patio.

She set Hope on the floor and held her finger to her lips. Careful to make no sound, she shut the door to the bedroom, then led Hope to the sliding door. On her first attempt the door didn't budge, then she realized she had to unlock it at the floor as well as the latch. Once it was fully unlocked, it glided open without a sound.

She led Hope through and shut it behind them. Moonlight relieved the darkness enough to show her the way along a flagstone path that wound past cacti and shrubs. If only she had keys to one of the vehicles surely parked in the three-car garage, but she and Hope had only their feet to help them escape. This ranch was miles from anywhere. They had no water, no food. There was a road but no place to hide along the barren stretch of asphalt. Her best chance of escape was to strike off into the desert, then wind back toward the road farther down and hope to find help. And she should pray.

"Mommy, I'm thirsty," Hope whispered.

"I know, sweetheart. I am too." She didn't dare start into the desert without water in August.

Leading Hope by the hand, she approached the back of the barn. She heard a horse inside shuffle and whinny. Of course. The horses. She could get much farther on a horse. If she had the courage to ride one. Glancing at her daughter, she knew there was no other way.

"This way," she whispered.

She tried the back door to the barn and found it unlocked. Stepping inside, the scents of hay and horse assaulted her noses, and she nearly changed her mind. Hope clutched at her hand, and Gracie found the strength to move forward. First she got her daughter some water, then Gracie drank too. She saw no canteens around, but there was a half-empty water bottle. She refilled it. It might not be the most sanitary thing, but it was better than no water at all in the Sonoran Desert.

"Hold this for me, sweetheart," she said. Gracie's breath began to come in short, laboring pants as she approached the horse. A bridle hung on the stall, and she grabbed it, then stepped into the pen with the sorrel mare.

"Easy," she murmured when the mare shuffled.

Gracie slipped the bridle into place, then led the horse from the stall. Hope hung back, but Gracie motioned her forward, then lifted her onto the horse's back. The sorrel stood still for her, and she thanked God for it. When she led the horse through the rear of the barn, she heard shouts from the ranch house.

"They know we're missing," she said. Holding the reins, she climbed the wooden fence of the corral, then slid onto the horse's back behind Hope. "Hold tight, honey," she said.

She dug her heels into the mare's side and urged the horse into a canter away from the barn. Going in this direction, the barn would hide their silhouette, at least until someone came this way.

The night air should have felt refreshing, but Gracie couldn't stop shivering. She clung to the reins and rode like a sack of feed on the horse's back until her childhood training began to take over. Then the ride smoothed out, and her shudders began to ease. They reached a stand of paloverde trees, and she stopped the horse long enough to gaze back toward the ranch. No hoofbeats came to her ears, just the distant shouts from the house. She and Hope were far enough away now that they couldn't be seen from the house. Facing forward again, she glanced around the empty desert. With only the stars to guide her, she had only a vague idea of where to find the road. Better not to go there yet. Their silhouette atop the horse would be easier for the arriving cartel to spot.

She strained to see some twinkle of light, some indication of another dwelling in this wilderness, but she saw nothing but endless night. She and Hope were alone out here. No, not alone. Not now.

God was here. Gracie started north, praying she could intercept Michael in time.

Lights from the road approached. Maybe her prayers were about to be answered. She urged the horse to a gallop. The wind lifted her hair. Another few feet and she could see who was in the truck. She heard a voice.

"Mommy, I smell oranges," Hope whispered.

"So do I." Before she had time to turn away, the truck stopped and a man waved a gun at them.

She turned the horse's head, but bullets slammed into the sand by the horse's hooves. The mare snorted and reared. Gracie clutched Hope, but they both went sailing into the air.

MICHAEL PUT DOWN HIS BINOCULARS. "THERE'S A BIG TRUCK OUT FRONT. I can't see into the house." The two men stood on the road by the lane that led to Governor Wheeler's ranch.

"She might not even be there," Rick warned.

"If she's not, I don't know where to look next," he said. "I'm going in."

"What about your backup? Weren't they supposed to be here?"

Michael glanced at his watch. "Yeah. Half an hour ago. Maybe I'd better call Estevez again."

A voice spoke out of the darkness. "That won't be necessary." Gravel crunched, then a figure stepped onto the road. Israel Fishman held a gun in his right hand. It was pointed at Michael. "Estevez had to inform me to mobilize help, of course. He's safe at home, assuming I've sent men to rescue you. He's much too trusting."

The moonlight illuminated Fishman's grim stare. Michael glanced from that stern face to the gun, then back. "Not you. I thought you were one of the good guys."

"I am. Most of the time. Sometimes it pays to look the other way." He moved closer. "In fact, it pays *very* well."

"Did you turn your back on Phil too?" Michael had to ask, even though the answer stared at him in the form of a gun's bore.

"He never understood business. He could have joined the fun but refused."

Michael balled his hands into fists. "You killed him."

"Not exactly. I just stood back and let others do it." Fishman motioned with the gun. "Let's join the party. I believe they're expecting us. Hand over your guns, please."

"I don't have one," Rick said. He exchanged a glance with Michael.

"Let's just make sure, shall we?" Fishman kept the gun trained on Michael and ran his hand over Rick's back and legs. "Hand over your gun, Lieutenant."

Michael pulled his gun from its holster and held it out by the grip. Fishman took it and stuck it in his belt, then frisked Michael too. When he found nothing, he motioned with his gun. "Move."

Michael started toward the house with Rick at his side. "There are two of us," Rick muttered under his breath. "Our best odds are now, before he gets to his cronies."

"Quiet," Fishman barked. "My trigger finger is already twitching. Don't even look at one another."

Michael believed the warning in Fishman's voice. There was no way to make a plan. Besides, he didn't want to get Rick killed. It was his fault the other man was here. He should have waited for backup from the army. Or the Border Patrol. Though he realized now no backup was coming for them. Fishman would have seen to that.

Fishman would have no choice but to kill them both. The prognosis was grim, but Michael wasn't giving up. While he breathed, he would try.

The three men trudged up the asphalt drive to the house blazing with lights. Once he saw whether Gracie and Hope were all right, he'd figure out a plan to get everyone out alive.

The door opened before they reached the stoop. A swarthy man with a Beretta gestured for them to come in. Michael strained to see past him, but Gracie wasn't in the hallway.

"Stay out here," the man told Fishman. "Teo should be here any time with Vargas."

Vargas. This was a plot to free Vargas. Michael gasped at the sheer audacity of it.

"No trouble?" Fishman asked.

"Nothing we cannot handle." The man's eyes shifted to Michael.

"Then I think I'll come in." Fishman pushed his way into the house.

Michael followed the voices to the living room. His gaze landed on the woman who'd warned him to take care of Gracie. She didn't meet his eye.

"Where's my wife?" he asked.

A man with a gold chain around his neck sneered in Michael's direction. "What do you think we'd do with a pretty *señora* like that?"

Michael willed himself not to react. The guy was trying to provoke him. He strained to hear Gracie or Hope in the house somewhere but heard nothing. He didn't notice the older man, likely Sam Wheeler, until he spoke.

"She escaped," Wheeler said.

The man with the gold chain stepped in front of the governor and smacked him in the head with his gun. "You will shut up!"

Michael's pulse began to gallop, and he couldn't hold back a smile. "You let her get away," he said. "You have to be Cid."

The man's face went ruddy under his swarthy complexion. "Sit." He pointed at the sofa. "We will find her. She cannot escape me that easily." His dark eyes swarmed over Michael's face. "She belongs to me and has been mine since the first time I saw her."

Don't react. Say nothing. Michael's nerves jangled. He sat on the sofa. Rick joined him. They faced Wheeler. Three against three. He could wage a coup and win.

Cid glared at Wheeler. "Where is Vargas?" he demanded, pacing the rug. "He should have been here by now."

Fishman glanced at his watch. "I want to be gone by dawn."

"You will get your guns," Cid said.

"And you'll get your dad out of jail. We all win." Fishman strode to the window and stared into the yard.

Cid pressed his lips together. "Where are they?" he muttered. "Fraco, go outside and see if there are car lights coming." His partner nodded and stepped out of the room. "Try calling him again."

"There's no cell phone tower out here," Wheeler said.

"Your plans are about to come unraveled," Michael said. "I'd be cutting and running now. Gracie and Hope are gone, so you have nothing to hold over Sam's head."

"He is dead if my father does not show up," Cid said, his lips twisting in a snarl. "And you will shut up or your teeth will be on the floor."

Michael closed his mouth. The man was on the edge. One shove and he'd be firing bullets. While Cid paced, Michael glanced around for something to use as a weapon and noticed Rick doing the same.

Car lights swept the far wall. Fraco popped back inside the living room. "Someone is here," he said.

Cid spat an oath and went toward the door. "Watch them," he ordered.

Fraco's sharp eyes studied them. "I am not like Cid," he said. "I would rather shoot you now. He will want to taunt you. It is a mistake. Maybe I will save him from himself." He raised his weapon.

Michael stared down the barrel of the gun. Sam was the closest to the guy. If the governor would tackle the gunman, they might have a chance. The man's finger tightened on the trigger, and his eyes narrowed. Michael's muscles coiled to spring. Fraco's head turned at the commotion at the door, but Michael had no time to act before Cid thrust two figures into the room.

Gracie and Hope.

29

Gracie had tried to get Hope to run after they'd been thrown from the horse, but her daughter wouldn't leave. The two men in the truck had quickly overcome them. The one in an orange prison suit gave her chills. Even now, Vargas stood watching everything with cynical eyes as the other man thrust them into the house.

Gracie stumbled and went down onto the hardwood floor. Pain flared in her knee, already bleeding from its contact with the road after her horse threw them. Whimpering, Hope clung to her hand. "It's okay, baby," Gracie soothed, pulling her daughter into an embrace. Her gaze met Michael's over the top of Hope's head.

Though they couldn't have been reunited in worse circumstances, Gracie drank in her husband's face. If anyone could find a way out of this, it was Michael. His eyes told her to take courage.

The gun. Crouched on the floor with Hope blocking their view of her leg, she thought she might be able to get to it. Her fingers quickly found the holster and she slipped the tiny gun from its nest, then thrust it into the back of her waistband.

Vargas entered the room. He spoke in Spanish. "My son, you have succeeded. I knew you would not let me down."

Cid embraced the man in the jumpsuit. He answered in Spanish. "Papa, you are here. We must go. Quickly."

Vargas's cold gaze roamed to Michael. He spoke in English this time. "He must die. Give me a gun." He grabbed a gun from Teo's hand.

"No!" She jumped up, in front of Hope. Gracie whipped out her gun and held it in front of her. She remembered Michael's instructions and widened her stance, then tightened her finger on the trigger. A shot spat from the barrel and the man flinched. His gun fell to the floor with a clatter.

Before Gracie could fire again, Cid tackled her. "Let me go!" she screamed, trying to keep control of her gun.

His weight crushed the air from her lungs, and he ripped the revolver from her hand. She thrashed until his forearm pressed against her windpipe and cut off her air. Darkness hovered at the edge of her vision and she gasped.

Cid released her and stood. "I should kill you now!"

She held her hand to her throbbing throat. A sobbing Hope threw herself onto Gracie's chest, and Gracie clutched her. "It's okay, honey," she soothed. She struggled to her feet, then lifted her daughter into her arms.

Vargas glared at her, then glanced at Michael before starting for the gun again. Cid stepped closer to his father and whispered in his ear. She caught the words "accident" and "tonight" before Vargas nodded and turned away from Michael.

A cold ball formed in Gracie's chest. Cid had something planned.

Thunder rumbled outside, and a streak of lighting illuminated the yard. Flickering and growling, the promised storm moved nearer. Gracie moved closer to Michael until Cid noticed and pointed his finger at her.

"Do not move," he barked. "Say *adiós* to this gringo. You will never see him after tonight."

"Let Michael and Rick take Hope and go," she said, pitching her voice to be low and soothing. "I'll go with you wherever you say. I won't try to get away."

"Do you take me for a stupid man?" He stepped nearer. His hand lashed out and struck her face.

"Cid, no!" Zita screamed. She leaped onto her brother's back and he reeled. She fell away, and he whirled to shove her. She fell onto the floor.

Heat flared in Gracie's cheek. She palmed her stinging skin as Michael leaped from the sofa.

"Leave her alone!" he shouted.

Fraco clubbed Michael with the back of his rifle, and her husband fell to the floor, where he didn't move.

Gracie started for Michael, but Cid seized her arm. His fingers bit in hard enough to bruise.

He nodded toward Michael's inert form and motioned to the other man. "Tie him up, Fraco. The other one too."

Fraco tied Rick, then knelt by Michael and bound his wrists together behind his back. Michael groaned, then slumped back onto the floor.

"Michael!" Gracie tried to wrench her arm from Cid's grip so she could go to her husband. He had to be all right. Cid's hard hand hit Gracie's back. Pain radiated to her shoulder, and she fell forward on one knee but managed to keep Hope from slamming to the floor.

Sam grabbed her hand and helped her to her feet. "I'm so sorry to get you involved in this, honey," he said.

"It's not your fault," she said, pressing his hand. "Cid had this planned."

"I played into their hands," Sam said.

She stared at her husband's body on the floor. He wasn't moving. "Michael," she said again. She started toward him once more, but Cid blocked her.

"Do not count on your husband to save you," he said. "Everything is prepared. We will all walk to our truck now. We will tie your hands, and you will get into the back. Then we will drive across the border."

"Where are my guns?" Fishman asked. "They need to be in place in two days, or I won't get paid."

"In the other truck outside. Our business is ended after tonight." Cid grabbed Gracie's arm and propelled her toward the door.

"Let Hope go," Gracie begged. "Please, Cid, do what you want with me, but let her go."

"I will do what I want with you whether she is freed or not," he said. "She is a tool to make you behave, is she not?" His smile held only an unpleasant promise. "You will pay for your betrayal." Cid's fingers laced through Gracie's hair. "A pretty blond gringo like you will earn her keep in the bordello."

She flinched away. "I don't think so, Cid. You'll be lynched when I bite off the first ear."

His face darkened, and he raised his hand again, but she stared him down, putting every bit of contempt she could muster into her gaze.

"Please. Leave her alone," Sam said, stepping between them. "I've done all you've asked. You have everything you need. Don't hurt her or my granddaughter."

Fraco shoved him back into the chair, then tied him to it. Sam slumped back with trembling lips.

Zita got slowly to her feet. "You did what this man wanted," she said to her brother, gesturing to Vargas. "Let him go his way and we will go ours."

"He is my *father*, Zita. I cannot do that."

"I am your sister."

"Half sister."

"I see," she said. "If there are choices to be made, you will choose the man who will toss you aside when he reaches his country. We are Americans, Cid. What you are doing is wrong. Evil."

Vargas took the gun from Fraco and shot her. His face was expressionless when she fell onto the floor. He handed the gun back to Fraco. "Let us go on without more whining."

"Y-you killed my sister," Cid said. He knelt by Zita and rubbed the back of his hand against his eyes.

"She would only slow us down and pull you from your duty," Vargas said, his voice indifferent. "Leave her."

Gracie fought the nausea burning the back of her mouth. "She loved you, Cid. And he shot her like a dog. How can you let him get away with it?"

"You will shut up or I will shoot you next," Vargas said. He glanced at Cid. "The child will slow us down. Leave her."

Cid shuddered, then rose from his sister's side. His jaw

clenched, and he stared at Gracie. "You will do what you are told, Gracie, or we will come back and take the little one. Do you understand me?"

He meant every word. She could barely summon the energy to nod her head. Once she was in Mexico, it would take a miracle to get out. The only comfort she could find was that her compliance would protect Hope—and Michael.

Cid's fingers bit harder into Gracie's arm. "Move." He propelled her toward the door.

"Mommy!" Hope tried to go after her mother, but Fishman blocked her access.

"Stay with your father," he ordered. He pushed her toward Michael's inert form. "Get going," Fishman said to Cid. "I'll handle things here before I leave. The authorities and the media will be swarming over this place."

Handle things. Rick and Michael would be able to identify him. Unless they weren't around to do it. The air escaped her lungs. He wasn't going to let Michael and Rick live. And what about Hope and Sam? Any one of them could identify Fishman. He couldn't afford to leave *any* witnesses. She tore her arm from Cid's grasp and ran to scoop up Hope. With her daughter in her arms, she backed away from the men who stood glowering at her.

"Just leave me here, Cid. You have what you want. I know what's happening here. I have to be here for Hope. We have to be together."

"Put her down, Gracie."

Something passed behind his eyes—compassion or awareness—but she couldn't be sure. "You loved me once," she pleaded. "Hope too. Do the right thing, Cid. Let me stay with her." *And die with her.*

For a moment, she thought her words had touched him. Then the softness she thought she saw in his face vanished. She knew she'd lost when he came toward her.

He caught her arm. "Hope can come with you."

It was better than nothing. Where there was life, there was hope. She allowed him to propel her toward the door, though she turned for one last glimpse of Michael. What would happen to Jordan and Evan without either of their parents? Michael was bound and unconscious. He'd be no match for whatever Fishman had planned.

Cid pushed her through the door to the waiting truck. It was a military-type vehicle with a tarp covering the rounded frame over the bed. Diesel fumes belched from its exhaust, and she coughed as Cid forced her toward the vehicle. He took Hope from her, then pushed Gracie to the back of the truck.

"Get in there." After she clambered into the back, he handed Hope up to her, then climbed in himself. He pushed her up next to the truck cab, where he snapped a cuff on her wrist before exiting the vehicle.

It was so dark in here. With one hand tethered to the truck, she was able to move a few feet in each direction. Using her free hand, she felt along the floor and walls for something to help her escape. Her fingers grazed over bits of straw and sand that littered the floor. She grimaced when her hand touched a greasy rag. A piece of metal lay in the corner, and she fingered it until she identified it as a pipe wrench. Her exploration continued along the side of the truck, but she found nothing else and moved to the other side. Nothing there either.

"Hope, can you feel on the floor for something small and sharp? Like a hairpin?" Not that Gracie knew how to pick a lock, but she had to try something. She heard shuffling as Hope scooted on the floor.

"Will this work, Mommy?" Hope's voice came nearer, and her small hand pressed a nail into Gracie's palm.

"Good girl!" Using her right hand, Gracie inserted the nail into the cuff and began to worry it along the outlines of the lock.

A JACKHAMMER POUNDED INSIDE HIS HEAD. MICHAEL MOVED HIS NECK AND groaned. His vision stayed blurry even after blinking, until he managed to sit up and focus. He glanced at Rick, who stood near the window, with his arms tied behind his back. When Michael tried to get up, he realized his own wrists were bound as well.

Fishman approached. "You're stuck with us, it seems," he said. He prodded Michael with his foot.

"What now?" Michael said, his voice a hoarse whisper. "You're going to kill us, aren't you?"

The man studied him. "I wish I could let you go, partner. If you live to tell the tale, I'll lose everything. Nothing personal."

"Estevez will ask questions."

Fishman shrugged. "If he does, he might have to suffer an accident."

Michael dived behind the sofa as Fishman came toward him. Rick dropped to the floor with him.

Fishman laughed at their panic. "I have other plans for you instead of a bullet," Fishman said. His footsteps moved away.

The men turned their backs to one another and began to tear at the knots on their wrists. The ropes at Michael's wrists loosened, and he worked harder on Rick's.

Michael heard something splash to the floor, then he smelled gasoline. "He's going to set the place on fire," he whispered to Rick. "Hurry!" He renewed his efforts on Rick's bonds.

"Please, let us go," Sam begged. The chair he was tied to thumped with his efforts to free himself.

The fumes from the gasoline grew heavier, and Michael choked back a cough. Almost there. The bonds loosened again, then his hands were free. He turned and tore at the knots on Rick's wrists.

Rick strained at the rope, but it held. "Go. Stop him. We're out of time."

As Michael worked at the knots, he heard a *whoosh*. Light flared brightly. Fire crackled along the floor, then engulfed the curtains. He stumbled to his feet and yanked Rick up with him. A nightmarish glow lit the room and threw shadows of fire and smoke against the walls and window. Soot burned his nose and throat. He couldn't see Sam or Fishman through the blaze. Pulling Rick with him, he rushed toward where he'd last seen Sam sitting. His outstretched hand touched flesh, and he patted his way up Sam's arm to his face. Unconscious.

If he dragged Sam out of here, he'd have to let loose of Rick. "Can you stay close to me?" he asked.

"Get Sam out of here! I can walk on my own," Rick said.

The windows in the front of the house shattered from the heat, and the fire roared higher. Michael dragged the unconscious man from the chair and grabbed him under the arms. There was no clear path to the door. Fire burned in lines and patches along the floor. The choking smoke obliterated his vision and muddied his sense of direction.

"That way!" Rick jerked his head.

It was the opposite direction Michael thought they should go, but he followed Rick's lead and dragged Sam across the floor. The heat lessened a small degree, but fire still blazed around them. He'd lost all sense of where he was in relationship to the exit. More glass shattered, and the flames responded to the increased oxygen by raging higher. His vision dimmed, and he struggled for every searing breath as he fought to stay conscious. Sam's dead weight was harder and harder to drag across the floor.

A wall of flames separated him from a large picture window. He and Rick could run and leap through the window, but it would mean leaving Sam behind, and he couldn't abandon the older man. There had to be a way to save them all. He saw an unburned path and followed it.

His shin banged up against a chair, and he realized he was in the breakfast room. "Wait here with Sam!" he yelled to Rick. He left Sam on the floor and felt his way to the counter, then began jerking out drawers until he found a knife. He made his way back through the choking smoke to Rick, who stood guard over Sam.

Michael sawed with the knife against Rick's bonds, and the rope finally fell to the floor. "Can you help me throw him through the window?" he shouted.

"I've got his shoulders. Grab his feet," Rick said.

The men hoisted the older man off the floor. "On the count of three," Michael panted. "Swing him. His body weight will give us momentum."

Sam was sure to get cut, but it was better than dying in this inferno. He swung Sam's body.

"Say when," Rick panted.

"One, two, *three!*" Michael heaved the older man toward the window with all his might. The man's inert body slammed into the glass, and it shattered as he crashed through to the outside.

"Now you!" Michael shouted. "I'm right behind you."

Rick took a running leap and dived through the window. Michael waited a split second, then followed him. The heat of the fire scorched his legs as he sprang, and the blessed fresh air waiting on the other side of the choking smoke revived him. His face felt the first touch of cool air, then he was on top of another body.

"*Oomph*," Rick said. "That's me right here."

Sand and soot filled his mouth. Michael rolled off his friend and staggered to his feet. "Where's Sam?"

"There." Rick pointed to the motionless body of the older man lying by the foundation of the house.

Embers rained down on Sam, and his shirt was smoking. Michael grabbed the governor and pulled him away from the house, with Rick's help, then patted out the sparks on Sam's shirt. Every inhalation was like breathing cut glass. Various burns on his hands and legs began to make themselves known.

A roar sounded behind them, and Michael turned to see the roof of the house collapse. Embers flew into the air, and the flames roared like a fire-breathing demon. He turned and scanned the landscape illuminated in the garish glow of dancing light. Fishman was gone with his guns. And so were Gracie and Hope.

30

THE LOCK WOULD NOT BUDGE. GRACIE JAMMED THE NAIL INTO IT AGAIN and poked with all her strength. A rumble echoed along the canyons outside the truck, and through the open back she saw flames shoot into the air in the distance. Something was on fire or had exploded.

The house where she'd last seen Michael.

She doubled over, and a sob burst from her throat. Her eyes burned, and she couldn't hold back the tears. He couldn't be in that house. She wouldn't let it be so. Her heart would tell her if he was dead.

Hope touched her face. "Mommy?"

Gracie enveloped her daughter in a hug. "I'm okay, honey." The truck stopped, and the wind brought the stink of smoke to her nose. They weren't in Mexico yet. The border was a few miles away. She yanked on her handcuff and discovered it was bigger than she realized. Could she work her hand out of it? She remembered the greasy rag on the floor.

Dropping to her knees, she patted the floor of the truck until her hand sank into the rag. She picked it up and rubbed it on her hand and wrist. After two passes around her exposed skin, she began to squeeze her hand out of the metal cuff. If the level of pain was any indication, it had to be taking some of her skin with it, but she forced herself to ignore the burning. Her hand got slicker, probably from blood, but it was too dark to see. Still, the cuff stayed firmly around her wrist.

It wasn't going to work.

Gritting her teeth, she gave her hand one last twist. Something snapped, and the cuff moved. She nearly screamed as agony enveloped her hand. She'd broken something, but the cuff dangled loose. With Hope's hand in her good one, Gracie scurried to the back of the truck and peered out past the tarp. The vehicle was parked in front of a wash. Cid stood with his father, gesturing at the deep ravine. The path up the wash on the other side looked too narrow for the truck. Were they intending to try to drive over it?

Holding her finger to her lips, she jumped down, then lifted Hope from the truck. Thunder rumbled overhead again, and lightning ripped through the sky, leaving behind the sharp stench of ozone. In a crouch, Gracie rushed away from the truck. Sand bit into her skin, and small rocks cut at her feet. The open desert held no good place to hide, but if she could get far enough away, Cid would think she was still in the truck.

She glanced back over her shoulder. The men were still arguing. She scanned the dark landscape. There. A ditch. Before she dived for it, she stopped and glanced down as lightning ripped through the sky again. The flash of light revealed a nest of black widow spiders.

Grimacing, she backed away from it. If they'd hidden there, she and Hope would have been bitten several times before they realized what was happening.

Lightning rippled again, and she and Hope stood outlined in the brilliant light. A shout rose above the thunder, and she glanced back toward the truck. Pulling Hope with her, she crouched and watched Cid jump from the back of the truck. Their escape had been discovered. It wouldn't take long for them to find her and Hope. Staying low to the ground, though, might make him think their silhouette belonged to a cactus.

The sky lit up again, as bright as daylight. When the shout of discovery came, she grabbed Hope's hand and ran back toward the fire burning in the distance. She'd never make it before Cid overtook her. Her pace slowed as she grew calm. She stopped and turned to look. Cid would be here in a few minutes. The time for running was over.

Gracie pulled Hope tight against her leg. "I want you to run away, Hope." She pointed to the burning house. "There's probably a phone in the barn. Find it and dial 911. Then hide until you hear the siren. Do you understand?"

Hope clung to her. "I want to stay with you, Mommy." Her hiccup turned into a sob.

"You can get help for me, Hope. I can't get it myself. Only you can do it. Cid will let you go." She embraced her daughter and inhaled the scent of baby shampoo.

"I'm scared, Mommy."

It was all she could do to push Hope away and pat her little bottom. "Run as fast as you can, honey. Don't look back. Don't stop even if I call for you. Do you understand?"

Hope's wide dark eyes blinked, then she nodded. "Keep running.

Dial 911 and tell them you need help. That's right. Now run, honey. Run like King." She watched Hope until her daughter's tiny form winked out into the darkness, then she turned and walked back toward Cid. Lightning lashed the sky and thunder rolled over the arroyo to the mountain. No more running.

TWO SETS OF HEADLAMPS RACED IN OPPOSITE DIRECTIONS. ONE HELD hundreds of thousands of dollars in guns that would arm a Mexican revolution. If Fishman arrived back in Big Bend safely and delivered the guns to his partners, the violence might spill over into the States. The other truck held Michael's wife and daughter. A year ago he wouldn't have paused. He would have called for someone to intercept the truck holding his wife, and he would have stopped the guns himself, because he was closer to that truck, and its cargo impacted more people. Serving the greater good was his job, after all.

He didn't pause now, either. Running to the barn, he glanced around wildly for a phone and a vehicle. And found both. The keys to the four-wheeler were in the ignition. He leaped onto the seat and turned the key. The engine sputtered, then fired. It had been years since he'd driven a four-wheeler, but his hands remembered how to shift. The tires began to turn, and the vehicle rolled through the barn door as lightning cracked overhead.

"There's a phone in the barn!" he yelled to Rick. "Call and get that truck full of guns stopped. I'm going after Gracie and Hope." Rick nodded and ran for the barn. Michael cranked the engine as high as it would go, and the ATV rolled over the sand toward the truck lights in the distance.

This thing will never catch a truck.

Though the words played over and over in his head with every crash of thunder, he couldn't stop. He had to try, even if he was rolling forward at only twenty-five miles an hour. Gracie's face shone before him, guiding him on. He'd been so focused on saving her, he hadn't realized how she'd saved him. Her gentleness was the light he'd needed to find his way. No wonder Kate had divorced him.

He swiped at his damp eyes and steered the four-wheeler toward the taillights. He seemed to be closing the gap. "God, help me save her," he whispered. "I have to find her."

A movement caught his eye, and he squinted when the next flash of lightning came. The light illuminated Hope's panicked face.

"Hope!" He jammed on the brake and jumped from the four-wheeler.

Hope leaped into his arms. "Daddy, you have to save Mommy. She's there!" She turned and pointed to the left of the taillights. "Cid's coming. He'll hurt her."

Michael crushed her to his chest. "I won't let him, honey." He set her on the ground. "Mr. Rick is in the barn. Run to him and tell him what you told me. I'm going to go get your mommy."

She wiped her eyes and took off toward the barn. He leaped back onto the old four-wheeler. The engine sputtered as he pushed it as fast as he dared. Lightning slammed into a saguaro cactus nearby, and the sizzling stench made him grimace. Riding an open metal vehicle in a desert thunderstorm wasn't the smartest thing he'd ever done, but it was the most necessary. Sand spit from the four-wheeler's tires, but the old machine handled the uneven ground.

The first raindrop hit his forehead, followed by another. And another. Just when he thought the heavens would let loose, the sprinkles stopped.

"Thank you, God," he said, straining to see through the flashes of light that lit the darkness for only a few moments. Lightning drew his eye to the blond hair of a woman in the distance.

Gracie. He steered to intercept her.

31

SOMETHING HAD CHANGED FOR GRACIE. THE SCALES HAD FALLEN FROM HER eyes, and she couldn't keep letting fear and shame rule her life. If she was going to die tonight, at least she'd die with her head held high and her integrity intact. Running had solved nothing for her in the past five years. Evil always gave chase. She would see if confrontation could turn it away.

Thunder crashed overhead as she watched Cid approach. She walked the last few steps to meet him. The scent of rain added to her sense of setting out on a new pathway. Lightning suffused Cid's face with color. His narrowed eyes glittered when Gracie reached him.

He moved to take her arm, but she stepped back and held up her hand. "No more, Cid. I won't be intimidated by you anymore. I chose to come back and face you. I'm not running. You can drag me across the border. You can throw me in a bordello. You can beat me. But you will never break me again. Do you understand?"

His mouth sagged, and he blinked several times. "The mouse is roaring?" His laughter held a note of uncertainty.

Poor, poor man. Only Cid knew the demons that drove him, just as she was the one who had to face her demons. "I haven't always made the best choices in life. Neither have you. But we can change."

"What is this—a sermon?" He rolled his eyes.

"I can understand you wanting to help your dad. You've done that. He's free. You can start a new life now, Cid. Let me go. I have children to raise."

Listen, please listen.

His jaw tightened. "You nearly got me killed, Gracie."

"No, *you* nearly got yourself killed. You're the one who chose to get involved with the cartel. You're the one who laid a plan to use me to free your dad. And you're the only one who can walk away now."

"It is too late for that. I must take my place at my father's side."

She heard the regret in his voice. "Do the right thing, Cid. Let me go."

His gaze held hers, then broke away. He shifted his weight and glanced at her again. She held her breath while she awaited his decision. The moment passed when the glint returned to his eyes, and his lips hardened.

He grabbed her arm. "You will not confuse me, Gracie. The time for talk is past. Come."

Her failure to turn Cid from his course hit her harder than the realization that her life was in danger. She almost started to walk with him, then she stopped and plopped onto the sand. "I'm not helping you do this."

He yanked cruelly on her arm. "Get up."

She ignored the pain and sat down in the rough sand. Her broken wrist throbbed. Lightning lashed the sky again, and a few drops of rain struck her face. "No. You'll have to carry me."

He waved the gun in her face. "I could shoot you where you sit."

"You won't. Then you couldn't continue to punish me."

Cursing, he grabbed her under the arms and began to drag her toward the truck. "This is going to take all night," he said, panting.

She dug her heels into the sand as hard as she could and slumped with her full weight to slow down their progress.

"I'm more trouble than I'm worth, Cid," she said. "This won't be the end. I'll fight you at every turn."

His breath labored in his chest from her weight. He dropped her on the sand and glared down at her. "If you do not get up and walk, I will find Hope."

Glaring back, she said, "I won't let you use fear to control me anymore." The clouds let go overhead, and rain began to pummel the desert. The wind blew the drops in a stinging curtain against her face. "You'd better hurry or you won't get across the wash before it floods."

His eyes widened, and he glanced back toward the truck. Gracie prayed for a flash flood to thunder down the canyon. Or a bolt of lightning to distract him. Something to change his mind. Surprisingly, she found she wanted him to change his mind for *his* well-being, not just her own. Revenge and bitterness would consume him if he let it.

When she first heard the rumble, she thought it was thunder. Then Cid's head jerked to the right, and his face twisted into a snarl. She peered through the sheets of rain and made out something moving. A four-wheeler in this storm? Swiping the deluge from her face, she squinted at the form on the seat.

Michael clutched the steering wheel with both hands and rode the machine to intercept them. She wanted to leap to her feet and dance. He was alive. The fire hadn't taken him and Rick. Her joy was short-lived, though, when she saw Cid pull his gun from his belt.

She stumbled up from the sand and leaped onto Cid's back. "No!"

"Get off me!" He whirled in a circle, trying to dislodge her.

Gracie grabbed for the gun, but it was out of her reach. Cid fell on top of her onto the sand, and the impact drove the air from her lungs. She struggled to pull in oxygen. Her hands fell from his neck, and she lay gasping, with the rain running into her mouth and nose. Rolling to her stomach, she coughed up the river of water. She got to her hands and knees and flung her dripping hair out of her eyes. Where was Michael?

After she staggered to her feet, she found both men rolling in the sand. The gun lay nearly submerged in a gully made by the driving rain. She grabbed it and pointed it at Cid, but there was no opportunity to use it. The men were too close. The rain stopped as quickly as it had started, but lightning continued to rip the sky. The men rolled and grunted.

Michael was on the bottom, with Cid's hands on his throat. His knee came up and dislodged Cid, who rolled into a ditch.

"Black widows!" Striking at his shirt, Cid staggered across the sand.

Gracie winced. He would be in intense pain very shortly. She thought the spider bites would slow him down, but he leaped at Michael again, and the two rolled into a struggling heap. Stuffing the gun in the waistband of her jeans, she tried to find a large rock she could use to hit Cid with, but there was nothing but wet sand.

The truck. The pipe wrench. She ran toward the vehicle, pulling out the gun again for protection against Cid's father. On approaching the truck, she saw no sign of him. The vehicle had been abandoned in the middle of the wash, bogged down by wet sand. She splashed through the water, then climbed into the back and found the wrench. It would be heavy enough to knock out Cid.

Before she could exit, the truck started and rolled forward with a jerk. Gracie lurched and fell when the truck veered and accelerated. She crawled to the tarp and saw Michael running toward her. Cid must be driving. She gained her feet and grabbed the side of the tarp to steady herself.

She heard Cid moan, and the truck stopped. She stuck her head out and peered toward the cab. She could see his ashen face in the mirror. His eyes were closed and he moaned again. Even after all he'd done to her, she pitied him. Though she'd never had a black widow bite, she'd heard stories about the pain. He'd fallen into a nest and likely had multiple bites. Even with medical attention, he would probably die.

"Gracie!" Michael screamed.

She turned her head toward him and gazed into eyes filled with terror.

"Jump!" Michael pointed and waved to her left.

Gracie saw what caused the fear on his face. A wall of water bore down on the truck as it splashed through the wash. She had only moments to escape its massive power. Without stopping to think, she leaped from the back of the truck and hit the sand. Even as she ran for the bank, she knew she wasn't going to make it.

The roar of the approaching water barreled down the wash like water in a pipe. Desert mountains rose on either side. She'd be unable to climb out with the water tumbling her along. Flotsam rode the crest of the waves and the floodwaters would hold even deadlier missiles under the surface.

She caught a glimpse of Michael's panicked face and charged toward him with all her might. The wet sand sucked at her feet, and she seemed to be running in slow motion. Almost there. Stretching her hand forward as far as she could without tipping over, she snatched at his open palm. He reached down toward her. Her fingers grazed his, then his hand closed on hers. He yanked her up as the water encased her feet. They fell back on the bank. Struggling to catch her breath, Gracie lay on top of him.

The ground rumbled under them from the newly swollen river rushing by. She buried her face in his wet shirt. Tears choked her. Such a close call.

She bolted upright. "Hope!"

Michael sat up with her still in his arms. "I found her and sent her on to Rick. She's fine."

Gracie turned to stare down into the roiling waters. There was no trace of the truck or Cid. "He's gone."

"Yeah. Are you hurt anywhere?"

She shook her head, then laid her cheek on his chest. "I'm so tired. And so glad it's over."

He pressed his lips against her forehead. "I thought I'd lost you."

"I thought you died in the fire. No, scratch that. I was sure if you'd died, I would have felt it." She lifted her head. "I confronted him, Michael. I decided I wasn't going to run anymore. I appealed to his better side and told him he didn't have to keep making wrong choices."

"He didn't listen, did he?"

"No. But I knew I had to do it. I had to quit running. I had to take control of my life and face my own decisions. I did a sit-down strike."

His lips curved. "A strike?"

She laughed, remembering Cid's face when she refused to walk.

"He was dragging me to the truck when he saw you. When you came to save me."

He cupped her face in his hands. "You saved me, Gracie. Your sweetness, your love. I let the truck with all the weapons get away. You're all that matters to me. The battle will go on this year and next year and the year after that. We can live to fight another day as long as we're together. Let's go home."

His lips brushed hers, then his arms swept her into a fierce embrace. "Anywhere you are is home to me," she whispered.

EPILOGUE

Residents of Bluebird Crossing milled about the patchy lawn outside the church. Gracie stood with Michael at the cake table under the tent. Her wedding dress billowed around her in the hot breeze. She couldn't believe how many people from town had shown up. The church had been packed for the wedding, and best of all, her father was on hand to give her away when she and Michael repeated their vows in a real church.

The three weeks since their ordeal ended had flown by. Estevez had become suspicious when no one went with Fishman, so he'd called Fishman's superior. Fishman was apprehended just inside the Texas border. Sam had made two trips to see Hope, and he was in the crowd of well-wishers here today. Gracie had come to realize there was no such thing as too much love.

The only ache left in her heart was that they'd been unable to trace King. She feared the old horse had indeed ended his days in the rendering plant.

"No cake in the face," she warned.

His blue eyes crinkled. "I wouldn't think of it," Michael said.

He slipped a morsel of cake into her mouth, and she smiled as the sweetness melted on her tongue. Michael's gaze traveled down her dress, then rested on her face. The spark in his eyes warmed her. He wore his dress uniform, and she couldn't take her eyes off him.

"I decided to do it, Gracie," Michael said, sipping his punch.

"Do what?" she asked.

"I'm going to see if I can raise some money to start a helicopter paramedic unit here. It's going to be tight financially for a while. Are you okay with that?"

"Oh, Michael, I'm so glad." She leaned over and brushed a kiss across his lips. "We'll be just fine."

His gaze searched hers. "You were right, you know. I was doing it for all the wrong reasons. Trying to save the world to make my dad proud, and he's not even still alive."

"What about Vargas? He escaped. There's still the bounty on your head."

"I got a call this morning. His body was found in the wash along with Cid's. Someone else will rise to power, and he won't care about me. That battle isn't mine anymore. I'm weary of death and combat. I can focus on life for a change."

"I like the sound of that."

Just then, a cameras flashed in her face. She smiled at Rick and Allie as they approached.

Rick slapped him on the back. "That's a beautiful bride you've got there."

"I always knew she'd be a knockout in a wedding dress," he said. His eyes held a meaningful glint.

She poked him in the ribs. "Sh," she said.

"Did you tell her yet?" Rick asked.

"Not yet," Michael answered, his eyes still on Gracie.

"Tell me what?" She didn't trust the impish expression on his face.

"It's customary for the groom to give the bride a gift. You haven't asked about yours."

"I have you and the kids. What more could I want?"

Michael's grin widened. "I think there's one thing." His large, warm hand enveloped hers and he led her out of the tent. Rick and Allie followed them.

Hope waved to her from atop a horse. "Mommy!" Jordan held the horse's lead, and Evan walked with her. Caesar bounded beside the kids, with his ears alert.

Gracie clutched Michael's arm. She squinted into the sun. "I-is that . . . King?"

"What do you think?"

Her vision blurred. She ran for the horse and children. Michael stayed on her heels. The horse whinnied when he caught sight of her and began to walk faster. Gracie broke into a jog and reached the horse and children.

King thrust his nose against her neck and huffed a blast of warm air onto her skin. She rubbed his neck. "You're not dead," she whispered. She turned toward Michael. "Where did you find him?"

His grin faded. "In a rendering plant. I barely got there in time. Rick and Allie kept him until today so I could surprise you."

She leaned her head against the horse's blaze. "It's the best surprise

I've ever had. Other than the one when I opened my eyes on a train station bench and saw my hero for the first time."

He colored as he smiled. "God had a plan, didn't he?"

"One I sure couldn't see." She laced her fingers with his.

"I don't know about you, but I'm ready to go home and start that new life."

"*Home* is a beautiful word," she said, leaning into his embrace.

DEAR READER,

I HOPE YOU'VE ENJOYED OUR THIRD VISIT TO THE GORGEOUS BIG BEND area of West Texas as much as I have. I've been a little obsessed lately with marriage-of-convenience stories. Do you love them as much as I do?

The thing I adore about these stories is watching how love works out when it's a choice. It's the day-to-day choices to love and to sacrifice that make a marriage work. A good marriage doesn't just happen. All marriages are between flawed people who have to figure out a way to meld their differences into a relationship that works. It's about learning how to give when you'd rather take. It's about agreeing to watch golf when you'd rather watch *The Biggest Loser*. (Not that I'm too good at that one, mind you!)

Gracie's story developed when I pictured a woman getting off a train in a bedraggled wedding dress, without a dime to her name. Intriguing picture, isn't it? I knew I had to find out what made her run like that.

Judging from my reader mail, you have been enjoying these peeks into relationship building as much as I have enjoyed writing them. Be sure to let me know what you think of this one. I love to hear from readers! Drop me an e-mail at colleen@colleencoble.com, and check out my Web site at www.colleencoble.com. You can also follow me on Twitter at http://twitter.com/colleencoble, and I'm on Facebook as well. Thank you all for giving up your most precious commodity— *time*—to spend it with me and my stories.

Much affection,
Colleen Coble

ACKNOWLEDGMENTS

I am *so* in my sweet spot! It is such a joy to do another project with my wonderful Thomas Nelson family. Publisher Allen Arnold constantly comes up with new ways to build my brand. Senior Acquisitions Editor Ami McConnell (my friend and cheerleader) is never allowed to be gone for an edit again. I crave her analytical eye! Marketing Manager Jennifer Deshler brings both friendship and fabulous marketing ideas to the table. Publicist Katie Schroder is always willing to listen to my harebrained ideas. Fabulous cover guru Kristen Vasgaard (you *so* rock!) works hard to create the perfect cover—and does it. And of course I can't forget the editors, assistants, and sales reps who are all part of my amazing fiction family: Natalie Hanemann, Amanda Bostic, Becky Monds, Jocelyn Bailey, Ashley Schneider,

Heather McCulloch, Chris Long, and Kathy Carabajal. I wish I could name all the great folks who work on selling my books through different venues at Thomas Nelson. You are my dream team! Hearing "well done" from you all is my motivation every day.

Michael Wayne was named by Joe and Frances Schwartz. Their daughter Mary Ann Dynes bid and won on the honor of naming a character in my next book at a Taylor University auction. She let her parents have the fun of naming the character, since they were also a great resource for me when I wrote my Amish mystery *Anathema*. I liked the name so much, I chose it for my hero in the story. Thanks, my friends!

My agent, Karen Solem, has helped shaped my career in many ways, and that includes kicking an idea to the curb when necessary. Thanks, Karen. You're the best!

Erin Healy is the best freelance editor in the business, bar none. Thanks, Erin! I couldn't do it without you. Check out her upcoming solo novel.

Writing can be a lonely business, but God has blessed me with great writing friends and critique partners. Kristin Billerbeck, Diann Hunt, and Denise Hunter make up the Girls Write Out squad (www .GirlsWriteOut.blogspot.com). I couldn't make it through a day without my peeps! And another one of those is Robin Miller, conference director of ACFW (www.acfw.com), who spots inconsistencies in a suspense plot with an eagle eye. Thanks to all of you for the work you do on my behalf, and for your friendship.

Thanks to my husband, Dave, who carts me around from city to city, washes towels, and chases down dinner without complaint. Thanks, honey! I couldn't do anything without you. My kids—Dave and Kara (and now Donna and Mark)—and my grandsons, James and Jorden Packer, love and support me in every way possible. Love you guys! Donna and Dave brought me the delight of my life—our little granddaughter, Alexa! It's hard to write when all I want to do is kiss those darling, pudgy feet. She is the most beautiful baby ever!

Most important, I give my thanks to God, who has opened such amazing doors for me and makes the journey a golden one.

READING GROUP GUIDE

1. Why do you think Gracie wanted to cut up the wedding dress when she was able to change out of it?
2. Gracie's desperation drove her to extreme measures. What would you have done if you were in her situation?
3. Michael took his duty very seriously. Where is the line between duty and family?
4. Michael was a crusader, out to save the world. In what ways did he go too far?
5. Gracie ran from trouble while Michael faced it head on. What is your response to conflict and why is that your reaction?
6. Had you ever heard of synesthesia before? Have you ever experienced a touch of cross sensation?

7. Why didn't Jordan want to accept Gracie's love?

8. How easy is it for love to grow out of gratitude and how does it relate to our love for God?

9. Is love an action or an emotion? How are the different manifestations similar and how are they different?

10. Have you ever felt like a prodigal? Share this experience.

11. When you read the prodigal story, which brother do you most relate to and why?

12. Is there a relationship in your life that needs to be reconciled?

ESCAPE TO
BLUEBIRD RANCH

ALOHA
REEF
SERIES

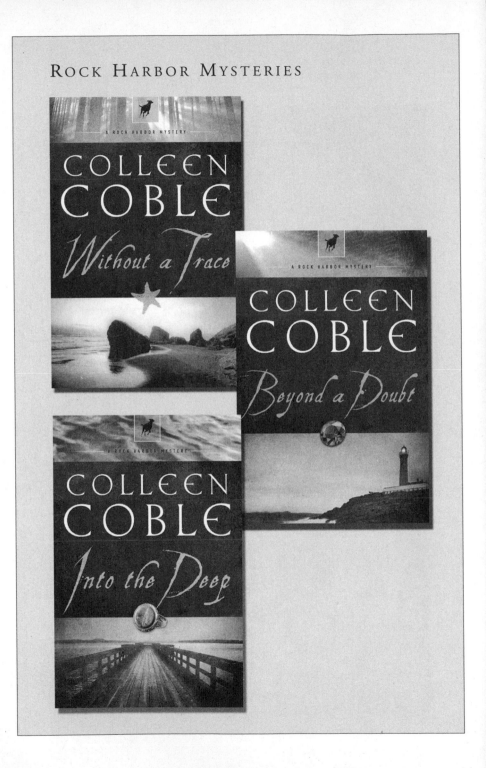